A GLADIATOR'S OATH

ROMAN HEARTS SERIES BOOK ONE

TANYA BIRD

Created with Vellum

For my Dad.
The best research assistant a girl could ask for.

FROM THE SATIRES OF JUVENAL

Who has not seen the dummies of wood they slash
at and batter
Whether with swords or with spears, going
through all the moves?
These are the girls who blast on trumpets in
honour of Flora.
Or, it may be, they have deeper designs, and are
really preparing for the arena itself.
How can a woman be decent, sticking her head in
a helmet, denying her sex she was born with?
Manly feats they adore, but they wouldn't want to
be men,
Poor weak things—they think—how little they
really enjoy it!
What great honour it is for a husband to see, at an
auction
Where his wife's effects are up for sale: belts,
greaves, manica, and plumes!
Hear her grunt and groan as she works at it,
parrying, thrusting;

See her neck bent down under the weight of her helmet.
Look at the rolls of bandage and tape, so her legs look like tree trunks.
Then have a laugh for yourself after the practice is over,
Armour and weapons are put down, and she squats as she uses the vessel.
Ah, degenerate girls of the line of our praetors and consuls,
Tell us, whom have you seen got up in any such fashion,
Panting and sweating like this? No gladiator's wench,
No tough striptease broad would ever so much as attempt it.

PROLOGUE

September 29, 199AD

It looked like any other sand-covered surface, but Mila knew the maze of tunnels below caged both men and beasts.

She raised her eyes to sixty-five thousand spectators, from the emperor to the plebeians, all awaiting the spectacle of death. She kept her gaze up so she would not have to look at the blood-soaked sand where criminals had been put to death just moments earlier. Instead, she focused on the feel of the sword and the weight of the shield. Libertas. That was what they called her, despite the fact that she was not free. They could hardly herald a gladiator as Mila the Slave.

She stopped walking to watch the reaction of the crowd. The sword turned in her hand as a rumble of applause pressed down on her. Not cheering—that would come later when the stakes were higher. It was a far cry from the arena at Ludus Magnus, where all she had heard was Remus's familiar voice and the clapping of wooden swords. She found herself searching for him, trying to find him amid a sea of blurry faces. Was he outwardly calm while breaking apart inside—like she was?

They called the Spaniard Hebe. The goddess of youth. She entered through the gate of life, striding towards Mila, chin up, her skin a polished contrast to the burned shoulders of a slave. Her breasts were partially covered with enough flesh on display to satisfy the men. She stopped a few feet from Mila, peering out at the crowd from beneath her helmet, and raised her shield to them. They responded with a roar that shifted the sand.

Mila wished her own helmet could shield her from the noise. She shuddered, adjusting her grip on the weapons. Damp hands were never a good thing.

The *summa rudis* approached, stick in hand, shouting instructions Mila could not hear amid the noise. Did her opponent hear? Unlikely. She was all but turned away from him, her sword hand resting on the curve of her hip. For a moment, their eyes met through the slits of their helmets. Strangers. In a moment, Hebe would try to kill her. In a moment, she would try to kill Hebe. That delicate skin would be bruised and broken, painted with sweat and blood.

Mila's gaze went to the crowd. Where was he? She did not know how to do this without him. Not entirely true—she just did not *want* to do it without him. 'Shield up,' he would shout, his tone sharper than a sword because he wanted her to live. Perhaps it was better he was not there. Whatever the outcome, she did not want to see his changed face in those final moments.

'Gladiators ready!'

Mila softened her knees, distributing her weight evenly. Was she ready? The thought alone was dangerous. Her opponent's shield was raised, her knuckles whitening around her sword. The stadium crackled to life in that moment, the sound vibrating around them before drifting up to the open sky, as blue as Remus's eyes.

Her opponent lunged, the tip of her sword colliding with Mila's shield.

Live or die.

She would not let the gods decide this one.

CHAPTER 1

Five months prior

The net snaked around Mila's ankle. She knew in a few moments she would be lying on her back, the wind knocked from her lungs and a trident pressed to her throat. If her sword had been sharp, she might have cut herself free, but even a street fight in an arena marked off with charcoal had rules. The fifteen-year-old referee had checked all the weapons before they began.

Thump. The air left her lungs. The swords fell from her hands, and the cool tips of a trident brushed the skin of her neck. Her opponent stared down at her, out of breath, a smug smile on his lips. The spectators clapped, and he stepped back from her. He looked to be around seventeen, a few years younger, but it was hard to tell as he was in need of a good meal. Mila sat up, watching as money exchanged hands, trying not to think about the extra coin she would have walked away with if she had just won.

She spotted Nerva coming towards her, the crowd dispersing at the sight of him. Disapproval was etched on his face.

'Did you forget you have feet?' he asked, coming to a stop in front of her.

She could not quite answer yet, her lungs struggling. He offered her his hand, and she took it. Dizzy, she folded over, holding onto her knees for a moment.

'What are you doing here?' she asked. 'If your father sees you—'

'If he sees *me*?' He shook his head. 'If he sees you fighting, you will be sold faster than you can say goodbye to your sister.'

She straightened, watching as he picked up her weapons, running a finger along the blunt edge of the blade.

'I must admit, you are better than some who trained me.'

She coughed, looking up at him. 'Given *you* taught me, that is a compliment aimed at yourself.'

He laughed, clapping her on the back. 'Let us go before the watch shows up and arrests you.' He glanced over his shoulder. 'Father is expecting me home.'

She nodded, falling into step with him. 'Another dinner party to recruit admirers?'

'Something like that. How else does one secure a place in the senate?'

At twenty, Nerva was about as interested in a political career as Mila was being a slave in his household.

'Does your father know about the new horse yet?'

Nerva looked around, frowning. 'No, and I prefer he hear it from me.' His grey eyes flashed at her.

She looked down.

Rufus Papias had big plans for his only living son—and they did not involve chariot racing. Well-bred, well-educated, and liked by all who knew him, it was expected that Nerva would follow him into the senate. Rufus was famous for saying that it took three successive generations to gain noble status, and one to lose it. And he liked to remind Nerva of the fact every day.

It was no secret that Mila and Nerva shared a father, but as Nerva's mother was domina of the house, and Mila's mother a slave, that made Mila property of her dominus—not his daughter. Having inherited her father's features and sharp mind, the blood connection did not go unnoticed. That was why her domina preferred to keep Mila hidden away in the laundry or kitchen. No one in the household spoke of it, nor did they mention the second daughter born seven years later. Even Nerva knew better than to bring the subject up, knowing his mother might one day insist the girls be sold.

'Nerva Papias?' came a voice behind them. They turned to see a large man wearing civilian clothes and cheap jewels striding towards them. Nerva relaxed at the sight of him.

'Yes?'

'Gallus Minidius,' he said, extending an arm.

Nerva hesitated before taking hold of it.

'This your slave?' asked Gallus, glancing past him to Mila.

Nerva studied the man. 'Yes.'

Gallus's gaze swept over her and he nodded, apparently satisfied with what he saw. 'Pardon the interruption. I sponsor the games in Caelimontium, a small arena, some entertainment for plebeians in the evenings.'

'*You* sponsor gladiatorial games?'

Mila blinked at his snobbery, remaining silent. Nerva let her get away with a lot for a slave. In return, she never embarrassed him by overstepping around people.

'Nothing fancy, I admit,' Gallus laughed. 'But we are always in need of entertainers.'

Nerva crossed his arms. 'What sort of entertainers?'

Gallus nodded towards Mila. 'All sorts, but especially women.' Seeing Nerva's sceptical expression, he added, 'Nothing too serious. The girls use wooden swords—'

'And roll about in the sand with their clothes off?'

Gallus smiled, shifting his feet. 'Sometimes, but your slave, your rules.'

Nerva cleared his throat. 'I am afraid my father would never approve of one his slaves being paraded bare-chested in front of drunk men.'

Mila stared down at her feet.

'They fight as hard as the men, and the winners are paid.'

Mila looked up, and Nerva chuckled.

'By gambling men?'

Gallus shrugged. 'I prefer to think of it as an entry fee.'

Nerva turned his back to the man and gestured for Mila to walk. 'Call it what you like. It does not change what it is. Nice to meet you, Gallus.'

'And you,' the man replied, watching them leave.

Nerva walked in front, shaking his head. 'Can you believe him?'

Mila looked around before speaking, ensuring there was no one within earshot. 'He thinks I am good enough to fight in an arena.'

Nerva scoffed. 'Hardly an arena. Besides, you lost back there.'

'Against a man.'

Nerva glanced over his shoulder. 'Against a *boy*.'

'It was my second fight for the afternoon. I was tired.'

Nerva turned to face her. 'Your second fight? Mila, this has to stop.'

'It will. When I have enough coin.'

He rolled his eyes and resumed walking again. 'Why not do what other slaves do? Hope and pray.'

She took a few fast steps to close the distance between them. 'Hope and pray? Why should I harass the gods when I can simply buy freedom for myself?'

They turned into another alleyway. Years of living in Rome had taught them to check their surroundings as they did so.

'You have romanticised freedom,' he said. 'Look around. This is what awaits you if you leave.' Violent coughing echoed through the narrow space. A man stepped into the alleyway, shouting at a woman who clutched her crying baby. They moved around them, continuing without a backwards glance. 'You have lived happily in our household your entire life. Have you not been treated well?'

'Of course.'

'Have you not eaten better than many of Rome's citizens? Slept in comfort every night?'

He did not understand. How could he? 'I am not complaining. I know I have been more fortunate than most. But I am still a slave, for no crime other than being born.'

'My father does not make the laws.'

That was not entirely true—his father was a senator with a lot of influence.

'And what crime did my mother commit?' she continued, ignoring him. 'Her father gambles away his wage, leaving the family destitute. Then along comes your father, taken with her, but unable to marry the daughter of a lowly teacher. So what does he do? *Buys* her. Not only does she become a slave by definition, she is also labelled a—'

'Save your breath. I know the story.'

She exhaled to calm herself. 'I am surprised that you cannot understand me wanting a different life. At least you can marry, have children—'

'Slaves have children all the time.'

If they had been alone, she might have tripped him. 'Children who are the property of their dominus, not their mother.'

He would not look at her.

She did not stop. 'If your father was to sell me, what would be my worth?'

Nerva picked up his pace, forcing her to do the same. Her legs ached from all the fighting.

'Five hundred denarii at the most, due to your laziness.'

'Nerva!'

He inhaled. 'All right, all right. Two thousand at a minimum.'

A mule came towards them. They moved into a doorway to get out of its way, and Nerva turned to her. 'If it were up to me, I would free you. If only to put an end to your complaining,' he added, stepping back into the alleyway and rounding the corner onto a wide street. 'Fighting boys on the street is one thing, but fighting in an arena in front of men is quite another.'

'Your slave, your rules,' Mila said, quoting Gallus.

'Exactly. It is time you listened before you find yourself in over your head, or worse, dead.'

'They use wooden swords,' she replied, keeping her voice low. 'I am not fighting to the death.'

The house came into sight and Nerva stopped walking, taking hold of her arm. 'Mila, you are my…'

He could not say it. *Sister.*

'We have known one another our whole lives,' she finished for him.

He let go of her arm. 'Stay away from people like Gallus. He only wants to exploit you, not free you. Understand?'

She stared at him a moment before nodding.

Looking to the house, he said, 'If anyone asks, I had

some business to tend to and asked you to keep me company.'

Another nod.

His eyes returned to her. 'Fix your hair and pray that shine on your cheek does not turn to bruising in the morning.'

CHAPTER 2

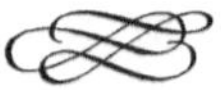

Mila was about to climb the wall when she heard Dulcia call to her in the dark.

'Please don't go.'

Mila turned, searching for her sister. She found her hiding in the shadows. 'Return to Mother. Quickly now.' She tried to keep her voice to a whisper.

Dulcia's gaze fell to the weapons hanging from her hips. 'Why are you taking your swords? You promised Mother you would stop fighting.'

'I promised Mother I wouldn't cause trouble for us, which means not getting *caught* fighting. If I stand here talking to you, we are both going to end up in trouble.' She watched as her sister sank deeper into the shadows. She kept praying that Dulcia would gain confidence, toughen up, but at age twelve, when other girls were being promised to greying men, her sister continued to hide away with the dolls Nerva bought her each year on her birthday.

'You're going to the arena. The one I heard you talking to Nerva about.' She looked suitably guilty for eavesdropping. 'You promised him you wouldn't go.'

Mila exhaled and walked over to her sister, looking around the garden before stepping into the shadows beside her. 'They need people to entertain the crowd, lighten the mood. It is not dangerous, only fun. I have a chance to earn some *real* coin.'

'You win coin all the time.'

Mila glanced at the wall. Soon it would be too late to go. 'Yes, fighting boys on the street for a few sestertii. Where I am going, winners are paid denarii.'

Dulcia only looked more worried. 'Because they will expect more. A fight to the death, perhaps.'

Mila smiled. 'Only in your imagination would that happen. I will be there by choice, and I have no intention of dying.'

Dulcia chewed her bottom lip as she thought it over. 'They will not let you in without an escort.'

She had already decided to cross that bridge when she came to it. 'The worst thing that can happen is I am home earlier than expected.'

'That is not the worst that can happen. What if you are injured? How will you explain yourself to our dominus?'

Mila pulled Dulcia close, hugging her. 'When we are free, we will explain ourselves to no one,' she whispered into her sister's hair. Arms went around her, holding tightly.

'Dulcia, are you out here?'

Mila stiffened at the sound of her mother's voice. 'Quickly now, go to her before she comes looking for you.'

'She will ask where you are. What shall I say?'

Mila gave her a gentle shove. 'Tell her I have a lover.'

'She will never believe that. Every boy you know is an opponent.'

'Dulcia?'

Tertia wandered out into the garden. Mila gave her sister a much harder shove before sprinting to the wall, scurrying up the thick vines and swinging her legs over the top. She dropped to the paved street below just as her mother's voice reached her.

'Mila!' Tertia called from the other side of the wall.

It was too late. She was already jogging away from the house.

IT WAS the exact type of spectacle that Remus tried to avoid. A small, hastily constructed arena filled with desperate men. He looked around the scraggly crowd in their threadbare tunics and coarse togas, faces red from drinking too much posca. He turned to his friend, sitting on the bench beside him. 'Tell me again why we come to these events?'

'Oh, stop complaining,' Felix replied, eyes on the entrance. 'You know as well as I that Brutus likes to buy the best men before they realise their worth.'

He knew, he just needed reminding if he was to endure an evening of amateur fighting. 'I feel as if the seating is going to collapse beneath us at any moment. My feet bounce every time someone takes a seat near us.'

'I will have to take your word for it,' Felix replied. He glanced down at his own feet, which sat a foot off the floor. 'Mine do not reach that far.'

'That explains your calm demeanour right now.'

It was a far cry from the arenas they were used to. Remus would have preferred to spend his evening at the tavern, or sleeping, or sleeping with a girl he met at the tavern. But what Brutus Julius wanted, Brutus Julius received. One of the necessities of a good gladiator school was good fighters—and good fighters had a tendency to die. Ludus Magnus had held its reputation as Rome's best school thanks to a long line of highly skilled gladiators that history would remember. One of those was Remus's own father, who had died at the hands of the very gladiator Remus killed eight years later during his last fight in the arena. It was the fight that had earned him his freedom. Instead of fleeing the city, he had remained as a trainer, preparing the younger men who found their way to Ludus Magnus, hopeful of freedom or fame.

The bench seats were filling up, and the growing noise combined with the stifling air made Remus more uncomfortable. 'I will be back in a moment,' he said, standing.

Felix nodded, knowing him well enough to not bother asking where he was going. Remus excused himself as he passed the spectators seated on the same bench and descended the timber steps towards the entrance, where he would be able to slip out for some much-needed air.

'Remus Latinius?' came a voice. He turned to see Gallus Minidius, the games' sponsor, coming towards him. 'Thought I had seen a ghost for a moment. I should have known you would be sniffing about the place.' He took hold of Remus's arm, looking past him. 'Is Felix with you?'

'Hiding inside, ready to poach the valuable ones.'

'Sounds about right.'

Remus examined Gallus's fine toga. 'Business is good, then?'

'Very good,' Gallus replied. 'I open most evenings now.'

Remus looked behind him. 'One would think people would tire of it all.'

A smile pulled at Gallus's mouth. 'Judging by your tone, one might assume you are becoming cynical.' He looked past him. 'Where are you going?'

'Need some air.'

Gallus scrunched his nose up. 'Yes, it gets rather stuffy.'

'That's an understatement.' It smelled like every animal in Rome had gone there to die.

'Yes, well, make sure you come back.'

Remus nodded, patting the man's arm before stepping out into the grey light. Going to stand in the shadows, just out of reach of the torchlight, he leaned against one of the support beams, conscious of his weight against it. As he watched Rome's poorest citizens arrive, eyes lit with excitement at what awaited them inside, he felt a familiar ache of discontent. It was not a logical feeling. He had what every man born into slavery wanted—freedom. And yet it felt as though his life were still not his own.

Taking a lungful of air, preparing to return inside where the smell of garbage, sweat, and human waste seemed to be tenfold to the rest of the city, he glanced behind to ensure the beam remained in place, then headed for the entrance. It was then he noticed a brunette woman standing at the gate, speaking with Gallus. She was looking past him into the arena, gesturing as she tried to explain herself.

Curious, and in no hurry to return inside, Remus stopped to watch the exchange. Judging by her simple braid and *stola*, he suspected she had become separated from her dominus and was being refused entry. She was a pretty thing, despite her scowl and unpainted face, the kind that made Remus think perhaps he did have a type after all. He stepped closer to listen, remaining in the shadows so as to not draw attention.

'Even if I were to agree, there is no one for you to fight,' Gallus said, crossing his arms over his inflated chest.

She seemed in no way intimidated by their difference in height, lifting her face to meet his gaze. 'I can fight anybody. It does not have to be another woman. A man, perhaps.' She bit down on her lip, realising her mistake. 'A smaller man, preferably.'

Remus smiled to himself. His eyes went to the swords flashing beneath her shawl every time she moved, likely stolen. So she wanted to be a gladiator. He was reminded of the woman they had recruited from a brothel after watching her beat a man who refused her payment. To this day she was still one of their best fighters.

Gallus narrowed his eyes and snatched her wrist. 'Does your dominus know you are here?'

That silenced her.

'I am here,' came an out-of-breath voice.

Remus's gaze shifted to the approaching man. Tall, sandy hair, strong jaw and handsome face—the kind that had never seen battle, but women loved all the same. His white toga was a startling contrast to the people he stood with.

Gallus glared at the girl before letting her go. She immediately stepped back. Extending a hand, Gallus said, 'Nerva Papias. Good evening to you. I feared the girl had come without your knowledge.'

Nerva glanced at her, struggling to disguise his annoyance. 'Mila would not dream of such a thing, for the punishment would be harsh.' The words came out through gritted teeth.

Mila. Remus let the name replay in his mind.

Gallus looked between them. 'She says she is here to fight.'

Nerva's eyebrows shot up, his annoyance dissolving into amusement.

'Only if that is your wish,' Mila replied, her hands brushing the handles of her swords.

Nerva shook his head and placed his hands on his hip. He stared at the ground as he thought while she shifted nervously next to him. 'You know, I think it might be a good idea to let her fight.'

Gallus seemed surprised. 'As I explained to her already, without notice, I don't have a suitable opponent.'

'What about an unsuitable one?' Nerva said, crossing

his arms again. 'A big retiarius with a trident and net, perhaps?'

Mila's face fell. 'My dominus is joking, of course.'

'You are not selling yourself very well,' Nerva said, his tone blunt and teasing.

Remus should have just continued past them and returned to his seat, but there was something endearing about her tenacity, and he suspected her dominus was keen to teach her a lesson, so he stepped out from the shadows and joined them. 'Gallus,' he said, placing a hand on the man's shoulder. 'What trouble has found you now?'

Gallus looked between the men, seemingly unsure. 'May I introduce Nerva Papias, son of Rufus Papias.'

The name was familiar. Remus watched as the girl stepped back from the men, her unblinking gaze on him.

'This is Remus Latinius. Remus used to—'

'I know who you are,' Nerva said, grinning. 'I watched you fight some years back. It was the only time in my life I considered becoming a gladiator.'

'Your father must have been thrilled, a fine educated man like yourself showing interest in the arena.'

Nerva laughed. The slave girl continued to watch him. Remus was used to women's attention, slave or otherwise, but he could tell she was not admiring him—she was assessing him.

'I believe he was the only spectator wishing you dead, so I might be put off the sport forever,' Nerva said.

Remus gave a small smile. 'He probably wasn't the only one. I can think of at least one more.' His gaze shifted to the girl, and her brown eyes narrowed on him. 'I couldn't help but overhear your dilemma. I might have a solution.' His eyes returned to the men. 'What if Felix gave the girl a workout?'

'Felix?' Nerva asked.

'Do not worry, he is only half a man,' Gallus said. 'But the dwarf can fight, and the crowd love him.'

'I will do it,' Mila agreed.

Everyone turned to look at her. Nerva cleared his throat.

'Are you sure you do not want someone bigger?'

She looked down. Remus could not tell if it was a sign of respect or if she was hiding a smile.

'Yes, I am sure,' she replied.

Nerva turned back to Remus. 'Would your friend be willing?'

'I can make it worth his while,' Gallus said, his own excitement growing.

'He's easily persuaded, and now I'm curious about whether the girl has any skill,' Remus said, looking at Mila. She raised her eyes to him, her expression giving nothing away. She certainly had a gladiator's stare. 'Leave your swords with your dominus. I'll have Felix meet you inside.'

Mila undid her belt and handed the weapons to Nerva, careful not to meet his stern gaze.

'Thank you,' she said.

'Don't thank him yet,' Remus warned. 'Felix won't care that you're a woman if you come at him with a sword.'

Mila stared up at him. 'That suits me fine. I am not in the habit of fighting gentlemen.' She turned and followed after Gallus, disappearing through a small door beneath the seating.

'Shall we break the news to your friend?' Nerva asked, gesturing inside.

Remus watched the door Mila had exited through for a moment. 'After you.'

CHAPTER 3

Mila had been ready for anything, except Nerva showing up. It was likely her sister had gone to him, worried about her. Now if anything went wrong, she was responsible for two people getting into trouble.

She followed Gallus through the dark passage, support beams appearing inches from her face and tripping her feet. Pounding sounded overhead as the arena continued to fill up. Her mind wandered to Remus, still suspicious of his willingness to help. She hoped she had done the right thing in accepting it. She knew Remus's type: more muscle than sense, conceited to no end. But there was something else about him.

Though perhaps he was more than a pair of blue eyes who made women swoon. She had noticed the silver scars beneath his trimmed beard, the one above his ear, the irregular shape of his nose which suggested it had been broken more than once. Yet none of those things took away from how handsome he was—as far as gladiators went. He was not insanely broad-shouldered like some, but had a good cover of muscle visible beneath his tunic. Perhaps he had relied on speed, as she did.

Blinking against the dark, she realised her evaluation of him had moved past the point of character assessment.

She wiped her hands on her clothes, the first sign of nerves, and kept her eyes on Gallus so she would not lose sight of him in the dark. A door swung open and they stepped into a torch-lit room filled with men. Not just men —gladiators. They turned to see who had entered, quickly losing interest in the slave girl. There were six fighters, three pairs, all in shackles.

'Wait here,' Gallus said, pointing a sharp finger at the ground between them.

A short while later, he returned with the dwarf. Upon entering, Felix stopped and looked around the room with disdain before his bored gaze settled on Mila.

Gallus gestured to her. 'That is her,' he said, in case Felix could not figure it out from the fact that she was the only woman in the room. 'The two of you will go on after the first battle.' He sniffed and called to her. 'Name?'

She was still studying the muscled dwarf. 'Mila.'

Gallus rolled his eyes to the heavens. '*Arena* name?'

'Oh.' She thought for a moment. 'What about Spes?'

Felix walked towards her, frowning. 'Spes? The goddess of hope? You are a slave girl fighting a dwarf with a wooden sword. It is hardly inspiring.'

Her eyebrows shot up, surprised by his voice. He sounded more like a nobleman than a gladiator. Not that she had ever met a real gladiator before Remus. 'Fair enough. What name would you give me?'

He let out a noisy breath. 'What about Nanus Slayer.'

She suppressed a smile. 'Dwarf slayer?'

His shoulder lifted in a shrug. 'It will make them laugh. People expect to laugh when I enter the arena.'

Gallus patted Felix's shoulder the way one did a goat

after taking milk from it, then disappeared back through the door.

Mila glanced at the bare-chested men seated on the benches, suddenly grateful she was fighting Felix. He began stripping down to his loincloth. Despite only reaching her stomach, he was muscled to the point of ridiculous, and she felt her confidence wane.

'Do not fret,' he said, taking in her expression. 'They are wooden swords, and I never hit a lady in the face.'

She did not know whether it was a joke. 'I should probably warn you that I will not hesitate to hit *you* in the face.'

He studied her for a moment. 'Why do you want to do this?'

She swallowed. 'For the coin.'

'Pfft. Gallus is as tight as a mule's arse. You would have been better off placing a bet.'

'Gambling is illegal.'

He let out a long whistle. 'Lectured by a slave. That is a first for me.'

She stiffened.

Felix walked to the bench and picked up the weapons, studying them. 'I assume you can actually fight,' he asked, turning and waiting for her answer.

She lifted her chin. 'Rather well, I have been told.'

There was amusement in his eyes. 'And who told you that?'

'The men I beat.'

His lips turned up. 'What are you wearing under that dress?'

Her arms instinctively wrapped her middle. She knew most female gladiators fought wearing nothing more than a loincloth and shield. 'I am keeping my breast cloth on.'

His expression did not change. 'The men will complain.'

'Let them complain. I am here to fight. If it is breasts

they want to see, they can visit one of the many brothels in the region.'

Another tug at the corner of his mouth. 'Very well, dwarf slayer. Now off with the rest of your clothes.'

She glanced at the other men who were now watching her. Shrugging off her shawl, she slipped her stola down to her feet and lifted her tunic over her head. She did not hesitate or cover her body with her hands; there was no point in being self-conscious in front of a handful of men before stepping out in front of an amphitheatre filled with them.

Felix appraised her, unaffected by what he saw. 'You are going to need a lot more muscle on you if you are planning on being a gladiator.'

She looked down at her arms, holding them out as she did so. 'You might be right. How long did it take you to get to that size?'

'That size?'

Her cheeks flushed. 'I was referring to your… width.'

A smile flickered. 'I knew what you meant. When you are as short as me, you have to compensate.'

'I suspect it is the same if you are a woman.'

They looked at one another for a moment.

Gallus entered the room with two men in tow. 'Let us move,' he said, signalling to two slaves. They stood and walked ahead of the men. The room went silent again.

'What is your weapon of choice?' Felix asked, gesturing to the bench.

She went to stand next to him, ignoring the stares of the other men. 'I am a dimachaerus.'

He snorted. 'Two swords? Women usually fight with a shield.'

'I fight better with two swords.'

He shook his head. 'Two swords it is.'

THE SCREECH of weapons did not invoke the same feelings in Remus as it did in other spectators. It was a sound he had heard every day of his life for the past twenty-five years. It was the sound of the everyday.

Two men were led out into the arena, not to die but to entertain. Though death was always a possibility if the injuries sustained were bad enough. New recruits were problematic, particularly if they were captured soldiers. Remus had seen them kill their opponents during training with one blow to the head. They only knew how to fight like soldiers, quick and clean, as they would have on the battlefield. A paying spectator would be most disappointed with a fight to the death lasting only a few moments.

'They must be saving the best for last,' Nerva said, glancing across at Remus. The first fight had ended with one of the men knocked unconscious while distracted by the crowd.

Remus leaned his elbows on his knees, smiling. 'They'll have come straight from the market. There's every chance they're all terrible.'

The victor exited to mild applause. Two men arrived, rolling the fallen man onto a long piece of wood and carrying him off.

'Where'd the girl learn to fight?' Remus asked.

Nerva leaned forwards also, eyes on the gate where Mila would enter. 'I taught her. I suppose I wanted someone to practice with. I do not have any living brothers.' He shook his head. 'I had no idea she would get such crazy ideas from it. If my father knew...'

Remus studied him, trying to figure out why he would be taking risks for an insubordinate slave. He glanced down at the swords sitting between Nerva's feet. 'She should not be walking the streets carrying weapons,' he said, nodding towards them. 'If she is caught…'

Nerva glanced down. 'Yes, I am beginning to regret giving them to her. They are blunt, but I cannot imagine the watch will care about that. They already live in fear of slaves rising up against them.'

Before Remus could reply, the gates opened and the crowd fell quiet. Gallus entered the arena, introducing Felix under his fighting name, Minui Spiculus, a joke that the crowd ate up, and then Mila as Nanus Slayer, after which the entire crowd burst out in laughter, including Nerva.

'The teasing will be relentless when we leave here,' he said.

Remus watched her enter the small arena behind Felix, her breasts covered. She held two short wooden swords. Remus's first thought was she needed a shield. He shifted in his seat, glancing at Nerva, who seemed relaxed. Mila drew a long breath as she took in her surroundings, reading the reaction of the crowd. Her gaze landed on Nerva and he nodded, a small gesture of encouragement. When her eyes went to Remus, she swallowed, and he saw that she was nervous. She turned away to watch Felix as he strolled casually around the perimeter, basking in the cheers and attention.

'Bare your breasts!' shouted the man next to Remus, cupping his hands around his mouth so his words would carry.

Remus saw Mila glance at the man. He had the urge to elbow him in the neck and watch him choke for a moment. Instead, he focused on Mila, finding himself unable to look away. His gaze travelled along her lean arms, down her firm legs. Her braid slipped over her shoulder as she crouched, face set with concentration. He straightened in his seat, holding on to the bench.

Felix was not ready to fight. He kept turning away from her, doing another lap of the arena, arms outstretched as though he were already their victor. Men cheered and laughed, and he pumped his swords at them so the cheering increased and the laughter died. Only once he had won the crowd over did he make his way over to Mila, swinging his swords to show off. Even Remus was losing patience.

'He is very entertaining,' Nerva said.

'He's a natural performer,' Remus replied, crossing his arms. He watched as Mila tired of the self-indulgent display, throwing one of her swords at his and knocking it from his hand. 'Was that a fluke?' he asked, glancing at Nerva.

He shook his head. 'No.'

Felix turned to her, a wry smile on his face.

'Are you done?' she called to him, feigning boredom.

He picked up his sword and stepped in front of the one she had thrown at him. 'Now you are down one sword.'

The crowd laughed, and she looked about. 'You think I cannot pick up my sword?'

'Not when it is behind me.' He spoke loudly so the crowd could enjoy the banter.

There was another wave of laughter.

She walked towards him, twisting her sword in her hand. 'Now that I have your attention.' She lurched forwards, the blow landing against one sword and immediately moving to block the second. They looked at one another, their expressions playful.

He spun around, his swords coming at her from different heights. Mila stopped the lower one with her foot and, gripping her weapon with both hands, blocked the other. Before Felix could make another move, she pushed him backwards with her foot and dove forwards into the sand, rolling once and snatching her second sword. The crowd cheered as she leapt to her feet, but there was no time to savour the moment as Felix lunged, swinging at her ankles. She jumped, and as her feet left the ground, she brought one sword down. He was ahead of her, blocking it and striking her side.

The sound she emitted made Remus flinch. Nerva must have noticed, because he turned to him. 'She is tougher than she looks.'

Felix stepped in to finish the job, but she whirled on him, her swords striking him from different angles. His weapon struck her arm and she yelped like a dog kicked.

The pair circled one another for a moment before clashing once again. That time, Felix knocked a sword from her hand. It should have been over in one more strike, but Mila dodged the next blow and rolled three times to snatch the fallen sword once again.

'She's good,' Remus said, not realising he had spoken the words aloud.

Nerva nodded, eyes remaining on her. 'She is stubborn, that is for sure.'

Some of the spectators were on their feet, shouting and waving fists. Mila lurched forwards again, trapping Felix's swords with her own when he went to strike. His foot went up to kick her but she caught it between her ribs and elbow, yanking it hard so he fell on his back. Her foot pressed down on his wrist, the other going behind her for balance. When Felix swung his other sword, she smashed it from his hand and pressed a wooden blade to his neck. They stared at one another, panting and trembling from their efforts.

Everyone stood, cheering her. She waited for Felix to drop the other sword before removing her foot from his arm and stepping back. Remus was torn between watching her and the reaction of the crowd.

'Crazy girl,' Nerva said, standing to applaud her also.

Remus took his time getting to his feet, bringing his hands together in a slow clap. He watched as she dropped her swords on the ground before extending a hand to Felix. She made no big display of her win, no victory pose. The dwarf glanced at her hand before taking it and pulling himself to his feet. Keeping hold of her, he lifted her arm as high as he could get it, encouraging the crowd to applaud her. She suppressed a smile as she looked around. Her gaze landed briefly on Remus before moving to Nerva. She gave him a cocky nod.

'What now?' Remus asked.

Nerva glanced at him. 'Now?' He frowned. 'Now I pray she sees sense before this all goes terribly wrong.'

CHAPTER 4

It was after midnight when they weaved through the alleyways of region four. Mila's shawl wrapped her body and head as she walked next to Nerva, eyes searching the dark nooks, her swords concealed. They were supposed to be a civilised society.

'Did you recognise Remus before he was introduced?' Mila asked, unable to contain her curiosity about the man any longer.

'He seemed familiar. I certainly did not need a family name.' He glanced at her. 'Why do you ask? Because he is handsome?'

She kept her eyes ahead. 'I can see how some might find him handsome.'

Nerva smiled. 'Every woman who lays eyes on him, noble or otherwise, believes Remus Latinius was hand-sculpted by the gods.'

'One of the vain gods, perhaps.'

He shook his head. 'If you are trying to deflect the attention from you, it will not work. You are lucky Dulcia came to me. What do you think would have happened if I had not shown up?'

'I would have returned home.'

'You would likely have been escorted to the front door by one of Gallus's men. It was careless and selfish.'

'Selfish?'

He stepped around a suspicious pool of liquid and she moved with him. 'Yes. Do you ever stop to think how your sister would cope with you gone? We all know you would be fine, but Dulcia depends on you. And your poor mother…'

She noticed he did not mention himself in the list of people affected by her hypothetical sale. Opening her hand, she showed him the five denarii she had earned. 'It would take a month to earn this on the streets. This is from one fight.'

He reached out, closing her hand. 'Do not wave it around. It is late, and you are easy prey.'

She held the coins against her chest. 'I am not easy prey.'

He looked about. 'Those men do not know that.'

She smiled. 'You know I will protect you.'

He let out a single laugh. 'Very comforting.' His eyes went up, checking the windows above them.

They walked in silence for a while, and Mila found her thoughts returning to Remus.

'You know, I remember that day a few years back, when you returned from the games. You told me you wanted to be a centurion, lead armies into foreign lands.'

He glanced at her. 'I was young and foolish.'

'Not that young,' she replied, leaving off the foolish. 'You have never once told me you want to be a senator.'

'What does it matter what I want? I do as I am told. You should try it some time.'

They rounded a corner into another alleyway.

'You gave me a blow-by-blow account of that fight.'

He checked behind them. 'Are we still talking about Remus?'

'I am talking about *you*.'

'You are talking about me talking about Remus.' He turned to study her. 'I knew you would take notice of men eventually, and I should not be surprised that the first man to capture your attention is a gladiator.'

Nerva had spent the last seven years warning her of the dangers of men, constantly reminding her that they could not be trusted, frightening her with stories of rape. She suspected the need for a sparring partner was not the only reason he had taught her to fight. He wanted her to be able to protect herself.

'They prey on virtuous girls,' he had told her.

Mila was not one to live in fear, so at age fifteen, she had taken matters into her own hands. She went to see a stablehand who she had fought on the streets many times, asking him to take care of the issue. He had stood in front of her, leaning on his pitchfork, a look of confusion on his face.

'You want to be rid of your… virtue?' He was unsure if he had heard right.

She had shrugged. 'I would prefer to give it away to a friend than have it snatched away by a stranger I failed to fight off.' Her virginity was not worth much as a slave, but the thought of it being taken without her permission did not sit well with her. While Rufus Papias had never claimed her as a daughter, every man in the household knew she was off limits. However, that did not help her when she left the house.

The boy had taken her by the hand and led her to a clean stall, doing as she had asked. She had followed his lead, and when it was done, had thanked him. The spent boy had stood, quivering, and awkwardly wished her a good day before she left. She had never mentioned the event to anyone.

A woman called to them as they passed a narrow alley, pulling Mila from her thoughts. She glanced at the woman in her red toga and quickened her pace.

'You cannot just sneak off and fight whenever you feel like it,' Nerva said, his tone serious. 'I will pay you five denarii to stay at home.'

'I am not taking your money. When I go to your father one day to buy my freedom, I cannot have him wondering if the money is in fact already his.'

Nerva did not argue the point.

'If I could just fight at some of the bigger arenas, I would have the amount I need in no time.'

He shook his head. 'Well you cannot. It is too risky. Father attends many of those events, and he would recognise you at once.'

'Not if I am wearing a helmet.'

He breathed hard through his nose. 'I always knew you would do something crazy like this. I blame myself for indulging you with stories of Mevia and her beast fighting. Perhaps it is not freedom you seek but fame.'

'You are wrong. Once I am free, I will never enter the arena again. It just happens to be the only skill I have to get where I want.'

He scoffed. 'Nonsense. You could earn your freedom via loyal service if you had any patience at all.'

'Loyal service?' she asked, turning her body to him as she continued to walk. 'Do you know how many years I would have to serve for that? I would prefer to leave while I still have use of my legs and a few teeth, if it is all the same to you.'

The scrape of ceramic against a windowsill sounded overhead and Mila took hold of Nerva, pulling him back just in time. Waste splashed onto the street in front of them. They covered their mouths and noses against the smell.

Nerva looked up, removed his hand, and shouted, 'People are walking down here!' An older woman peered sheepishly out of the window. 'Yes! I see you! Take it to the latrine, you lazy wench!'

A laugh escaped Mila and she grabbed a handful of toga, pulling him around the mess and away from the house.

They broke into a jog, Mila keeping her shawl over her head as she did so. Only when they reached the steps of the house did they stop to catch their breath, both sweating but thoroughly enjoying a few moments of something resembling their childhood. In those rare moments, they could be real siblings.

'Thank you for tonight,' she said. 'I promise I will not do that again without speaking to you first.'

He was leaning on his knees, panting. 'If you do, I will sell you myself.'

She glanced at the door, which remained closed to them. 'Just to be clear, that does not include the street fighting, does it?'

'Mila.'

'It is harmless fun between children.'

He stood and took hold of her shoulders. 'You are in your nineteenth year. You are not a child anymore.' He released his grip on her. 'Anyway, such amounts will seem insignificant now that you have tasted sand.'

A cart came towards them and they moved onto the bottom step to get out of its way. The driver bounced in the seat, a cushion tucked beneath his buttocks. In the back were cabbages and a crate packed so tightly with chickens that wings sprouted from the gaps.

'I wish I could give you what you want—the coin, the freedom.'

She felt pure affection for him in that moment. 'You need all the coin you have to keep those fancy horses hidden from your father.'

He studied her. 'What do you need from me, then?'

She smiled. 'One fight, in a proper arena.'

'One fight will not earn all that you need.'

She bit down on her top lip before speaking. 'It might if I give you everything I have saved so far and you take it to Gallus.'

He narrowed his eyes. 'You want me to gamble all of your money?'

Her eyes went to the door and she leaned forwards. 'It is a sure win.'

He shook his head, staring at her as though she had completely lost her mind. 'You would be fighting trained gladiators.'

She shrugged. 'I am trained.'

'No, you are not.'

She looked insulted. 'I fight almost every day.'

'One, you should not be telling me that, and two, that is not training, that is practising with equally untrained boys.'

She crossed her arms. 'You just said we were not children anymore.'

'I take it back. You are behaving like one right now.' He turned to leave and she reached for his arm.

'Please,' she said. He turned back, his patience gone. 'One fight.'

His hard expression turned to resignation. 'I will look into it.' When she smiled, he raised a hand. 'I am not saying yes, I am saying I will make some enquiries and see what is possible. If I find out you have so much as touched your swords in the meantime, I will forget the whole thing.'

Her expression fell. 'I will need to practice if I am to win.'

'Then you will do so with me and stay off the streets. Are we clear?'

She nodded. 'We are clear.'

CHAPTER 5

If there was one thing Mila dreaded, it was Balbina getting sick. Whenever her domina's body slave became ill, Aquila Papias would send the woman off to bed for the day.

What might appear to be a kind gesture was in fact one borne of fear. After burying all of her children except Nerva, Aquila feared even the most common of colds. Because their domina behaved like she was incapable of dressing herself, or even reaching for a cup, it meant such tasks then fell to Mila. There were few slaves the woman trusted with the task of being her hands, and unfortunately she was one of them. That did not mean she liked Mila—quite the opposite—but nineteen years under the same roof had gotten them to the point of mutual tolerance when absolutely necessary. Aquila was hardly going to request Tertia, her husband's harlot, to follow her, dress her. The only reason living in the same house had worked for so long was due to the fact that they existed separately within it.

'Why do I have to do it?' Mila whined at her mother.

Tertia was forced to have the same conversation with

her daughter she had every time Balbina took to her bed. 'You know why.'

'Dulcia is old enough now.'

They were standing in the laundry, voices low, while Tertia lay a garment flat, inspecting its hem. 'Your sister all but cowers in her presence.'

'Can you blame her? She threw a cup at me last week because the baker did not have the bread she wanted. Throw a cup at *his* head.'

'You told me the cup missed you.'

Mila leaned on the bench, immediately shooed back by her mother. 'The point is that she was aiming for me.'

Tertia let out an exhausted breath, looking up at her daughter. It was late in the afternoon, and she had to get the dress ready for the dinner party Aquila and Rufus were attending that evening. 'Help her dress, accompany her to the dinner and pour her wine. It is rather simple, and you seem to have plenty of free time.'

Mila rested a hand on her hip. 'What do you mean I have plenty of time? Am I to be ridiculed for finishing my chores in half the time it takes others?'

Tertia knew better than to argue with her daughter when she was in a mood. 'Balbina will be better by morning.'

Shaking her head, Mila replied, 'Better or not, I will drag that woman from her bed if she does not rise tomorrow and relieve me of my suffering.'

Her mother reached up, tucking loose hair behind Mila's ear. 'Go and fix yourself up, and put something clean on. You are representing the household tonight. It will not do to have you looking like a—'

'Slave?'

Tertia's mouth pinched with disapproval. 'You might be interested to know there will be a gladiator display this evening.' She turned back to the dress.

Mila eyed her mother suspiciously. 'That is awfully convenient. You never mentioned it before.'

'Well I am mentioning it now.' She sifted through reels of cotton. 'I am safe to do so now that Nerva has put an end to your indiscretions.'

Mila raised her eyebrows. 'Indiscretions? Mother, you make me sound like a common whore.'

Tertia turned to her daughter, pulling her close and kissing both cheeks. 'I love you, but there is a fire in you that terrifies me. Do not mess up your life chasing things you do not understand.'

Mila stared at her mother. 'Why does everyone make such a big ordeal of a few fights.'

'A few? That is laughable.'

'Even upper-class women are taking to the arena nowadays, and they have much more to lose.'

Tetra squeezed her daughter's hands. 'Be obedient and meek this evening and you will be fine. Off you go.' She turned her daughter towards the door and gave her a push.

'Perhaps they will need an extra gladiator for the display,' Mila called over her shoulder.

Her mother shook her head, eyes returning to the dress. 'Go.'

THE HOUSE BELONGED to Jovian Fadius and his wife, Prisca. Jovian had recently joined the senate and was keen to show off his new status to his peers. One way to do this was an elaborate dinner party. The second way was to serve up *tetrapharmacum* at the dinner party, a dish both expensive and complex. The four key ingredients were pheasant, wild boar, ham in pastry and sow's udders. The problem was, in order to get udders large enough to be stuffed with the other ingredients, the sow needed to be suckling piglets, and finding someone willing to part with a breeding sow before her piglets had even weaned was no easy feat.

Mila stood against the wall, staring at the tray brought out to noises of appreciation. Even Aquila joined in the fuss, despite the fact that she did not care for the dish. All the food was laid out on the table. Mila knew most of it would return to the kitchen because, as always with these occasions, there was far too much of it.

'Afterwards, we shall move out to the garden for a special treat,' Prisca said. She gestured for a servant to cut the *tetrapharmacum*, a ritual where the udder was slit open so the other ingredients tumbled out.

'What a treat,' Aquila said to her host. She brushed imaginary lint off her new garment. Her face was painted, eyes darkened, her auburn hair half up and glossy. If she were anyone else, Mila might have thought her pretty.

A servant girl carried the tray around to each guest, attentive to their fussy requests. Once everyone was settled with food, then came the clicking of fingers, waving of hands, and tapping of cups, causing servants to arrive from all directions to tend their domini.

'What a pretty girl,' Prisca said to Aquila, as Mila stepped up to the table to remove her domina's shawl.

Aquila wore the same frozen smile she always wore when someone paid the girls a compliment. She did not like to be reminded that the daughters born of her husband's indiscretion were as beautiful as the woman who birthed them. 'She is a hard worker' was all she said on the subject.

'Good help is not easy to come by,' Prisca replied, but there was not much sincerity behind the words.

Aquila nodded with enthusiasm. 'Is it just me, or does it feel like slaves have more rights than their domini nowadays?'

'We have Emperor Nero to blame for that,' one of the men chimed in.

Mila stepped back from the table and returned to the wall, aware of her dominus's gaze on her. A more naive, younger her would have hoped Rufus might speak up in defence of his slaves, given he fathered two of them, but she knew better. The best she could hope for was his silence.

Prisca did not seem interested in continuing the conversation, emptying her cup and giving it a gentle wave. A servant stepped forwards to fill it again.

More food was brought out, and Mila felt her own stomach groan as new scents filled the room—fish, honey cakes and, her favourite, fruit tarts. She kept her eyes on the ground in front of her, wondering when she would be permitted to escape to the kitchen and eat something. There was every chance she would not eat until late that night after her domina was tucked away in bed, her belly full.

Jovian stood, a grand gesture that commanded the attention of the room. 'Fill your cups, then let us move out into the garden.'

Prisca seemed to perk up at the suggestion. She was the first to stand.

Mila stepped up to the table and ladled the watered-down wine into her domina's cup.

'The air is cooling. I will need my palla,' Aquila said, standing.

Mila fetched the shawl and draped it over her domina's shoulders before stepping out of the way. The servants followed the slow-moving guests out into the large garden where torches burned, casting light across a paved area which would act as the arena for their entertainment. Despite the company, Mila could not stop the stir of excitement as she stepped back into the shadows to watch.

'Remus!' Prisca cried, looking far more alive than she had moments earlier. 'Look at you. You are as fit as you were when we watched you at the Flavian Amphitheatre last year.'

Mila saw Aquila exchange a knowing look with one of the other guests, but her eyes quickly returned to Remus Latinius, who strolled over to the gushing host.

'Lady Prisca,' he said, giving a slight bow. 'That was *four* years ago, and yet you haven't aged a bit.'

It was a shallow compliment. No doubt part of the performance.

Prisca waved a modest hand. 'I am an old bat in comparison to the young beauties I have seen hanging from your arm.' Her tone was a pitch higher suddenly.

'My wife adores the games,' Jovian said, covering the awkward silence that followed. 'If she were a pleb or a slave, she might have fought herself.'

Light laughter tinkled in the small area at the same moment Remus spotted Mila in the shadows. A flash of recognition passed over his face, replaced by a look of question. She looked away, but not down. There was no way she was going to let him think she was intimidated by him.

Entertainers were sourced from gladiator schools throughout Rome, and yet it had never occurred to Mila that Remus might be there. It seemed beneath him. He was Remus Latinius, undefeated in the arena.

'Tell me it is you fighting this evening,' asked one of the men. 'It would be such an honour.'

Rufus cleared his throat before speaking. 'Yes, I took my son to watch your final fight. Afterwards, Nerva spoke of nothing else.'

'What boy does not dream of being Remus Latinius?' Prisca said. Up went her cup.

'I'm glad I won, if only for your entertainment,' Remus said to Rufus.

Prisca laughed. 'You won *every* battle. That is why you stand before us a freed man.'

There were hints of bitterness in her tone.

Remus glanced at Mila but did not let his gaze linger. 'I've two excellent fighters for you tonight. If you'll all be kind enough to remain in your seats during the performance, there is less chance of someone losing an arm.'

'What a tease you are,' Aquila said, 'parading yourself before us and then serving up mere slaves.'

Despite his smile, Mila saw the change in Remus's expression. He had been a mere slave once.

'I fought enough in my younger years to last a lifetime. Now I'm forced to leave the fighting to the younger men.'

'Forced by whom?' Prisca asked. 'You speak as if you are an old man. I happen to know for a fact that you are only twenty and five.'

'That *is* old for a gladiator,' laughed one of the guests. 'The fact that he stands here alive at all is a miracle.'

'Yes, yes,' Jovian said, shifting in his chair. 'Enough embarrassing the man. As he is no longer a slave of Rome, we cannot force him. We are a civilised people, are we not? Now then, tell us, will this be a battle to the death?'

All the guests laughed, and Prisca tutted.

'What a gruesome dinner party that would be,' Aquila said.

'Not one guest here would forget it,' Prisca replied.

More laughter.

Mila ran her fingers along the wall, allowing herself another glance at Remus, surprised to find him looking back at her. She acknowledged him with a discreet nod, and he walked over to her. He did not say a word as he came to stand beside her, focused on the show that would soon begin. Mila straightened and folded her hands in front of her to keep them steady.

A drum, hidden among trees, beat slowly. Everyone fell silent, waiting. The beat quickened, matching the tempo of her heart. It was a performance in every aspect, building suspense amid the guests who searched the shadows, waiting for the men to appear. Finally two gladiators burst from the side, causing everyone to jump and then laugh at their own reactions. Swords and shields clashed, the noise deafening to those unfamiliar with the sound of warfare.

Mila studied the guest's faces. They were like children passing a dead mule on the street, repulsed and yet fascinated, unable to look away even if they wanted to.

She snuck a sideways glance at Remus, who leaned on the wall a polite distance from her.

'Which one is your domina?' he whispered, not looking at her.

She turned, nervous that Aquila would hear them talking. Thankfully the clang of swords meant no one was paying attention to what was going on behind them.

'Does she know you're sneaking about Rome with her son?' When she did not reply, he probed, 'I've been trying to figure out if Nerva is your lover.'

Her face screwed up in disgust. 'No.'

Remus looked at her, eyes lit with mischief. 'I'm guessing she isn't aware of your secret gladiator escapades.'

Another glance to check no one was listening. 'And I would prefer to keep it that way.'

He smiled, facing forwards again. 'I was wondering when I might run into you again.'

She hated how pleased she was by that comment. He had been thinking about her.

Before she could reply, Aquila glanced over her shoulder, waving her empty cup. Her gaze landed briefly on Remus before returning to the fight. Mila walked over to her, careful not to impede anyone's vision in the process. There was a small table next to the lounge with a jug of wine and a platter filled with colourful fruits. Mila picked up the jug and began to fill the cup held out to her.

Halfway through pouring, she heard Remus shout behind her, 'Down!' She looked up to see a sword spinning towards Aquila and knew there was no way the woman would move in time. Without thinking, she lifted the jug like a shield against the runaway sword. Of course, ceramic stood no chance against steel. While she did manage to stop the weapon from colliding with her domina's face, there was nothing she could do to stop the spray of shards and wine that covered both Aquila and herself, as well as the expensive fabric covering the lounge and one side of her dominus's robe, which her mother had bleached for the occasion.

The drums ceased and everyone went still, even the gladiators. Mila's stomach fell as she took in the sight before her: Aquila, sprayed red, with shards of ceramic peppered through her hair. From the moment her domina looked up, she knew she was not going to be praised for her quick reflexes.

Aquila shot up, slapping Mila's face with such force that they both lost their balance. It was much harder than usual due to the humiliation fuelling her foul mood.

'You stupid girl!'

The thing Mila hated most about being hit was not the pain but the fact that she had to take it without complaint or retaliation. She could easily grab the hand hurtling towards her, twist it at an angle that would make her domina cry out. But to what end? Instead, she took the blow and had the good sense to keep her gaze down afterwards.

Out of the corner of her eye, she saw Remus take a step towards her and then stop himself. Rufus did not move, knowing better than to get involved when there was an audience.

'Aquila,' Prisca sang. 'Do not beat the girl. You would have been complaining of more than a ruined dress had she not done something.'

Aquila looked about, as though suddenly aware of everybody watching. She straightened, attempting to calm herself.

Prisca waved two servants forwards. 'Find our guests some clothes and show them where they can get cleaned up,' she said to one, then turned to the other. 'Take the servant girl to the laundry and bring her something clean also.'

Mila did not raise her eyes to her domina, not trusting herself to hide what was in them. She felt Rufus watching her as she turned and followed the woman back inside. They walked through the house, not speaking, because anything they said would be heard by someone. That was how it worked in large households.

'Wait in here,' the woman instructed. 'Take off your clothes and I will bring some water for you to wash.'

Mila nodded and undid her belt, stepping out of her stola and slipping her tunic over her head. She rolled them into a ball and looked down to assess the damage to her undergarments. Just a few spots, but as luck would have it, her mother had been blessed with extraordinary stain removal skills.

The servant returned with clean garments, a towel and a basin of water.

'What is your name?' Mila asked, taking the items from her and placing them on the wooden bench top.

'Sabina.'

Mila smiled. 'Thank you, Sabina. I shall have everything laundered and returned to you as soon as possible.'

Sabina lingered. 'Your domina would have been very sorry had the weapon marked her face.'

Mila glanced at her and nodded. She knew better than to share her own thoughts with a stranger.

'I better go help with the clean-up,' Sabina said before leaving.

After she had gone, Mila cupped her hands in the water and brought it to her face, watching the liquid turn red from the wine as it passed through her fingers. She touched the cheek Aquila had struck. It was likely red, but probably would not bruise. It was nothing compared to the knocks she received when fighting, and yet the sting lingered for other reasons. Every time that woman struck her, it fanned the fire within her, the one her mother was afraid of. She placed her hands palm down on the bench and stared into the red water.

'You know, this is the second time I've seen you with your clothes off in a matter of weeks,' came a familiar voice.

She turned to see Remus leaning in the doorway, watching her. She did not give him the satisfaction of covering up; instead, she picked up the towel and dried her face and hands. 'That must be very distressing on your sensibilities. I know how fragile you gladiators can be.'

His grin widened, and he continued to watch as she dressed. Everything was too big, so she tried to disguise the problem with her belt.

'How's your face?' he asked, stepping into the room.

She continued to fasten the strap. 'Rosy, I imagine.'

He came to a stop in front of her and placed a finger under her chin, raising her face so he could inspect it.

The angle of her head made her feel short, and she realised as they stood close that she only came to his chest. His broad frame did not help matters either. She held her breath as his eyes moved over her face.

'You might have a mark tomorrow.' His hand fell away, and he stepped back from her.

She watched him. 'A slave with a marked face is a sign that all is right in the world.'

He laughed at that. 'Is that so?'

She took a step back as well, finding he was still too close. 'Reflections on earlier dinner conversation.' She looked past him to the door, conscious that she might be overheard.

'I think I should get my men out of here before they're accused of conspiring to kill.'

She could not stop the small smile that formed. 'That is probably wise.'

He tilted his head, studying her for a moment. 'I've figured it out. Nerva is your brother.'

'He is not my brother,' she said, much too fast.

He held up his hands. 'Then I'm sorry. Maybe it's chance that you share the same eye colour and handsome jaw as Rufus Papias.'

She narrowed her eyes. 'What do you mean handsome jaw?'

Satisfied with her reaction, he turned to leave and then stopped. 'Where will you be popping up next?'

She shrugged. 'Probably nowhere you would find yourself. I usually fight in alleyways. Though not the ones with thriving brothels you would be familiar with.'

He nodded his appreciation at her wit, eyes never leaving her. 'I probably shouldn't tell you this, but you're good. Not great, because you're untrained, but you are good.'

She lifted her chin. 'Thank you. That means a lot coming from a retired gladiator past his prime.'

Light danced in his eyes, and he continued to watch her for much longer than was polite. 'Good to see you again, Mila.'

Something in the way he said her name made her brain freeze up. She dug around for some intelligent words. 'I shall try to keep my clothes on next time we meet.'

And then that came out.

He winked at her before heading to the door. 'I wasn't complaining, by the way.' He left without so much as a glance behind him.

Mila gripped the bench and watched the empty doorway, suddenly aware of the heat in her cheeks and dampness of her palms. She turned back to the basin and splashed more water on her face, waiting for it all to pass.

CHAPTER 6

Squatting, Mila swept leaves in the garden while Nerva stood in the shade of the loggia. He watched her, all the while trying to extract information. She was not making it easy for him.

'I am still trying to understand what he was doing in the laundry.'

She glanced up, her hands continuing their work. 'I told you, he was being polite, seeing if I was all right.'

'Why? It is not as if the sword hit you in the face.'

She rolled her eyes. 'No, the *sword* did not hit me.'

He laughed at her sulky tone. 'I have seen you hit with far worse than my mother's hand, and I am not convinced you even felt it.'

'If you are referring to the time you punched me in the face with the hilt of your sword, then yes, that was far worse.'

Another laugh. 'If I recall correctly, you *fell* into the hilt of my sword. You cannot ask me to train you as though you are a man and then react like a girl.'

That time she stopped sweeping. 'My nose was bleeding, but did I complain?'

'You are complaining now.'

She stood. 'Perhaps Remus followed me into the laundry because he is a better man than you.'

Nerva crossed his arms, a smirk on his face. 'Or perhaps he fancies you.'

She felt colour rush to her cheeks. 'That is… ridiculous.'

He narrowed his eyes on her. 'Are you blushing? I do not believe I have ever seen you blush before. You must have it bad for the man.'

She threw the small broom at him at the same time Rufus stepped into view. A small gasp escaped her.

'What is going on here?' he asked, looking to Nerva for an explanation.

Mila swooped down to retrieve the broom laying at Nerva's feet. His smile was long gone.

'I was just asking Mila about the dinner party last night.'

'The one you were too busy to attend?'

Nerva cleared his throat. 'That would be the one.'

Rufus glanced at Mila, who stood behind her swept pile of debris. He was far more tolerant of her than he would be with any other slave, if only for the sake of her mother. He liked to keep her happy.

'As you were,' he said, gesturing to the broom.

'Yes, Erus.' She bowed her head and crouched, grateful for his turning a blind eye. She hated being struck in front of Nerva, the way he turned away, unable to watch. It always left her pride in tatters, despite there being no place for pride in her life. Not that Rufus took a hand to her very often.

She pretended not to listen to their conversation, noting Rufus's insistent tone as he laid out his son's social plans for the evening. Nerva nodded, despite the fact that he hated spending time with his father's political friends. The invitation was not optional.

Only once Rufus had left did Mila look up again.

Nerva let out a breath and leaned against a pillar. 'Do not fear. I will say nothing to Father of your gladiator love affair.'

She shook her head. 'Do you not have expensive horses to tend?'

He smiled and pushed off the pillar. As he turned, he noticed Dulcia standing behind him, waiting to speak with Mila. He strolled over to her.

'Make sure your sister does not jump the wall tonight,' he said as he passed her.

'She does not listen to me,' Dulcia replied.

Nerva stopped walking and gave her plait a gentle tug. 'Then we will have to toughen you up so you can stop her.'

Dulcia looked down, blushing. Once he had disappeared from sight, she went to her sister. Mila watched her, frowning at her timid frame. What would become of her if one day their dominus sold her to another household? She was neither strong nor confident, and judging by the duties and tasks she was given, everyone knew it.

'I am going to the market,' Dulcia said. 'Germana wants lemons.'

Germana had been the household's cook for more than twenty years. Due to that fact, and her much-sought-after culinary skills, she was given free rein over the other servants and often sent the girls on errands to fetch last-minute ingredients. They had once been forced to comb the city in search of quail despite an abundance of available chickens that would have sufficed.

Mila blew at the loose hair falling over her face. 'I went to the market this morning and she said nothing of lemons.'

'She is making a tart,' Dulcia said, as if that answered every possible question that might follow. 'And I thought I might stop at the temple to pray.'

Mila eyed her sister. 'All right. Let Mother know where you are going before you leave.'

Dulcia's hands were clasped in front of her and she did not move.

'What is the matter?'

Her sister hesitated before speaking. 'I thought you might come with me.'

Tilting her head, Mila replied, 'You are twelve, more than capable of buying lemons and praying alone.'

Dulcia nodded, chewing her bottom lip. 'I thought you might like the walk,' she lied.

Mila exhaled and glanced down at the leaves by her feet. 'Help me finish here and I will come with you.'

A smile spread across her sister's face, and she bounded forwards like an excited pup.

IT WAS mid-afternoon as they headed to the *macella,* the indoor market on the other side of the Caelian hill. The girls preferred to shop at the *nundinae,* which was closer, cheaper and fresher, but the street market only ran every ninth day, which meant they usually spent a great deal of time shopping elsewhere for ingredients.

The sun pounded down on them, and the heat from the pavement made their feet swell in their sandals. The market was at least quiet at that time of day, with all the sensible people having visited in the morning. All that remained was tired merchants, a few stray servants fetching last-minute dinner items and some wilted vegetables. When they finally found a vendor selling lemons, Dulcia paid with the coin Germana had given her. It was not uncommon for servants to pocket the occasional change given them, but as luck would have it, their cook knew the exact value of every available food item.

Lemons in hand, the girls stood for a moment in the shade across the street, working up to the long trek home. It was then that Mila spotted Remus walking down the road towards them. She went still at the sight of him, afraid any movement would draw his attention.

'What is the matter?' Dulcia asked, looking up at her sister with a confused expression.

'Nothing,' Mila whispered, ushering her in the other direction. She made the mistake of glancing back at Remus and found him staring at her. She froze, and then, feeling foolish, raised a hand in greeting. 'Go,' she said, giving her sister a shove.

Dulcia squeaked, objecting to the rough treatment.

Mila noticed that Remus had started to cross the street and was walking towards them. She took hold of Dulcia's arm to stop her, and her sister came to an abrupt halt.

'Are we going or staying?' Dulcia asked, exasperated. She followed Mila's line of sight to Remus. He came to a stop in front of them, and she immediately stepped back into Mila's shadow.

'Well, this is a surprise,' Remus said, his blue eyes on Mila. 'You following me?'

'You flatter yourself.' She tried not to stiffen beneath his gaze. 'Are you really so surprised to see a slave at a market?'

His gaze moved over her. 'I'm surprised to see you clothed. Almost walked straight past you.'

Mila did not take the bait, glancing instead at her bewildered sister, who looked positively terrified. 'This is my sister, Dulcia.'

Remus looked at the cowering girl and nodded. 'Hello.'

Dulcia studied him, wide-eyed. 'Are you one of the men my sister fights?'

'No,' Mila answered for him. 'I do not fight men.'

'You fight men all the time,' Dulcia said.

'Boys,' Mila explained. 'And the occasional dwarf.'

His amused gaze moved between them.

'Remus used to be a gladiator. Now he is a trainer at Ludus Magnus,' Mila explained to her sister.

'Remus? As in Remus Latinius?'

Remus beamed at Mila. She was annoyed that her sister, who knew nothing about gladiators, had somehow heard of him.

'You a fighter like your sister?' Remus asked.

Dulcia recoiled at the suggestion.

'My sister has no desire to hold a sword. Though I have seen her become rather aggressive while kneading dough.'

Remus laughed at that, and Mila found herself pleased by his reaction. She took in his face before looking down at her sister. 'We better get these lemons back before the cook sends a search party.'

'Will you be going to the games at Amphitheatrum Neronis with your domina?' he asked, stopping her with his words.

She looked up at him. 'Unlikely. I do not normally accompany Aquila out of the house. The only reason I accompanied her last night was because her usual slave was ill.' She hesitated before asking the question burning her throat. 'Do women fight at Amphitheatrum Neronis?'

'*Trained* women do. Our emperor isn't a big fan of women fighting, but he gets that the people like it.'

They watched one another for a moment.

'Will you be attending?' she asked.

He nodded. 'Ludus Magnus provides many of the fighters.'

She was annoyed at herself for asking such a stupid question. 'Nerva is looking into opportunities for me. Perhaps I will suggest the event to him.' She spoke to his chest.

'You beat one dwarf. Now you think you're ready to fight a trained gladiator?'

'Felix was trained.'

'As a *paegniarius*. He is a performer.'

She looked up. 'You told me I was good.'

'For someone with no training.'

Dulcia spoke up at that. 'I have seen my sister beat men your size.'

Mila was torn between muzzling the girl and hugging her. 'Not men, boys,' she repeated.

Remus watched her. 'Come as a spectator first, see what you'd be up against.'

She swallowed down her disappointment, though she did not know if it stemmed from the lost opportunity or Remus not believing she was up to the task. 'You have forgotten what it is to be a slave. I cannot go where I please.'

He glanced at Dulcia and then at his feet. 'I haven't forgotten.'

After a long silence, Mila said, 'We should go.'

He stepped back from them, then looked at Dulcia. 'Keep your sister out of trouble.'

'You are the second person to say that to me today.'

Remus raised his eyebrows, looking to Mila for confirmation.

She shook her head. 'Nerva was speaking of something else entirely.'

'No he was not,' Dulcia protested. Mila's response came in the form of a push to start walking.

Remus remained where he was, a smirk on his face. 'Good day.'

'Good day,' she mumbled to the pavement, hearing laughter in his tone.

She was down the street when she finally worked up

the courage to look behind her. He stood in the same spot with his arms crossed in front of him, smile gone, still watching her.

CHAPTER 7

The early morning sun was warm on Remus's bare arms. He stood in the middle of the arena at Ludus Magnus, eyes moving between the pairs, assessing their fitness, their technique. Two men would be selected for combat at Amphitheatrum Neronis in five days. It was his responsibility to pick the best and ensure that they walked away with all their limbs intact while fighters from other schools did not.

He glanced over to where Fausta trained with Titus, a former gladiator who had recently been promoted to trainer and had been abusing the privilege ever since. After twelve years of being pushed to the breaking point, it seemed he was eager to inflict harsher training methods on the gladiators in his charge. Even more of a concern was his reputation for ensuring "women knew their place" among men. That meant Remus was forced to keep an eye on Titus whenever he trained Fausta. The former prostitute understood men, and she had learned early on how to handle them. But she could not match them in strength, and Titus liked to remind her of that fact.

Pressing his toes into the sand, Remus's thoughts went

to Mila. That was happening a lot lately, and it did not matter how many women he snuck into the barracks late in the evenings—nothing was enough to rid him of her.

'Remus,' Felix called, striding across the sand towards him.

Remus looked up. The dwarf pointed to the *cavea* where Nerva Papias was seated alone, watching the men train. An irrational surge of panic pelted his insides. 'What's he doing here?'

Felix shook his head. 'Want me to find out?'

Seeing that he had been spotted, Nerva raised a hand in greeting.

'Have him meet me beneath the portico,' Remus said, raising a hand also. Once Felix had left, he turned to the new recruits in his charge. 'Swords down!' he instructed. 'Get some water.'

Walking towards the exit, dismissing his illogical anxiety, he watched as the young nobleman approached, his relaxed expression easing his fears of bad news. 'Nerva,' he said, extending his arm. 'Good day to you.'

'And you,' Nerva replied, gripping his wrist and then letting go.

Felix was standing with his arms folded, feet wide, watching the exchange. 'Nerva has come to ask your help with something.'

'Oh?' Remus asked, the uneasy feeling returning.

Nerva nodded. 'I apologise for interrupting. I am afraid I do not have many contacts in gladiator circles.'

Remus glanced at the men being served water by a slave girl. They drank greedily. 'That's enough!' he called to them. 'You'll only bring it up again!' His gaze returned to Nerva. 'What do you think I can help you with?'

Nerva exhaled. 'Mila.'

One word and the nobleman had his full attention. 'The slave girl?' As if it needed clarifying.

'Yes. I foolishly agreed to let her fight again, on the condition that it was one time only. She has the crazy idea that she can earn enough money to buy her freedom.'

Remus frowned. 'From one fight?'

Nerva looked around. 'She assures me it is one *win*.'

Felix spoke up at that. 'Even if she wins, it will not be enough to buy her freedom, unless your father is particularly generous.'

Nerva looked between them. 'She has a little coin saved and has asked me to give it to Gallus Minidius to invest. She is fighting at the Amphitheatrum Neronis next week.'

Remus was afraid of that. 'So she's backing herself and trusting Gallus with everything she has?'

Nerva nodded. 'She is a creative thinker.'

'I would go with naive,' Felix said.

The men glanced at him and he raised his hands, signalling his silence.

'Why don't you give her the difference?' Remus asked. 'You care enough to indulge her insanity.'

Nerva crossed his arms and glanced down at his feet. 'Because she cannot buy her freedom with my family's money. My mother would never allow it.'

'So don't tell her.'

'Ha! You do not know my mother. If she wants to find something out, she will.'

Remus considered this for a moment. 'What happens when they learn how the coin *was* raised?'

Shrugging, Nerva replied, 'It will be too late then.'

'Your father might say no to the sale.'

'He might.'

Remus rested his hands on his hips. 'And what if she loses? She have an answer for that?'

'One fight. That is her promise. If she loses, it is over. She has been fighting on the streets for nearly four years, and she has given it all to Gallus. It seems she knows something we do not.'

Felix shook his head, and Remus stared at his feet.

'She is certain she will win,' Nerva added.

'She's wrong,' Remus said simply, looking up. 'There's every chance she'll be matched with one of our own.' He gestured to Fausta. 'I trained that one myself, and she'll beat your… slave.' He did not dare say 'sister'.

As Nerva stood processing those words, Brutus wandered out to check on things. Seeing the gladiators in Remus's charge were resting, he made his way over, his gaze moving over Nerva as he came to a stop in front of them.

'Why are your men not fighting?' he asked, not bothering with introductions.

Nerva took in the greying *lanista* with more scars on his face than fingers and shoulders the width of an ox.

'I am afraid I am to blame for that.'

'And who are you?' Brutus asked.

'Nerva Papias.'

Recognising the name, he extended an arm. 'And what's your business here?'

Remus glanced at Felix, knowing Brutus would agree to anything for the right price. Nerva explained the situation. When he was done, Brutus asked, 'What is it you want Remus to do?'

Nerva held a hand to his forehead, blocking the low sun hitting his face. 'I am to attend the games with my father. I would like him to keep watch over her on the day, take her to and from the arena, and whatever else you do for your own gladiators. I will not pretend to know what is involved.'

Brutus nodded. 'Remus will take care of the girl, for a fee.'

And there it was.

Nerva did not seem surprised by the request. 'Of course. I would never assume your time to be free.' Noticing Remus's reluctance, he said, 'One fight. Win or lose, that is it. She has given her word.'

Remus wanted to refuse, but he knew Brutus would simply give the task to another trainer—Titus, perhaps. If Mila was going ahead with her crazy plan, she would need someone to help navigate her through it, and it was better if it was him.

'She doesn't know you're here?' Remus asked.

Nerva smiled. 'I am not sure if you have noticed this about her, but she is rather independent.'

Remus nodded. 'I might've guessed that about her.'

Nerva readied himself to leave. 'Send word with your fee and what time you need her, and I will ensure she gets here.'

He nodded a farewell to them all, and the men watched him walk away towards the exit.

'An untrained slave girl won't last more than a few moments in the arena,' Brutus said with a sniff. 'It'll be an easy win for Fausta. I'll make sure they're matched.'

'You should've said no,' Remus said. 'Anything happens to that girl, we'll be to blame.'

Brutus did not look the least bit worried. 'We can't control what happens in the arena. Even pompous fools like Nerva Papias know that. All you have to do is take his coin and throw her in. Return her in pieces if you have to.' He looked at the men slumped in the shade, their skin slick with sweat. 'Get those men on their feet,' he added before leaving them.

Remus ran a hand through his hair.

'It is one fight,' Felix said, trying to reassure his friend. 'It is on Nerva if anything happens to her.'

Remus glanced at him. 'I told her about the games. I put the idea in her head.'

Felix frowned. 'When?'

'Saw her at the macella a few weeks back. Suggested she go as a spectator.'

Narrowing his gaze, Felix asked, 'That is three encounters in a matter of weeks.'

'So?'

Felix raised his hands again. 'It was just an observation. You never see a woman more than once, and you never remember her name.'

'Nerva used her name.'

Felix followed Remus's gaze to where Fausta had been paired with one of the more experienced gladiators and was fearlessly fending him off despite the man being three times her own weight.

'It is one fight, and it might teach the girl a few hard truths,' Felix said.

The dwarf spoke sense, and yet the entire thing had Remus on edge.

'It is one fight,' Felix said again.

Remus looked down at his feet. 'One fight.'

CHAPTER 8

Mila waited in the tunnel, a leg bouncing as she listened to a man tied to a post being torn apart by a small bear. *Damnation ad bestias* was a popular form of punishment used on runaway slaves. She refused to watch. The screaming told her everything she needed to know about what was happening. Heaven forbid the man die with dignity and the people not be entertained by his final moments.

The Amphitheatrum Neronis was small in comparison to the Flavian Amphitheatre. The wooden structure had been built in place of the Amphitheatrum Statilii Tauri, which had burned down one hundred years earlier. While less impressive, it still held thousands of spectators who had gathered to watch the one-day spectacle. The noise made Mila's head pulse.

She turned her sword in her hand. In the other, she held a green shield, to contrast Fausta's blue one, and a bronze helmet. She wore a matching green loincloth and a breastplate held in place with leather straps. She was ready—whatever that meant.

Nerva had seen to everything, even paying the lanista

of Ludus Magnus to manage her for the event. She insisted on paying him back, but she needed to win in order to do that. He told her he did not care about the money. Once he made the decision to help her, he had been all in, even making a public display of sending her off to "run errands" around the city for the day so she could disappear without raising suspicion.

She had arrived at Ludus Magnus early in the morning and found an irritated Remus waiting for her.

'If I'd known you were coming alone, and on foot, I'd have collected you,' he had snapped.

'What were you expecting? A litter dropping me at the gate?'

He was clearly not in the mood for jokes, barely looking at her as he waved her into a cart where the others were waiting. He had gestured to the only remaining seat on the bench, but it was not appropriate for a slave to sit while a free man stood.

'I will sit on the floor,' she had said.

'You'll sit on the bench,' he had replied, crouching in front of her.

Everyone watched her take a seat, saying nothing.

As the cart lurched forwards, Remus had looked at her properly for the first time, as though sensing her discomfort.

'That's Brutus Julius, lanista at Ludus Magnus.' He gestured to the man at the far end. Keeping his voice low, he went around the rest of the group: a trainer named Titus, three male gladiators, and a blonde woman named Fausta who had looked rather pleased at the sight of her opponent.

Upon arriving at the amphitheatre, Brutus had gone to his seat while Remus and Titus led the others through an archway. There was no procession, just a single guard escorting them. The chink of the iron chain attached to one of the men unsettled Mila. She had tried to distance herself from the noise, but Remus kept glancing back to check she was still behind him.

Once they had reached the torch-lit room where the gladiators prepared, Fausta stripped down to nothing but a blue loincloth and her armour.

'Here,' Remus had said to Mila, holding out a breastplate. He turned his back to her. She dressed quickly, fumbling with the straps until he eventually turned back round, stepped closer, and took the straps from her, his fingers brushing her back while she held her breath.

'Thank you for the breastplate,' she said, not looking at him.

'Shall I wear one also?' Fausta asked, a smile on her face.

Glancing at her, Remus had replied, 'It might be a little late for modesty.'

The others had laughed, helping Mila relax.

The crowd cheered, pulling Mila from her thoughts. She watched the disembowelled criminal being dragged across the sand by a hook while two bestiarii tried to contain the bear. She glanced down at her shield, wishing she had two swords instead of one.

'You need a shield,' Remus said, emerging from the dark and apparently reading her thoughts.

She looked up. 'I can fight with anything.'

'Except a net?'

She gave a small smile. 'Except a net. Or any form of rope, really.'

He held out a piece of cloth for her.

'What is that?' she asked, laying her weapons and helmet down and taking it from him.

'It goes under your helmet, extra padding. The swords might be blunt, but they'll still hurt.' She nodded. 'Not too different from your street fights. You need to disarm her, and you need to do it quickly, before you tire. She's fitter and stronger, and that'll be a big advantage if the fight goes on too long.'

She frowned at him. 'Should you be helping me? I mean, I am fighting one of your own.'

He looked around, his expression serious. 'The moment you think you've lost, let her knock your weapons from your hands. There's no point getting injured if the outcome is hopeless.'

Mila stared at him. 'Nothing is lost until it is. I am not surrendering to avoid a few knocks.'

He looked out into the arena, his jaw working. 'Suit yourself. If you lose, you exit via the Porta Sanavivari at the other end of the arena. The victor returns to this gate.'

'The Porta Triumphalis,' she said absently. 'The gate of life.'

He looked at her, his expression still tense. 'Watch Fausta's shield,' he said, voice low. 'She'll use it to stun you, distract you. Her sword will follow.'

Mila looked at him. 'Are you a gambling man?'

He shook his head. 'No.'

She studied him. 'If you were, who would you bet on?'

Before he could answer, Titus and Fausta entered the tunnel, gazes going briefly to Mila. Remus took a few steps back, keeping his eyes forwards. They all stilled to listen as Fausta was introduced as the fiercest female to grace the arena since Mevia, the beast hunter. A guard on the other side opened the gate and Fausta jogged through it, the applause growing as she came into sight. Mila placed the cloth covering on her head and then wiped her hands on her loincloth. She bent, snatching up her helmet and sliding it on before grabbing her weapons. Her heart raced and her fingers flexed against wood and ivory. She barely heard her introduction, her nerves ringing in her ears.

Remus turned and straightened her helmet. 'Good luck.'

She looked up at him. 'The editor, what did he call me?'

'Libertas,' Remus replied, crossing his arms.

She had not told him a name. 'Goddess of freedom.'

He nodded. 'I thought it was better than dwarf slayer.'

She gave a weak smile and faced forwards again. One foot in front of the other, she stepped beneath the archway and squinted against the harsh sun. She kept her gaze on Fausta, who paced, swinging her arms to loosen her muscles. Mila tried not to look around the full amphitheatre, aware of the curious gazes on her and the modest applause. She wondered where Nerva was and if his heart was pounding as hard as hers in that moment.

'Gladiators ready!' boomed the referee.

REMUS WATCHED from behind the gate as the women circled one another like beasts before a kill.

'Haven't seen you this nervous before,' Titus said, amused. 'Your jaw's doing that thing where it pulses.'

Remus forced his mouth to go slack. 'Fausta will be fine. She's beaten women twice that size with six times that girl's experience.'

Titus smiled. 'Yes, she has. But you're not nervous for Fausta, are you?'

Remus stiffened. 'Shut your mouth before I do.'

Titus laughed, shaking his head. 'It's always the pretty ones who soften you.'

He was bracing for the first blow. 'She's here to earn coin, buy her freedom. Have you forgotten what it feels like to be a slave?'

Titus shook his head. 'There are easier ways for a pretty thing like that to get her freedom. Does her dominus prefer cock?'

'Enough.'

The women ran at one another, weapons clashing.

'I know you'd like to see every slave freed, but the truth is Rome would fall apart without them,' Titus went on, ignoring the warning.

The roar of the crowd quietened him. The only thing Remus heard from that point on was the clash of steel and wood. He could have predicted every one of Fausta's moves; after all, he had taught them to her. When her shield hit Mila, she was ready, blocking and then thrusting her body weight forwards to throw Fausta off balance.

Remus shifted, his body tense as Fausta fought back, going through a sequence of movements he knew well, the ones he had drilled into her daily for the past two years. They were moves designed to swiftly flatten her opponent. Mila did not so much block the blows as dodge them, and he knew she would eventually tire—and lose.

It did not take long for his prediction to come true. Mila slowed, only a little at first, but it threw her rhythm. She missed the cue of the shield as it smashed into her head and shoulder, the force of the blow sending her helmet flying. Remus saw fear in her eyes as her gaze swept the crowd. She was not afraid of Fausta, but of being exposed in front of her dominus. It was the distraction Fausta needed to end it. Her sword came from the side, and Mila turned, blocking it with her own while striking back. But Fausta was two moves ahead, ducking below Mila's shield and then thrusting hers up into Mila's face. Remus gripped the gate as blood sprayed from her mouth and her eyes rolled back in her head. Her legs gave out and she sank down into the sand, face up with her legs twisted beneath her. The crowd erupted, standing and cheering, the noise deafening.

'Easy win,' Titus said.

'Open the gate,' Remus called to the guard.

The guard looked over, hesitated, and then seeing his expression, stepped up to open it.

The heavy feeling in Remus's gut grew the more the crowd cheered. As the gate separated, his eyes went to Fausta, assessing her.

'Where're you going?' Titus asked.

But Remus did not hear him. He watched as Fausta lifted one foot and looked around the crowd—they wanted more. His legs propelled him forwards, but it was too late. Fausta brought her foot down on Mila's chest, and he could almost hear the crack of bone amid the cheering. His eyes widened at the sight of the slave girl, still and broken on the scalding sand.

He broke into a run.

CHAPTER 9

The first thing Mila heard when she woke was arguing. She blinked against blinding light, her head pounding as she tried to figure out where she was. Her vision blurred and cleared, then blurred again. She gave up, closing her eyes. A memory surfaced: Fausta's face, fierce and covered in sweat, her blue shield like a bolt of lightning against her. She tried again, forcing her eyes open and taking in the familiar surroundings of the room she shared with her mother and sister. Through the curtain she recognised Nerva's silhouette, softened by the fabric, gesturing as he spoke. He only ever gestured when he was worked up.

'You knew!' Rufus shouted.

That was when she noticed a second silhouette. Her dominus. Her father. It was also the moment she realised how much trouble she was in. Her eyes sank shut.

'How long has this been going on?' Rufus hissed.

She opened her eyes, focusing on the sharp shadow of her dominus's finger, pointed at Nerva's face. She was not the only one in trouble.

'It was one fight, and we agreed it would end there.'

'You *agreed*?' He was quiet a moment. 'Is this your way of rebelling? Of living a life you cannot have?'

Nerva shook his head. 'Through Mila? That is ridiculous.'

Silence for a moment. 'Did her mother know about all this?'

Mila held her breath.

'She knew nothing of today,' he replied, keeping his answer honest.

Mila tried to move her tongue in her mouth but everything was stuck in place. That was when she became aware of the pain in her cheek, jaw, and gums. She slowly reached a hand up, feeling her swollen face and running a finger along her teeth to ensure they were still in place. Satisfied, she turned to look at the small table next to the bed where a jug and cup sat. Her mother always made sure they had fresh water available to them. She tried to sit up and a searing pain shot through her chest. She pressed her teeth together to stop from crying out. Looking down at her bandaged chest, she tried to recall how the injury happened. Nothing came.

'This is on me,' Nerva said, his tone calmer that time. 'And you have my word it will not happen again.'

Rufus exhaled, and Mila watched him shake his head. His resignation meant Nerva was almost in the clear. She pushed herself up into a seated position, wincing the entire time. Footsteps approached at a fast walk. She knew from nineteen years in the house that they did not belong to her mother or sister, that they were the footsteps of her domina—and she was not in a good mood.

'Rufus, I will not have it,' she said, coming to a stop next to her husband. 'The entire city is laughing at us.'

Mila watched them move like shadow puppets behind the fabric, but her thirst was distracting.

'I am sorting it out,' Rufus said, his tone tired. Conversations with his wife often had that effect on him.

Unable to ignore her thirst any longer, Mila reached for the water, holding her breath in hope of minimising the pain. Her fingertips brushed the rim of the cup.

'She is gone from this house,' Aquila said, her tone like a knife. 'The only reason she remains here is out of some twisted sense of obligation to her mother. Well, our kindness ran out the moment she brought shame on our household.'

Mila froze, her heart skipping a few times.

'Mother, you cannot be serious—'

'I am perfectly serious. Dulcia can remain here, because the gods know no one else will take the useless girl, but Mila is gone the moment her worth is restored.'

Smash.

The cup fell to the floor and Nerva pulled the curtain back. The three of them took in the shards of ceramic sprayed across the floor, reaching all the way to their feet.

Mila swallowed. 'I will clean it up,' she said, her voice hoarse. The wounds in her mouth reopened and she tasted blood.

Aquila turned on her heel and left.

CHAPTER 10

Boredom was the worst form of torture. Four weeks Mila was forced to remain in bed, amid the stifling July heat, tended by her mother and sister. They brought her porridge and apricots, and sat by her, humming while they sewed. When Mila complained about being confined, they showed no pity, instead bringing her small chores she could do sitting up in bed, like basic mending she could not mess up. Tertia left the garments in a pile on the table by the bed, never meeting her daughter's gaze. Mila completed the work without complaint, knowing her mother's harsh indifference stemmed from the pain she felt at losing one of her daughters. They were weeks away from being separated—and it was Mila's fault.

The moment she was fit enough to return to work, Mila was to be sold to Jovian Fadius to serve his wife, Prisca. Mila recalled the dinner party Prisca had hosted some weeks back. She had seemed disengaged, erratic, though pleasant enough. Most women of superior birth were in public; only time would tell. As much as she tried not to worry about what lay ahead, tried to be brave for the sake of her family, there was a heavy feeling in her gut that would not go away.

To distract herself, she gave in to thoughts of Remus, replaying private moments in her mind, from the time in the laundry to their final words before she had entered the arena. She had not heard a word from him since.

Her sister swept through the curtain carrying a tray of soup and a chunk of coarse bread. She placed it on the table next to the mending and sat at the foot of the bed, staring down at the floor.

'It is not so bad,' Mila said, swinging her legs carefully over the edge of the bed and picking up the bowl of soup. 'At least I remain in the same district. I will probably run into you at the market.'

'Only if Prisca Fadius sends you there,' Dulcia said, her voice barely audible.

'Dulcia, look at me.' Her sister dragged her gaze up, eyes already brimming with tears. 'It is a small hiccup in our plan, that is all. We *will* be free—'

'I heard Nerva tell Mother the coin is all gone. Everything. Four years of savings, gambled away.'

Ah, Nerva and his enormous mouth. Her own disappointment was bad enough without everyone else's crushing her. 'Like I said, it is a hiccup.'

Dulcia shot off the bed. 'I know you think me a child, but I am not. Stop telling me stories.'

Mila rocked backwards, her ribs aching from the tension. 'I do not think you a child,' she lied.

'You do.' Her sister's gaze fell. 'But the fault is mine. I just assumed we would always be together, that you would be grown up enough for both of us. I was wrong—I see that now.' A tear betrayed her and she brushed it away with an angry finger.

Mila put the soup down on the tray, then stood and pulled her sister to her, ignoring the pain. 'They are not stories. I am buying my freedom, and then I am coming back for you.'

Dulcia's arms went around her, squeezing much harder than Mila could cope with. She was about to mention it when she felt her sister's chest expand, the way it did before releasing a giant sob.

'Promise me,' Dulcia said, sucking in a breath. 'Promise me you will come back for us. We will leave Rome. Go and find our uncle, just like we planned.'

Mila pulled back and wiped at her sister's cheeks. The uncle Dulcia was referring to was their mother's brother, a legionnaire who had left Rome the year before Tertia had been sold. 'The uncle who likely does not even know of our existence? He never came looking for her.'

Dulcia's eyes closed. 'As long as we are together, it will not matter where we are. We will find work. Every noble house needs a seamstress.'

Mila smiled. 'You are quite right. Mother would be much sought after with her skills.' She glanced at the unfinished pile of mending. 'Me, not so much.'

The thought of finally being free, to then go on suffocating in the same city that had confined her all those years, did not sit well with Mila. She had always imagined fleeing its walls first chance she got. Their mother had told them endless stories of quaint villages, open fields painted with flowers, peach trees bursting with fruit and air so clean it could heal a dying man. That was one of the worst parts about being born a slave—Mila had no *before* life to be nostalgic over, relying solely on her mother's childhood memories.

The sound of a throat being cleared made them both turn. Nerva's head poked through the curtain, his eyes going to the tray where the soup and bread sat. Not the white fluffy kind he enjoyed, but the *panis sordidus* brought for the rest of the household.

'Is your sister still bringing you food? You really are taking advantage of her.'

Dulcia smiled. 'I do not mind. But I do have other chores to do.' She looked shyly up at Nerva. 'Someone has to do Mila's share of the work.'

Mila went to swat her and winced as pain shot through her chest.

'Serves you right for trying to hit her,' Nerva said, stepping into the small room. 'Run, Dulcia. I can spoon-feed your sister.'

Dulcia rushed from the room, smiling at her feet.

When she was gone, Nerva turned to look at Mila. 'I am not actually going to spoon-feed you by the way, but I will sit here and watch you spill it all over yourself.'

Mila sat on the bed and picked up the bowl. 'I can eat just fine,' she said, shovelling the soup into her mouth.

Nerva sat also, studying the rug that hung on the wall to cover the cracks that were growing on it. 'The physician says tomorrow you will be all right for light duties.'

'Thank the gods,' Mila said, scooping up the last of the hot liquid. 'I am going out of my mind cooped up in here.'

Nerva looked at her then. 'How are you feeling? I am not referring to your broken ribs, or your hideous facial injuries. About leaving?'

She shrugged. 'Probably how you imagine I am feeling. I will be fine, but I worry about Dulcia.'

He hesitated. 'How much do you know about Prisca Fadius?'

'Only what I have seen of her.' The truth was she did not want to know any more because she was struggling to keep herself together as it was.

He frowned. 'She is a very powerful woman from a very wealthy family with a rather scandalous past.'

Mila placed the empty bowl on the tray. 'Lucky she is wealthy, then.'

'Prisca Fadius is the daughter of Celcus Heius.'

She thought for a moment. 'Am I supposed to know who that is?'

Nerva shook his head. 'I will spare you the lesson in politics, but Celcus is a former magistrate. He has since retired to the country.'

'Great, perhaps I might finally glimpse the countryside after all. So what was the great scandal?'

'Everything is hearsay. Best I not repeat it.'

She rolled her eyes. 'Of course it is.' She studied him. 'Will you really not tell me?'

A smile flickered. 'I will tell you one thing involving Remus.'

Mila felt something pinch inside of her. 'Remus?'

He leaned his elbows on his knees, glancing at the curtain. 'It is only rumour, and he was a slave at the time.'

'At the time of what?' She gripped the edge of the bed.

'Of their affair.'

She swallowed. 'Oh.' She tried not to let her disappointment show. 'Well, that makes sense. He was a gladiator, and she is beautiful. What man would say no to her?'

'One with honour?' Nerva suggested.

She did not know why, but she felt defensive on Remus's behalf. 'We cannot enslave men and then lecture them on honour.'

Nerva exhaled. 'All right, I take it back.'

She thought for a moment. 'I am surprised Jovian lets Remus into his house if he is aware of the rumours.'

'I do not have all the answers, but he would not be the first husband to turn a blind eye to his wife's indiscretions.'

A question rose in Mila's throat. She fought against it and failed. 'Does Remus still… visit her bed?'

Nerva smiled. 'Why? Does it bother you?'

'Why would it bother me?' she shot back.

'Because you like him, and I suspect it is mutual.'

She blinked. 'A man like Remus is not going to look twice at a slave girl like me after tumbling about in Prisca Fadius's fine… bed linen.'

Nerva laughed. 'Look at you, so plainly jealous.'

'I am not jealous. I just do not fancy the idea of Remus being invited into her bed and having to fan them in the act. Or any other man, for that matter.'

'Honestly, the vulgarity that comes from your mouth.'

She looked down.

Noticing, he said, 'For the record, Remus *would* look twice at a slave girl like you. Why else would he harass me with messages enquiring after you?'

She looked up at that, searching his face for signs he was teasing. 'He has sent you messages?'

He nodded. 'Many.'

She waited, and when he did not offer anything further, she asked, 'And did you reply?'

Nerva tilted his head in a manner that suggested she should know better. 'Of course I replied. He asked after your injuries. I told him your face now resembles the man who had been half-eaten by the bear prior to your big moment in the arena, and that both your front teeth are missing.'

She would have hit him if she had not been in so much pain. 'You paid him a fee to look out for me. I suppose it is part of his service to ensure I lived through it.'

'I paid the fee to Julius. I doubt Remus saw any of it.' His face turned serious. 'You know, he was the first person to reach you. He carried you out of the arena himself, waiting for no one. I am grateful.'

It was the first time she had heard of any of this. 'Oh' was all she said.

Nerva cleared his throat. 'So now when you are fanning him in the act, perhaps you could show some gratitude.'

She picked up the pillow behind her and hurled it at

him. A sharp intake of breath followed as a stabbing pain shot through her ribs.

'The physician says you are ready for light duties, not combat.'

She breathed through the pain. 'Be thankful I will not be around once I am healed.'

Nerva's smile faded and he looked down at his hands. 'Jokes aside, it will be rather dull around here without you. Who will get me into trouble?'

Mila studied him. Though they would never admit it, they were siblings being separated, and she felt the pain of it as much as she did with her sister. 'Is that your way of saying you will miss me?'

He looked at her, his mouth turning up. 'I suppose it is.'

She leaned forwards and covered one of his hands with her own. 'Will you take care of Dulcia for me?'

He nodded. 'Of course.'

Removing her hand and straightening, she said, 'I will come back for them. I will buy their freedom as soon as I am able.'

He drew a long breath. 'You never stop.'

'I will stop when I am free or dead.'

He watched her. 'Have you ever asked your mother if she wants to leave?'

She narrowed her eyes. 'What do you mean? Of course she wants to leave. She is not here by choice.'

'I know. But your mother has lived in this house since she was fifteen years old. She has had a good life here, has been well provided for by my father—'

'I know all this, but she is still a slave.'

His expression was conflicted, as though unsure whether to continue the conversation. 'I am not sure you actually understand how it is for common people in this city. It is not an easy life. Your mother would need to marry or work twice as hard as she currently does in order to afford housing and food and all the other expenses that she never has to worry about.'

Mila stood. 'Listen to yourself. We slaves have it easy in your household, is that it?'

He stood also. 'That is not what I am saying.'

She let out a slow breath to calm herself. 'I thank you for your insights. I will be sure to keep them in mind when I am weighing up whether a free life is the right choice for my family. Now if you do not mind, I have mending to finish before I am sold off like a fine pig.'

Nerva stared at her, his expression one of pity, before turning and leaving the room.

Mila felt her face collapse but caught herself before it turned into anything more. She lowered herself onto the bed, already missing him, and Dulcia, and her mother. Perhaps even the cook, who, despite her vile nature, had always given Mila the outer layer of bread because she knew Mila loved the crust.

Staring at the gently swaying curtain, she drew a shaky breath and reminded herself that everything would be fine.

It was just a small hiccup, and she had a plan.

CHAPTER 11

It was the middle of the day. Remus and Felix sat in the mess hall, eating poached fish and stale bread. They did not complain, because food at Ludus Magnus was prepared by someone else, and they were free to go elsewhere if they wished.

The gladiator school was home to hundreds of gladiators, trainers, and slaves who kept the place running. Remus knew many of them, trained some of them and drank with a few of them.

Felix was one of those people, and he could hold his drink better than men four times his size. The dwarf had come from a noble family, turning his humiliating existence into a life he rather enjoyed. People still laughed at him, but in the arena it was different; he controlled people's reactions and had a steady stream of women visitors to show for it. While his family had been quick to disown him, he was still a civilian, free to come and go as he pleased. He took the oath he had made as seriously as any other man, despite the fact that he had no intention of ever fighting to the death. Luckily for him, he was too difficult to replace, and the crowd adored him. No spectator would wish him dead.

'You were rather harsh on Fausta this morning,' Felix said.

Remus did not even look up from his food. 'She likes to be pushed.'

Felix tore a piece of bread and soaked up the liquid on his plate. 'Perhaps I am getting soft in my old age.' Looking at Remus, he added, 'Or you are getting meaner.'

Remus pushed his plate away and looked up. 'You done?'

A slave girl stepped up to the table and snatched up the empty plate.

Felix put his bread down and rested his arms on the table. 'All right, let's have it. What is the matter with you?'

Remus glanced at the noisy table of men next to them. 'Why would you ask that?'

'Because this morning you had everyone running laps, something you do when you are angry.'

'No, it's something I do when our fighters are unfit. Maybe I should have *you* run laps.'

'Run laps?' Felix's face twisted in horror. 'What? In case the others do not have enough reasons to ridicule me?' He exhaled. 'I think you have taught Fausta her lesson. Time to move on.'

Remus pretended not to understand. 'Who says I'm teaching her a lesson?'

'You are punishing her for doing her job, and doing it well. It is not her fault she was matched with the slave girl you have taken a fancy to.'

'Are you drunk already?'

'I wish I were.'

Remus stretched his neck from side to side. 'Fausta didn't have to break her ribs. She'd already won.'

'There you go. Was that really so difficult?'

Remus cast a warning glance at him.

'So she got carried away,' Felix continued. 'Ribs heal. I would know, since I believe I have broken every one of mine.'

'That's your reply? Ribs heal?'

Felix shrugged. 'What do you want to hear? Do I think it was dirty? Unnecessary? Sure.'

'Exactly. I should've said no to the whole thing.'

'It was not up to you. She is not your slave.' Felix studied him. 'How is the girl? I know you have made enquiries after her.'

'That was weeks back,' came his reply. 'Nerva told me she was confined to her bed, complaining but healing nicely.'

The truth was he had thought of nothing else since the day it had happened. He could not shake the memory of standing over her unconscious body, too scared to touch her. Then remembering how rough the men on their way over would be with her, he had bent and scooped her up in his arms.

Too light for the arena.

Something had shifted inside him as he carried her lifeless body across the sand. A floodgate had opened, and he had been trying to close it ever since. He found himself looking for her every time he visited the market. Perhaps he had even visited the market for the sole purpose of running into her.

'I imagine Rufus Papias is not happy about the whole thing.'

Remus's foot bounced beneath the table. 'Nerva said nothing of it.'

'Unsurprising, as it is family business. Hopefully they skipped the lashings upon seeing the state of her face.'

Felix picked up the bread and began eating again while

Remus blinked away the vision of Mila's bloodied face and hair.

'Does Brutus know you have been sending his slaves to the Papias household for updates?'

'Probably.'

Brutus let him do as he pleased because he knew Remus could leave any time he wished, and he wanted to keep his best trainer happy. It was no secret that lanistas from other schools came sniffing around the tavern he drank at, hoping to poach him.

'I see the attraction,' Felix said, finishing the last of his bread and pushing the plate away. The young slave reappeared next to them, and the empty plate vanished. 'She is like you when you first entered the arena, unhinged with something to prove.'

'Fausta's just doing her job, but I'm unhinged?'

The men at the table near them left and the room fell quiet. Remus stood suddenly, staring down at the table as he thought.

'What is going on inside that head of yours?' Felix asked.

Remus stepped over the bench seat and headed for the door.

'Where are you going?' Felix called after him.

'Tell Brutus I've business to take care of,' Remus replied over his shoulder.

THE PLAN WAS SIMPLE: he would visit the Papias household, under the pretence of needing to see Nerva, and check on Mila. Nerva seemed to like him, had even admired him at one time, so he was confident he would not be turned away.

He made his way through the busy streets, manoeuvring around merchants and children darting about, ignoring the pleas of their exasperated mothers. Where possible, he took shortcuts through alleyways most people avoided, finally arriving at the Garden of Sallust. From there, he asked a slave for directions and climbed the hill towards the great house.

He stood out front, taking in the wide door and high walls. After a few moments, he ascended the steps and took hold of the iron knocker, tapping it a few times before stepping back. The door swung open and Dulcia appeared from behind it, struggling with the weight. She peered up at him, recognising him but not daring to mention the fact. Too many ears in homes that size.

'May I help you?' she asked.

Remus looked past her into the vestibulum, searching for Mila. Empty.

His gaze returned to the girl. 'My name's Remus Latinius. I'm hoping to speak with Nerva.'

'Remus?' came a voice behind him.

He spun around to see Nerva standing on the bottom step, looking up at him.

'Are you here to see me?' Nerva asked, not seeming too surprised.

'Yes, if you've a moment.'

Nerva climbed the steps towards him and glanced at Dulcia. 'You may close the door. I will be in shortly.'

The girl glanced at Remus before pushing the heavy door closed.

'That was Dulcia, Mila's sister,' Nerva said, coming to a stop next to him.

'I see the resemblance,' Remus replied, not wanting to raise questions by admitting they had met before.

'I thought having her answer the door would help her shyness.'

'How's that working out?'

Nerva smiled. 'Visitors struggle to hear her, so they lean closer to listen, and that only makes matters worst.'

'Contrast to her sister, then.'

'We would never have let Mila near the door. She would have scared away all our guests.'

He was speaking of her in past tense, and that made Remus nervous. 'How is she?'

Nerva studied him. 'Is that why you are here? To check on her?'

Remus glanced over his shoulder at the closed door, unsure how to answer.

'She is not here,' Nerva said, letting him off the hook.

Remus nodded. 'Where is she?'

A man had stopped in front of the house to flog his tired mule. They both watched for a moment before continuing their conversation.

'My father sold her to Jovian Fadius. She was handed over yesterday.'

Remus kept his face neutral. 'Sold,' he repeated, getting used to the word. 'What's Jovian Fadius want with an unruly slave?'

A smile tugged at the edges of Nerva's mouth. 'It is nothing untoward as far as I can tell. She is to serve his wife.'

He was afraid of that. 'Makes more sense.'

'I too have been trying to figure out the whole thing. Do you have a theory?'

He laughed through his nose. 'That woman's unpredictable at the best of times. Who knows?'

Much to Remus's relief, the flogging stopped and the mule began walking again.

'I won't keep you,' he said, extending an arm. Nerva took hold of it briefly.

'I imagine I will see her at some point. Shall I tell her you came by to check on her?'

'No,' Remus replied, much too quickly. 'Thanks for your time.' He stepped around Nerva and walked down the steps.

'I never thanked you for helping her,' Nerva called to him. 'Your kindness will not be forgotten.'

Remus paused on the last step and turned. 'Hopefully she walked away with some sense.'

Nerva laughed. 'Hardly. I spent the best part of my childhood knocking that girl to the ground. I learned very early on that she just gets back up.'

Nodding, Remus turned away and began his descent down the hill.

CHAPTER 12

'It will not do to have you dressed in such a way,' Prisca said. She was seated on a lounge in the *tablinum*, her finger tapping on the fabric as she assessed Mila. 'My servants wear only the finest fabrics. They are representing me and this household.'

Prisca had a number of personal servants, including a mute bodyguard she had bought from the market, despite her husband's protests. According to Sabina, Prisca liked the look of him. The fact that he could not speak was seen as a bonus. He was without a doubt the tallest man Mila had ever laid eyes on, his shoulders filling the average doorway. When she asked why his tongue had been cut out, Sabina had told her that no one knew because he was unable to tell his story, could not write, and was not one for charades.

Her domina had recently granted freedom to one of her body slaves who had served in her father's household for more than fifty years. While the story should have offered hope, Mila felt only pity for the old woman who, with no living family, had been exiled from the grand house on account of her unsteady hands, under the pretence of reward.

'I will wear whatever pleases you,' Mila said, keeping still beneath her domina's scrutiny. It was only day two in the household, and she was still trying to figure her out.

'Mmm. Sabina,' Prisca called out, gesturing to the woman standing by the wall. 'Send for the seamstress to come measure her. Tell her I want something bright. Look at that pretty face, washed out by dreary fabric. No, it will not do.'

'Yes, Era.' She glanced at Mila, indicating that she should follow.

'Off you go,' Prisca ordered, winding a thread of hair around her finger and then letting go. 'I think I shall have a lie-down.'

A lie-down? Mila had never met a person who slept that much. She had only risen from her bed a few hours earlier.

'When you are done, come wait at my bedside.'

Mila bowed her head. 'Yes, Era.' She followed the woman out into the atrium where a young boy lingered.

'Go and fetch the seamstress,' Sabina instructed him.

The lanky boy looked up at Mila. 'Are you going to live here?'

'I suppose I am,' Mila replied, attempting a smile.

'I'm Nero,' he said, trying to appear a little taller.

Mila took him in. 'That is quite a name.'

'He wasn't born with that name, but we had to call him something. The women at Latebra used to call him Rat. When I met him, it was the only name he knew.'

Latebra was a well-known brothel in region three. Staring down at him, Mila asked, 'Does your mother work there?'

'I don't remember my mother.'

'Likely dead,' Sabina added. 'He showed up there one

day looking for work in exchange for food. One of the girls gave in and fed him, so he kept coming back.'

Mila watched the boy, who was taking her in, assessing her. 'Well, I definitely prefer the name Nero.'

'Some of the men here still call me Rat,' he said, shrugging. 'Except when Albaus is around.'

'Albaus?'

'The bodyguard,' Sabina explained. 'The mute. Albaus is fond of the boy. Not his real name either, but we couldn't go on calling him the mute.' She glanced at Nero and waved. 'Now off you go.'

The boy strode from the room, and Sabina turned to Mila. 'He was caught stealing from a vendor at the market one day and I made the mistake of speaking up for him, even paying for the stolen bread. He must have followed me home, because the next day when I emerged from the house, he was waiting for me. That was two years ago.'

'How old is he?'

Sabina shook her head. 'No one knows. I would guess around eleven.'

'And our dominus just let him stay?'

They began walking.

'It wasn't that simple. He had to prove he could work first, that he could be trusted. He works as hard as any man here.'

Mila knew he was one of the lucky ones. 'And he does not know what happened to his parents? Perhaps he has other family in the city. He might be freeborn.'

'Maybe, but without even a first name, what are we to do?'

Sabina stopped walking and turned to Mila, folding her arms across her small bosom. 'I hear you're a gladiator, that you almost died in the arena.'

Mila looked around before speaking, a habit formed

over a lifetime. 'I fought *once*, with blunt swords. I was quite safe.'

Sabina studied her. 'You have certainly captured the attention of our domina. She is drawn to rebellious types.'

Before Mila had a chance to respond, Nero returned, out of breath, forehead shiny from his efforts.

'She's on her way,' he puffed.

'Good,' Sabina said, shooing him away again. 'Go see the cook. He will make you some porridge.'

'With honey?'

'I dare you to ask him.'

The boy jogged off towards the kitchen. Sabina waited until he was out of sight and then turned back to Mila.

'Are you ready?'

'For what?'

Sabina exhaled, shrugging. 'Whatever our domina has in store for you.'

Mila glanced about at the expensive furnishings, plush pillows, mosaic floors and life-size sculptures. 'I suppose I will soon find out.'

MILA SLEPT on a thin mattress on the floor next to Prisca's bed. It was the first time in her life she had slept away from her mother and sister for an extended period, and something resembling panic pounded in her gut. She did not really sleep—she lay awake, listening to the sounds of strangers breathing. She wondered how her domina fell asleep with such ease, confident Mila would not stab her in her sleep.

Sabina slept on the other side of the bed, clean water and chamber pot at the ready. It was as though Rome existed only for the upper class.

There was no privacy, no mother to hum familiar

tunes, no sister nestled against her, fists tucked beneath her chin as she slept. There was no escaping to the garden, no Nerva to make jokes with, no fighting, no freedom in any sense of the word.

What have I done?

She always fell asleep eventually, only to be woken early by Sabina. They had to rise before their domina, then wash, dress, and eat the porridge that would sustain them until evening if the day proved busy. Mila would dress in her new tunic and tangerine stola, belting it in the fashionable way the seamstress had shown her. Next the women prepared their domina's clothes for the day, brought fresh drinking water, and sat in silence by the window, waiting for her to wake.

Prisca Fadius liked her sleep. For a woman who did little, she was always exhausted. In the mornings, she would stir, ask for water, drink it with her eyes still closed, and then lie back down and sleep some more. During that time Mila fidgeted, unable to keep still, not used to being idle. So much silence. Not enough work. She would sit next to Sabina, watching her embroider, foot tapping incessantly, the air in the room too thin.

Two weeks into her new life, she sat in that same chair, heel bouncing as she pictured her sister helping in the kitchen back home. There was that punch to the gut again. The dull routine and self-destructive thoughts were enough to make her question her survival in the Fadius household. She thought she might lose her mind to it all.

The sun was already high in the sky when Prisca finally climbed from her bed, enquiring after her husband.

'He left early this morning,' Sabina replied.

'And my sons?'

'At their lessons.'

Mila was brushing Prisca's hair with far more caution than she normally showed her sister. The thick, dark hair felt like silk, and she could not shake the thought of how it would have felt in Remus's callused hands.

'Good,' Prisca replied. 'I would like to see Mila fight this morning.'

The brush stilled in Mila's hand. 'You want to see me *fight?*'

Sabina held the polished bronze up so Prisca could see her reflection.

'Of course,' her domina replied, meeting her eyes briefly in the reflection. 'I knew the first time I laid eyes on you that you had skills beyond that of a household slave. I have an eye for these things, and I was right. Your reflexes when that sword almost hit Aquila'—she shook her head —'it was like poetry. And her face?' A smile. 'Absolutely priceless.'

Mila placed the brush down and began to braid the hair.

'My question is,' Prisca continued, 'when does a slave girl have time to learn such skills? I cannot imagine Aquila permitting such a thing.'

Mila did not want to bring Nerva into the conversation, but there was no other viable explanation, and she had to be honest if she were to be trusted. 'Nerva Papias is a year older than me and used to invite me to spar with him when we were children.'

A mischievous smile tugged at Prisca's mouth. 'Only when you were children?'

Mila swallowed. 'And more recently.'

Prisca laughed, her brilliant teeth flashing. 'There is no need to be shy about it. I too started with my brothers. Then suddenly you come of age and everyone is frowning and telling you your behaviour is disgraceful.' Her smile lingered but it changed form.

'Would you like to dress now?' Sabina asked, not reacting to the information.

Prisca got up from the stool and waited to be undressed. Mila went to fetch the clothes laid out on the bed while Sabina lifted Prisca's tunic over her head. Mila waited, taking in the firm, naked body in front of her. If it were not for a few faded stretch marks around the hips, one would never suspect she had given birth to two sons. She noticed a small, angry scar above Prisca's left breast.

'Even a blunt sword can do damage,' Prisca said, running a finger over the scar.

Embarrassed at being caught staring, Mila's gaze fell and she stepped closer to help Prisca into the lower *subligar* and upper *strophium*. When Mila reached for the tunic, her domina stopped her.

'That is all I need for now,' she said, her glowing skin on display.

Mila glanced at Sabina before asking, 'Do you wish to eat before dressing?'

Prisca's eyes shone at her. 'No, I wish to *fight* before dressing.'

Mila stared a moment before shaking her head. 'I cannot… that is… it would not be appropriate for me to… hold a weapon to you.'

Prisca laughed and waved a dismissive hand. 'Nonsense. It is entirely appropriate if I deem it so. Nero,' she called, glancing at the empty door.

The boy appeared as though he had been waiting for the mention of his name.

'Yes, Era?'

'Fetch the wooden swords and shields. Meet us in the garden.'

Mila stiffened and looked over at Sabina, who gave a small shrug.

'Right away, Era.'

He left at a run, incapable of walking anywhere it seemed. The fact that he knew where these items were kept suggested it was not the first time he had been sent to fetch them.

Prisca's eyes swept over Mila, the glint in them matching her smile. 'Are you ready?'

To fight her domina? No. She most definitely was not ready.

MILA FELT LIKE A PELL, the ones gladiators used for practice. She stood, seemingly anchored to the spot, while her half-dressed domina lunged forwards to beat her with a wooden sword. She blocked a few of the blows, but she could hardly fight back. That would never end well for a slave.

Thump, thud, thump.

Mila winced as pain shot through her chest. She might have recovered from her injuries, but her ribs did not take kindly to being thumped in the same spot they had broken.

Prisca lowered her shield, straightened, and exhaled.

'I am assuming you did not fight at this standard against a gladiator trained by Remus Latinius. You are holding back.'

Of course she was holding back. If she injured her domina, she would be locked up. Slaves had been killed for less. 'I am afraid I am not as fit as I was.'

Prisca gave her a hard whack with her sword, watching her flinch, noticing the tightening of muscles when she did it. She smiled and softened her knees. 'Nonsense. You are just afraid. I understand why, but as your domina, I order you to put in the effort. Do not make me fetch Albaus,' she added, smiling coyly.

Mila nodded. 'Ready?'

'Do you normally ask your opponent if they are ready before you strike them?'

Mila swung her shield and then plunged her sword at Prisca's thigh. Her domina blocked both attempts, and then her sword came to a stop against Mila's ankle.

'There goes your foot,' Prisca said smugly.

Mila stared down at the sword. She really was out of shape, and she was not enjoying it. 'Did your brothers teach you that?' she asked, meeting Prisca's gaze.

'My brothers taught me in the beginning. When I overtook them in skill, I found a real trainer.'

Mila was silent for a moment. 'How far did you go?'

Prisca retracted her sword and straightened. 'Not far enough. Do you know what people say when women like me take to the arena?'

She knew very well. She had heard Aquila weigh in on the topic a number of times—and she had not held back. 'Yes' was all she said.

'When you have money, everything comes at a higher cost.' She glanced over at Sabina, who stood with Nero against the wall. 'I was good, you know—very good. If I had been a man, I might have been my father's favourite son.'

Mila should have been thrilled at this revelation, except she suddenly understood why Prisca had bought her.

'You do not know how lucky you are. No father or husband to hold you down. No social responsibilities.'

Nothing to hold her down? The woman must have been deluded to say such things to a slave. How was not being allowed to marry being listed as an advantage?

She looked down to hide her feelings on the topic, but she could feel Prisca studying her.

'How would you like a chance to earn your freedom?'

That made Mila look up. Prisca had spoken the words so slowly, so gently, that she thought she may have imagined them.

A smile spread on Prisca's face as she pushed her hair over one shoulder.

'I thought so,' she said, satisfied by Mila's reaction. 'Again, but this time I would really like to see what you are capable of. Impress me and I will give you a chance to fight in the greatest amphitheatre in Rome. Disappoint me and the swords go away forever.'

Mila regarded her for a moment. 'I could be put to death if I hurt you.'

Prisca shrugged. 'I will not make you. You get to choose. Gladiator or slave?'

'And if you get hurt?'

Laughter. 'You have a very high opinion of yourself.'

Mila raised her sword and shook her head. Gladiator or slave. It was not really a choice. 'All right. I will fight you.'

She saw the same fire in Prisca's eyes that she had heard her mother describe many times. Perhaps they were not that different after all.

She did not ask her domina if she was ready that time—she attacked.

CHAPTER 13

The sun was low in the sky when the *essedari* left the arena on foot. The horses were unharnessed and led away, the chariots locked up. Slaves were running about collecting horse manure when Remus stepped into the arena with Titus. Remus liked to keep fit and strong. He wanted the men he trained to know he could put them flat on their backs if the need arose. While he did not like Titus as a person, he liked him as a partner. He was one of the few men who challenged him—and he liked to be challenged.

Felix sat in the cavea, watching them. Afterwards, Remus would wash and they would go to the tavern to eat, drink cheap wine, and hopefully return with some women who went there in search of gladiators. But first he would teach Titus some manners.

Before they had even begun, Brutus appeared beneath the portico.

'Remus.'

Remus waited for his opponent to step back before glancing over at the lanista. He was surprised to see Prisca Fadius standing with him. His gaze went past her to where Mila stood with Prisca's mute bodyguard, watching him with that famous guarded expression of hers. He straightened and looked at Felix to see if the dwarf knew something he did not, but his friend just shook his head. Normally, if Prisca wanted gladiators to entertain, she would send someone else to make the arrangements. His gut told him she was not there to book a show.

'I need a few moments,' he said to Titus, dropping his weapons on the ground.

'Don't sell yourself short,' Titus said with a wink. 'Take as long as the lady needs.'

Remus ignored him and walked over to the waiting party, trying not to look at Mila. 'Lady Prisca, what a pleasant surprise. If you're here to watch the men train, you're too late.'

She wore that devilish smile she reserved just for him. 'I could always watch you.' She gestured to his tunic. 'Though I am most disappointed to find you all covered up.'

Remus's gaze went to Mila, who was no longer looking at him. 'To what do we owe the honour?'

'I need a trainer, a good one.'

Remus looked at Brutus to gauge his reaction. The lanista was clearly ahead on this one. 'A trainer for who?'

Prisca turned and gestured for Mila to step forwards. 'You remember Mila?'

Actually, he had spent a great deal of time trying to forget, without success. 'Yes.' Their gazes met. 'You look better than the last time I saw you.'

'Honestly,' Prisca said, tutting. 'Matching a slave girl against the best female gladiator in Rome. Rather mean-spirited of you. Though smart business, I imagine,' she added, glancing at Brutus.

Remus's hands rested on his hips and he continued to

stare at Mila. Her expression did not change. 'What are you training her for?'

'The upcoming games at the Flavian Amphitheatre,' Brutus said.

Remus looked at him. 'The games are in six weeks. That's not enough time.' The idea was insane, and he would do whatever he could to shut it down.

'That's enough time with the right trainer,' Brutus said. 'You've trained men in less.'

Men who could be replaced, not Mila. But of course, the lanista had already agreed. Prisca had probably offered him a ridiculous sum to do it.

'You agreed to this?' Remus asked, managing to keep his voice calm and his body still.

Brutus nodded.

His jaw worked. 'And how will it work, exactly?'

'The girl will come every afternoon for the next six weeks, and you will train her as hard as any other gladiator.'

'Harder, I would hope. We do not want a repeat performance of last time,' Prisca laughed.

Remus was not laughing. 'You want *me* to train her?' He already had his answer. He was just buying time while he came up with a good reason to shut it down.

'Lady Prisca's asked for you, but we've plenty of good trainers who could work with the girl. Titus is getting good results from gladiators in his charge at the moment,' he said, turning to Prisca.

'No,' Remus said, shaking his head. 'I'll do it.' There was no way in hell he was letting Titus near her.

'Excellent,' Prisca said, clapping excitedly. 'You will not be disappointed. She is good, but I suspect you already know that.'

He looked everywhere but at Mila. 'For someone with

no training, she has raw potential.' He thought he saw her flinch. 'And what do you get out of this, Lady Prisca?'

Brutus crossed his arms and rocked on his feet. Prisca kept her gaze trained on Remus, her smile unfailing.

'You know better than anyone how easily I bore.'

If she was trying to suggest that she had eventually bored of him, she could save her lies. Everything else, sure. He had visited her bed enough times, heard enough complaints about her husband, her children, her empty life. Problems of the wealthy. 'So she's your muse?'

Prisca shifted, drawing attention to her round hips. 'I need *something* to look forward to.'

'He'll train her,' Brutus said, wrapping up the conversation. 'Have her here tomorrow afternoon. No time to waste.'

Remus had no choice. It was him or Titus. 'Of course.'

Satisfied, Prisca turned to Brutus. 'May I have a private word?'

The lanista nodded and the two of them stepped away to speak in private. The others remained where they were, with plenty of distance between them. Remus took in Mila's colourful stola and carefully braided hair. She looked tiny next to the large man keeping a trained eye on his domina.

'You all right?' he asked. It was the first question that came to him.

She clasped her hands in front of her. 'Fine, thank you.'

'The ribs?'

'Healing.'

He nodded and looked away for a moment. 'You ready for this?' When she did not immediately reply, his eyes returned to her. 'You'll work harder than you ever have.'

She regarded him. 'I am not one to shy away from hard work.'

He took a few steps towards her. 'How much do you know about her?' He nodded in Prisca's direction.

'Why does everyone keep asking me that?'

'Didn't wonder why she bought you?'

She glanced at her domina. 'I know now.'

Remus moved even closer. 'The only daughter amid an army of brothers. All centurions. The living ones, anyway. Names of the dead won't be forgotten.'

'She wanted to be like her brothers?'

'She wanted the glory. The attention. So she entered the arena. Disgraced her family.'

'Was she any good?'

'Maybe the best female at that time.'

'And her father put an end to it?'

He nodded. 'He married her off to Jovian, to be tamed.'

'I do not think it worked.' She swallowed. 'Did she train here?'

Another nod. 'Brutus trained her.'

'Is that how the two of you met?'

She knew about the affair. He shrugged. 'I was ten at the time.'

'Oh.'

He did not need to explain himself to her, but he did anyway. 'We met again during my fighting years. The best get invites to all the fancy parties.'

'I imagine you met a lot of women in your fighting years.'

Her cheeks burned despite the tenacious remark. He suppressed a smile. 'I think she misses the thrill and attention.'

'I can see that.'

'I'm talking about fighting.'

Another burn of the cheeks. 'So was I,' she lied.

He watched her squirm. 'What's she promised you?'

Her guard went up again. 'What makes you think she has promised me anything? I just do as I am told.'

'Pfft. When?'

'When there is no choice.'

A small smile, and the guard slowly came down.

'Can I… trust her?' she asked.

That scowl on any other woman would be unflattering. Not on her. 'Why do you ask?'

She looked up at Albaus before replying. 'She has promised me freedom if I win.'

He frowned. 'She did?' He was grateful the bodyguard could not repeat their conversation.

'Just one fight. If I win, she will give me my freedom.'

'After one fight?' That did not sound right to him. All that coin spent, time invested, for one battle.

'Is she telling the truth?'

He looked over to where Prisca was watching them. 'Time will tell.' His gaze returned to Mila. 'I'm going to train you hard.'

'You said that.'

'You'll end each day hating me.'

Her shoulders lifted in a shrug. 'If I walk away a freed woman, I will be quick to forgive.'

He smirked, but then it faded. 'She's chasing the fame she missed out on—the thrill of a win.'

Mila swallowed. 'I know.'

They stared at one another.

'You might get injured. Maybe worse than last time.'

'I know.' Silence. 'Will you help me win?'

His eyes moved over her face. 'Yes.'

Before another word could be exchanged, Prisca and Brutus returned, her coin pouch no doubt a little lighter, or a lot lighter if Brutus had his way.

'Let us leave Remus to his training,' Prisca said, glancing at him. 'Ensure you push her. By the time she enters the arena, I need her to be the best Rome has to offer.'

'I understand.'

Only once Prisca had passed him did his eyes return to Mila. He nodded once, and she returned the gesture. The bodyguard gave him a cold stare as he passed.

When they were out of sight, he linked his hands on top his head and closed his eyes.

CHAPTER 14

The device was similar to a training pell, but it had a wooden blade at head height and another at ankle height. Remus held a rope that made the blades turn.

'Ready?' he asked.

Mila looked around the arena, aware of the glances from passing men. No actual fighting, Remus had told her. Not until her skills and fitness were at the level he wanted. She wondered how long that would take.

'Ready,' she said, shaking her arms in an attempt to let go of some tension.

Remus pulled the rope and the blades began to spin. She ducked, jumped, ducked and jumped. It was going well, until the blades changed direction. She jumped, then ducked, but took too long getting up. The lower blade crashed into her ankles and she fell backwards onto the ground. Remus stopped the spinning blades with his foot.

'You all right?' he asked.

Laughter reached her from the cavea where some of the men had gathered to watch. Even Fausta sat among them, a broad smile on her face.

'I am fine,' she replied, getting to her feet and brushing sand off her hands.

Felix strolled over to stand beside Remus. She had not seen the dwarf since she had fought against him.

'If you have come to laugh, then just keep walking,' Mila said.

Felix held up his hands. 'I just got here.'

Satisfied he was not there to mock her, she glanced at Albaus and Nero, who were leaning against the wall. Thankfully, neither was laughing. Prisca had insisted she take the bodyguard into what she described as a "den of desperate men", and as Nero was supposed to be learning from Albaus, he had tagged along also.

'Again,' Remus called to her. 'Stop worrying about everyone else and focus.'

She took in his stern expression. He had not said one friendly word to her since she had arrived. 'Ready.'

They continued for most of the afternoon. Mila compared the experience to a person tied to a horse and forced to run behind it. It was relentless. Her tunic clung to her skin, and her lungs hurt every time she drew breath. Remus said little, occasionally handing her the waterskin when she was close to collapse. She clutched it with both hands, closing her eyes to savour the cool water against her burning throat.

'Small sips or it'll come straight back up,' he said, pulling it from her hands.

She stood, panting, wanting to empty it and then fall down. But she would never let that happen.

'You did all right,' Remus said, observing her. 'Especially without a rest.'

She leaned on her knees, willing her legs to stop trembling. 'Was resting an option?'

His eyes creased at the corners. 'No.' He glanced at the sun. 'You're done for today.'

She thanked the gods and wiped her face with her hand. 'Is there somewhere I can wash?'

'I'll have someone bring some clean water.'

She pushed off her knees. 'I can get my own water.'

'We've workers who tend the gladiators.'

'Slaves?'

He crossed his arms. 'Some. Mostly boys who wouldn't last in the arena. Making them useful keeps them alive.'

'Oh.'

'Feel foolish now?'

She stiffened. 'No. Do you feel superior?'

He shook his head but continued to watch her.

She cleared her throat. 'Nero can help me.'

Remus glanced at the young boy standing in Albaus's giant shadow. 'Is he like a pet or something?'

She could not stop her smile. 'Sort of. I think Prisca wants Albaus to teach him a thing or two, but he is a few years off being much of a protector.'

Remus nodded. 'It's good that Prisca sent Albaus with you.'

'Why?'

He hesitated. 'Keep you safe.'

'From you?'

'From this city.'

She studied him. 'You know, the biggest threat to a slave is usually in the house they reside in.'

He shifted. 'Is that true for you? Are there threats in the Fadius household?'

'Not yet.'

He blinked. 'Then your argument doesn't stand. The men you pass on the streets don't care if you're a civilian, slave, or whore. All they see is a pretty girl.'

She wiped her hands on her tunic. 'Is that what you see?'

He glanced back at Felix, who wore an amused expression. 'I see a gladiator not fit for the arena.'

She was glad her face was already red from exertion, because she felt a burn in her cheeks and wished she could snatch the question back. 'It is early days, Remus Latinius,' she said, turning away and heading for the water. She could feel him watching her.

'See you tomorrow,' he called.

She nodded, not daring to turn around.

THE FOLLOWING DAY, the entire city complained about the heat. Horses walked the streets with their heads inches off the ground, people moved at half the regular speed, and the merchants sat in the shade fanning themselves while whinging to their customers.

'Come, Nero. I cannot be late,' Mila said to the boy who had fallen behind. Albaus turned, waiting for him to catch up. They weaved between a group of old men who stood shouting at one another, something about geese, the words swallowed by the dense air.

'It is too hot,' Nero said.

Mila had never heard the boy complain. She glanced over her shoulder at him. Sweat dripped off his face and his cheeks were flushed. She stopped and placed a hand on his head. He was feverish. 'Do you feel unwell?'

'Just hot,' he said, unable to tell the difference due to the weather choking him.

Mila walked over to the closest shopfront and asked the merchant for water. At first he said no, but then Albaus stepped forwards and he begrudgingly went to fetch some.

'Thank you,' she said, handing the cup to Nero.

He emptied it and handed it back to the man.

'Are you all right to continue?'

The boy nodded. He never said no to anything. Albaus crouched down and gestured for the boy to climb onto his back. Nero collapsed against the man, wrapping his arms around his thick neck and closing his eyes.

Mila touched a hand to Albaus's arm. 'Thank you.'

He nodded and began walking.

When they arrived at Ludus Magnus, Remus was waiting in the arena looking agitated. Catching sight of Mila, he uncrossed his arms and marched towards them, eyebrows drawn together, ready to reprimand her. Then he spotted Albaus carrying Nero and his expression softened.

'What happened?'

Mila glanced over her shoulder. 'I think he has a fever. Hard to tell in this weather.'

Remus nodded and watched Albaus pass. 'Lay him in the shade. And get some water into him.' He looked at Mila. 'He the reason you're late?'

'It is this heat. Everyone is moving a bit slower today.'

Remus looked around, everywhere but at her. 'I want you to run laps until I tell you to stop.'

She glanced up at the smouldering sun. 'You want me to *run* in this heat?'

'We've less than six weeks to get you ready. Do you think you'll only fight if the weather is pleasant?'

'No, I was—'

'Start running.'

She crouched to slip off her sandals, aware of his shadow covering her. When she stood, she removed her belt and stola, noticing the way he averted his eyes when she did so. Her tunic, which she normally left on, was already soaked, so she pulled it over her head.

'What are you doing?' he asked, eyes returning to her.

'Minimising chafing,' she said, rolling the garments into a ball and tossing them aside.

His gaze fell to her chest, her bare legs, then away. He cleared his throat. 'Fine. Go. I'll be back shortly.'

'What?'

'Off you go.'

'You are not going to stay?' If she was expected to run in the heat, the least he could do was stay in the arena with her.

'Too hot for me,' he said, turning away.

She stared at his back.

'Go!' he shouted without turning around.

She broke into a jog, moving to the outside of the arena. He had told her she would end each day hating him. Instead, she was beginning the day hating him.

Within moments she tasted sweat on her lips. Daring a glance at Remus, she saw that he had wandered to stand beneath the portico. Her hands tightened into fists. A man walked over to speak to him, and they had a relaxed conversation about something. At any moment she was about to fall down while he stood under cover, keeping himself cool, probably complaining about the heat. He did not even glance in her direction. She doubted he would even notice if she stopped. But she would not stop; she would keep running even if it killed her.

The sun continued on its path and her undergarments acted as sponges for the sweat pouring off her. Every breath started to feel like a punch to the chest. Her thirst grew until it was all she could think of. Still, he did not offer water or tell her to stop. He even disappeared out of sight for a while, returning with someone else, pointing to some men who were being marched from the arena.

Only after he had spoken to every person in the vicinity did he bother to return. He stopped in the middle of the yard with his arms crossed in front of him.

'All right,' he called to her. 'That's enough.'

If he was waiting for her to collapse at his feet in gratitude, he would be waiting a long time. She continued at the same pace. 'I can keep going.'

He shook his head and looked at the ground. 'Mila, stop before you faint.'

Her feet pounded the sand. 'You want me fit. I have plenty left.'

Remus glanced over at Albaus, who frowned back at him. He let out a breath before trying again. 'You've made your point. Come here and drink.'

She stopped, hands going to her knees, determined not to be sick in front of him. Her body shook, threatening to give out. Before it could, a hand slipped beneath her arm, pulling her upright. She looked down at it, large and firm against her bare skin. Enough pressure to take the weight of her, but not enough to hurt.

'Drink,' Remus said, holding the waterskin up to her lips.

She closed her eyes and obeyed, her mind moving between the sensation of the water and the hand still wrapping her arm. When she was done, she opened her eyes and turned her head to look at him. 'Thank you.'

He nodded and let go. 'Rest for a moment.'

Mila shook her head. 'I am fine. We can begin now.'

He searched her face, as if trying to read her, then stepped back. 'Suit yourself. Let's begin.'

She felt something bordering on disappointment as he turned away. She watched his hands curl into fists and open again, the gentle swing of his arms, the muscles on his back shifting beneath the fabric as he moved. For a moment, she was blind to everything else. Remus seemed to fill her vision.

He bent, picking up two training poles, and turned to

face her. He tilted his head and she worried her thoughts were transparent.

'You all right?'

She nodded, focusing hard on the poles in his hands.

'Ready?'

'Ready.'

CHAPTER 15

'Mila!'

Mila turned, searching the busy street for the familiar voice. 'Nerva?'

He stepped into view, his hand clasping Dulcia's, pulling her between two women who had stopped in the middle of the road to talk. A smile spread on Mila's face and her sister broke into a run.

'Dulcia,' she breathed as her sister hit her at a run. 'What are you doing in this part of the city?'

'Looking for you,' she said, smiling up at her. 'Remus sent word to Nerva, suggested we might be able to catch you on your way to training.'

Mila looked at Nerva who stopped beside them. 'Remus sent word to you?'

He wore a worried expression. 'He told us Prisca is training you for the games.'

Mila smiled, mostly for the sake of her sister. 'Did he also tell you she has promised me freedom if I win? It is just one fight.'

'I have heard that before.'

'So it is true, then?' Dulcia said, beaming. 'Soon you will be free? Then you will come for me?'

'It is not that simple,' Nerva said. 'Mila will need coin to buy your freedom.'

'Whatever the wealthy throw down will be mine to keep.'

Nerva frowned. 'Do not encourage your sister's excitement. You know as well as I that the only gladiators who earn any decent coin are those fighting for their lives. You will just be there to warm up the crowd.'

Mila looked down, then at Nero. 'Nero, come and meet my sister.' After a lengthy illness, the boy was finally back on his feet.

Nerva took Mila's arm and pulled her away from the others. Albaus took a step towards her and she shook her head, letting him know it was all right.

'We need to keep walking,' she called behind her. 'Remus gets moody when I am late.'

Nerva looked back at Dulcia, who fell into step with Nero. The pair began to chat quietly. His gaze returned to Mila. 'What was that?' he whispered, keeping a hold of her arm.

'What?'

He shook his head. 'I have known you your whole life. Do not play games. Why did you look away when I mentioned about those fighting to the death earning the coin?'

'Did I?' He squeezed her arm and she yelped. 'You know, one signal to Albaus and he will crush you underfoot.'

He ignored her threat. 'Are you fighting in the morning or the afternoon?'

'What does that matter?'

Another squeeze.

'Ouch!' She pulled her arm free. 'Afternoon.'

His feet slowed for a moment. 'You are fighting to the death.'

She glanced back at her sister, then to Albaus, who followed behind them, scowling. Lowering her voice, she said, 'It is only to the death if the crowd wishes it so.'

He released her arm. 'You agreed to fight to the *death*? What is the matter with you?'

'Keep your voice down,' she said, smiling again over her shoulder to reassure Dulcia. 'Did you hear the part where I am free at the end?'

'If you live.'

She picked up her pace. 'I have the best trainer in Rome and every motivation to win.'

'So does your opponent.' He stared at her, and she continued not to look at him. 'Remus failed to share that important detail with me.'

She glanced at him and swallowed. 'Remus does not know.'

Nerva stopped walking and then ran to catch up. 'What do you mean he does not know?' he hissed. 'He is your trainer. You do not think it was important to tell him you need to kill?'

A young boy ran out onto the street and they stepped around him. 'Prisca does not want her husband finding out all the details just yet.'

'Because he would object to the entire thing?'

'Because he agreed to let her buy me on the condition that she was discreet. Women fighting to the death tends to send tongues wagging.'

He shook his head, mouth tightening. 'Can you hear yourself? There is every chance you will die.'

She looked at him then, head shaking. 'I think sometimes you forget I am a slave, and slaves do not make decisions. We follow orders.'

He was not buying it. 'Since when do you follow

orders? You could go to her husband and beg for your life, and he would put an end to this insanity at once.'

'I do not want to beg, and I do not want to put an end to it,' she snapped. 'I have a chance at freedom, and I am taking it.'

Nerva threw his hands up. 'The truth at last. Admit it, Prisca dangled freedom in front of you and you snatched it up like a greedy little slave without thinking it through.'

'Without thinking it through? You cannot actually believe that.'

'I know it, because if you actually stopped to think it through, you would see how selfish you are being. Better to have a mundane life than no life at all.'

Her glare cut though him. 'So kind of you to shine some perspective from up high.'

He continued to match her pace. 'Gods, give me strength.'

They both turned to check on the others, finding them smiling secretively, Dulcia's arms swinging. She was never that relaxed with people she did not know. Mila's body softened at the sight.

'What am I meant to tell your sister when you die in the arena?'

She tensed again. 'I will not.'

'You might.'

'If I fight well, the people may insist I live.'

'It does not work like that. They spare the big names they have grown attached to. No one knows who you are. No one will care if you die. Are you ready for that? A sword driven through your neck? A hammer following to ensure you are in fact dead?'

'Stop it. If Dulcia hears you, there will be no consoling her.'

'If you *die*, there will be no consoling her.'

Mila inhaled and looked at him. 'Say nothing of this to anyone, not even Remus.'

He faced forwards. 'He will find out eventually. Your fight is in four weeks. What are you going to do, take down the notices?'

'I will tell him, just not now.'

They both fell silent.

'How is my mother?' she asked, changing the subject.

Nerva glanced around at the vendors. 'Well enough.'

'Good.'

He looked at her. 'Am I to keep this from her also?'

She turned to him, pleading. 'It is just for a little while. Prisca is just being cautious.'

'To protect her interests.'

'Which happen to be in line with my own.'

He did not respond. They walked shoulder to shoulder, the others laughing and chatting behind them all the way to the entrance of Ludus Magnus.

Nerva turned to face her, his expression finally softening. 'You are beginning to look like a gladiator. Getting a little bulk on you.'

'She *is* a gladiator,' Nero said, coming to stand next to her. 'You should see her fight.'

Nerva smiled down at the boy. 'I have seen her once or twice. And who are you?'

'Her bodyguard,' Nero replied, glancing at Dulcia as he spoke the words.

Nerva's eyebrows rose with surprise. 'Are you now?' He looked at Albaus. 'Is he your backup?'

Nero laughed.

'He might be small, but he is fierce if provoked,' Mila said, keeping her face serious.

Nerva turned to Dulcia. 'Say goodbye to your sister.'

'I YIELD.' The wooden sword dropped from Mila's hand the same time her knees gave way. Remus took a step in her direction and then stopped himself. She looked up at him, panting and wheezing.

'You'll not get to yield in the arena,' he said, throwing his own sword on the ground between them. 'You drop your sword like that and you'll lose.'

He was only slightly out of breath, with a shine of sweat on his forehead. This annoyed her to no end as she sweltered like a pig at his feet. 'Just give me a moment.'

'Is that what you'll tell your opponent?'

She glared up at him, too exhausted for words. It was her third week of training, and every session ended the same way. The day before, she had stood retching in front of him, possibly the most mortifying moment to date. He had just waited for her to finish and handed her the waterskin to rinse her mouth. At least there was cloud cover providing much-needed relief, though no promise of rain.

'Get up,' Remus said. His tone was gentle despite the abruptness of his words.

'I do not think I can.'

He stepped over his sword and took hold of her arms, lifting her to her feet. The moment her legs took her weight, he let go and picked up the swords, handing one to her. He did all this without looking at her.

She gripped her sword as best she could and brushed loose hair from her eyes. He was crouched and ready. She waited for him to strike, desperate to prove herself. That was all she seemed to care about. She wanted him to tell her she was getting better, that she was good enough. That she could win.

They stared at one another for longer than normal. She saw his gaze fall to her bare legs, saw the movement in his neck as he swallowed. Suddenly, he straightened, lowering his sword.

She frowned. 'What is the matter?'

He shook his head, turning away. 'We're done. Get yourself cleaned up.' He began to walk away.

'What?'

'You heard me. Go before I change my mind.'

Felix, who had joined them halfway through the session, stepped out of Remus's way. Mila stared after her trainer as he strode across the sand towards the pail of water in the shade.

'What did you do?' Felix called to her, half a smile on his face.

She held her hands up. 'I have no idea. I can do no right with him.' She threw her sword down. 'When I am begging the gods for strength to stay upright, he tells me to keep going. When I assure him I am fine, he tells me to go home.'

Felix wandered closer. 'I gave up trying to figure him out years ago.'

'I was worried he was only like that with me.'

Felix studied her. 'I suspect he is worse with you.'

She rested her hands on her hips to help her balance. 'Does he really loathe me that much?'

Felix chuckled. 'He does not loathe you. He is hard on you because he wants you to win.'

'Because it will reflect badly on him if I do not?'

He glanced at Remus, who had poured half the pail over his head. 'It will, but he will not care about that. Remus wants to see you free. If he had his way, he would free every slave in this city.'

She watched as Remus placed the pail down and brushed water from his hair. As much as she hated to admit it, his carved frame and glistening skin were rather pleasing to the eye at that moment. 'Well, whatever his opinion of himself, he is no Spartacus.'

The dwarf nodded. 'You should tell him that.'

Mila studied the blisters on her hands. 'He has a funny way of showing that he… cares.'

'What would you have him do, go easy on you?'

She stretched out her fingers, wincing as she did so. 'A kind word occasionally would not kill him.'

'It is his job to toughen you up, not comfort you.'

'I am not asking for comfort. Just… never mind.'

'Kindness? Friendship?'

She sniffed. 'You make them sound like diseases.'

Felix shook his head and glanced up at the sun. 'He is trying to get you out of that arena in one piece. That is all he can focus on right now.'

They watched Remus jog across the sand and disappear beneath the portico.

'The best thing you can do is win. Walk away with your freedom, and I think you will find a very different Remus waiting for you at that gate.'

CHAPTER 16

It was the one part of the day Mila did not mind so much. The Fadius family would come together for dinner, the boys supposedly on their best behaviour, hiding mischievous smiles while kicking one another beneath the table. Jovian and Prisca had two sons, twelve-year-old Seneca and fourteen-year-old Varius. They were little clones of their father with their round noses, sloping eyes, and thin lips. The only feature they had inherited from their mother was her thick brown hair.

'Poetry,' Jovian said, waving a servant away from his plate. 'Of all the things for Varius to excel at.'

'Yes, but have you read any of it?' Prisca asked. 'It is quite lovely.'

Jovian glanced at his son. The boy had stilled to listen to the exchange. 'I do not doubt it. Poetry written for leisure is a perfectly acceptable pastime.' He looked between his sons. 'But a man must first master the sword.'

Mila thought that was a rather hilarious comment coming from a senator who had never seen battle. She glanced at Sabina, who was pouring Prisca's wine. That was how they communicated, small glances here and there.

'The person you employed to train them is not very good,' Prisca said.

'He is a legionnaire.'

She laughed and sipped her wine. 'How he has remained alive this long I have no idea.'

'And for the last time,' he continued, 'you will not be teaching them.'

Her hand went to her collarbone. 'Me? I would not dream of it. To betray my gender by picking up a weapon… it is unfathomable. And just imagine what all our loyal friends would say on the subject. We might even be shunned. Imagine, no more stuffy dinners fuelled by dull conversation.'

'All right.' He shook his head.

'I gave you my word, and in exchange, you gave me Mila.' She glanced over her shoulder to admire her. 'Perhaps she could teach them.'

'Absolutely not,' Jovian replied, signalling for more bread. 'You assured me you would be discreet.'

'Have I not been?'

His expression was tired when he looked at her. 'She spends more time training at Ludus Magnus than serving you.'

'We are not lacking in servants.'

'As long as you are not hanging about that place.'

'And bring shame on my family by mixing with the dregs of society? Never.'

'Sarcasm does not become you.'

'Nor does snobbery.'

Jovian's knife screeched across his plate. 'That is enough of that talk.' He tore some bread and dipped it into the oil on his plate. 'Did the seamstress bring the fabric today?' he asked, attempting to change the subject to something more befitting of a lady.

Prisca, who always seemed to muster a smile when

required, did not seem to have it in her. 'Yes, it is lovely. I wonder if she could make a new dress in time for the dinner party.'

'Splendid idea,' Jovian said, chewing his food. 'To think, Nerva Papias, a senator at twenty and one.'

Mila's breath caught at the mention.

Nerva. A senator. The news must have been very recent. He had said nothing when she had seen him the week prior.

'Are we to join you, Mother?' Seneca asked, face hopeful.

'No, my love. Besides, there are no children in the Papias household for you to socialise with. Aquila is as barren as she is rude.'

Another screech of the knife.

'But I want to see the gladiators.'

Jovian raised a hand to silence his son. 'There will be no gladiators at this dinner party. Aquila Papias is a woman of class and chooses not to indulge in such pastimes if she can help it.'

'Goodness, a snob and a bore.' Prisca dropped her spoon onto her plate. The noise made everyone turn. 'Does she think herself above entertaining her guests? Perhaps she will give us all a weaving demonstration instead.'

'Aquila is a fine example of what a Roman wife ought to be.'

Prisca pushed her plate away. 'I am afraid I do not have much of an appetite this evening.'

Mila marvelled at the woman's ability to maintain a composed face despite the violent thoughts no doubt racing through her mind.

Prisca stood. 'I think I shall retire early.'

Sabina stepped forwards to pull her chair back in one silent motion. Prisca walked over to her sons, kissing them before leaving the room.

Mila helped Prisca undress while Nero ran to fetch water so they could wash the paint from her face. Angry energy radiated from their domina, and when the boy returned with the water, Prisca's eyes locked on him in a way that made the others turn and look at him also.

'He is too old to be running about in a lady's room. He is meant to be with Albaus undertaking real work. Can he even use a dagger?'

Mila stared at the boy, a year younger than her sister, expected to be a man. 'A dagger for what?' she asked.

'To drive through the stomach of any person who poses a threat to this household,' Prisca snapped. She narrowed her eyes on him. 'From now on, you are to remain with Albaus and leave Sabina to her work.' She turned away. 'And for heaven's sake, have him teach you how to use a weapon.'

Nero looked bewildered, no doubt wondering what on earth he had done wrong. Sabina chewed her bottom lip.

Clearing her throat, Mila said, 'The men in the stables tend to treat him unkindly.'

'All the more reason for him to learn how to use a dagger.' She waved the boy away. 'Go on now. Find Albaus.'

'He grew up in a brothel,' Sabina said. 'He's desensitised to the naked form, if that's your concern.'

'As a boy, that might be true, but soon he will be a man.'

When Nero hesitated, Mila gestured to the door. Albaus would take care of him. It was not the time to try and negotiate.

Sabina picked up the basin of dirty water and left the room. Mila began combing Prisca's hair, leaving the subject alone.

'How goes it with Remus?' Prisca asked, once they were alone.

Mila kept the brushstrokes even. 'My fitness continues

to improve. We are now using weapons, so that is a good sign.'

Prisca stared ahead. 'Is he still bringing those cheap whores back to the barracks?'

More even strokes. 'Remus?' She wanted her domina to say another name.

'Yes, Remus.'

Mila wished she had taken the basin of water. 'I would not know. We barely speak, and never about such things.'

'Does he speak of me? Perhaps he wishes to know who visits my bed nowadays?'

Mila blinked, practising steady hands. 'He has not asked, and if he did, I would never tell him.'

'I would be happy for you to tell him if there was something to share. Obliging my husband on occasion is not particularly newsworthy, is it?'

She had no idea how to answer. 'I can tell him whatever you like.'

She pushed Mila's hands away. 'Anything you offer will be taken as construed, a tactic to make him jealous. I shall not give him the satisfaction.'

Mila stepped back.

'It is still hot. I will need two fans this evening until the air cools.'

It took the longest time for the room to fade to black. The women stood on either side of the bed, a lotus leaf in hand, not speaking. A slave disturbing their domina was unthinkable.

Mila wondered how she might secure a place at Prisca's side for the dinner party. To lay eyes on her sister in that familiar house, to hear Nerva's laugh, to listen to her mother's familiar hums. If she closed her eyes, she could almost feel the stroke of her sister's fingers through her hair.

She felt her body jolt as sleep tried to take her. The

training tired her in a way she had never experienced before. Not only did every muscle ache, but she had developed the ability to fall asleep in an instant. It was a blessing during lonely nights and a curse when she was supposed to stay awake fanning her domina.

She looked across at Sabina, finding her in a similar state, blinking away sleep. Perhaps she was missing her family too. Many of them had died back in Armenia; the others she would likely never see again. The only family she had was the woman she served and a young orphan she was not allowed to keep.

Mila's arms began to cramp. She had given everything to Remus that afternoon. 'Go to bed,' she whispered to Sabina. 'The air is cooling. I will stay a little longer.'

Sabina nodded her thanks and went to wash. Mila stared down at her sleeping domina, remembering the conversation she had with Nerva before she was sold. An image formed in her mind of Prisca and Remus, a tangle of limbs beneath her fan. She wondered how often Remus had laid in that bed, bathing in the soft hair Mila brushed every day. She had no right to feel the way she did, but jealousy coiled within her.

As far as she knew, their affair was over. But what about all the other women? He was probably with someone at the barracks that very moment. Many women went searching for good-looking gladiators like him. He was the ultimate prize.

Sabina returned to the room, pulling the small bed out from beneath Prisca's large one. Within moments, soft, even breaths filled the room. Later, when the air had cooled enough to sleep in comfort, Mila did the same. Sleep should have swallowed her, but the moment she closed her eyes, Remus played in her mind. She opened her eyes so it would stop, holding them open for as long as she could. She tried to think about her family, her training, the upcoming fight, Prisca's volatile mood. Anything but him. Finally, she was rewarded with sleep so deep all thoughts left her.

In the morning, she opened her eyes to grey light, and Remus flooded her mind once again. In her half-asleep state, she saw his steady gaze on her, heard his voice, soft that time. She felt his hands. She shifted beneath her blanket and reminded herself that those hands were for other women, not the one he was preparing for the arena.

She closed her eyes again, willing sleep to return, but it was no good. Remus Latinius had woken something within her, and she had no idea how to rid herself of him.

CHAPTER 17

One thing that really got under Mila's skin was the ease with which Remus moved and fought while she struggled to avoid the precise blows of his sword. The few times she did make contact, she did not hold back.

'Good,' he said, breath even.

But she saw the questions in his eyes, no doubt wondering where her newfound energy stemmed from.

'All right, stop,' he said.

When she did not listen, he knocked the sword from her hand. It landed in the sand some distance away. He lowered his shield and studied her.

'What's the matter?'

They were training amid other gladiators and had to speak up to hear one another.

She dropped her shield and rested her hands on her hips, trying to catch her breath. 'What do you mean?'

'You're angry.'

'I am trying to beat you. You want me to smile?' The truth was she did feel angry, but she had no right to be.

Remus exhaled and looked to the heavens for strength to continue the conversation. 'I've been doing this a long time. I've learned a thing or two about people.' She refused to meet his eye. 'Something I've done?'

'No,' she said, finally looking at him. 'You want me to fight harder, and when I do, you stop me to talk about it.'

'Because you're angry.'

She felt like she was losing her mind. She was supposed to be focused on the fight, on her freedom, on anything but him. If she could just find a valid reason to hate him…

'I'm trying to figure out what has you in such a foul mood. We can use it to our advantage.'

'*My* advantage.'

He frowned. 'What?'

'Use it to *my* advantage. You said "our".'

He shifted, amusement in his eyes. 'You've a problem with me saying "our"?'

Why had she said that? 'It is a bit misleading. When the time comes for me to fight, there will be no *us* in the arena, only *me*, the slave you beat up for a few hours every afternoon.' She sounded like a child and wished the gods would strike her down in that moment. Anything to shut her up.

He regarded her for a moment before walking over and picking up her sword. 'All right, *slave*. Won't make that mistake again.' Coming to a stop in front of her, he took her hand and closed her fingers around the weapon, then collected the shield and did the same.

Heat pulsed through her as his hands wrapped hers.

'You've had your moment. Ready to get back to work?' he asked, looking down at her.

He was so close she could feel his breath on her when he spoke. She did not look up, concentrating instead on the task of not trembling.

'Yes,' she replied, trying to bring strength to her voice.

He stepped around her, his fingers dragging along her arm and settling against her elbow. His other hand held her shoulder, his lips coming close to her ear. 'See how easily I disarmed you before?'

Yes, she had seen. She nodded. He slid the hand on her left shoulder down to her wrist, making the hairs on her arm stand on end. He raised her shield so the top of it was level with her chin.

'You're going to keep it at that height.'

His voice hummed in her ear, and she worried that if he asked her to move, her limbs might not obey. His fingers slid down to meet hers.

'Open your hand so your fingers tip the shield flat.'

She did as she was told.

'Get used to the weight. Practice balancing it.'

She moved her arm, focusing on keeping the shield horizontal. He leaned closer.

'In a moment, you're going to grip the handle nice and tight and thrust it forwards as hard as you can.'

He released her hand and elbow, stepping back from her. She released the breath she had been holding and focused on the shield, not the cooling parts of skin where his hands had been.

'Now,' he said in a firm voice.

She gripped the handle and thrust it forwards.

'Again,' he shouted. 'We're breaking noses, not dancing.'

There was that "we" again.

She thrust harder, feeling the force of it in her bones.

'Again!'

A growl formed in her throat, escaping as she thrust one last time.

'Good,' he said, stepping into her vision.

They looked at one another, and she saw something in his eyes, in the way his gaze fell away. Whatever physical reaction she was having to him, she was fairly certain it was mutual.

A clap sounded nearby, and they both turned to see

Prisca and Sabina sitting in the cavea, watching them. Prisca sat with a straight back and an amused smile on her face. Sabina wore a worried expression.

'Heavens, Remus, your methods have evolved a great deal. More… hands on.' She stood and Sabina rose also.

Remus managed to hide his surprise at seeing her. 'Lady Prisca. Didn't know you were here. Checking up on me?'

Her teeth flashed. 'Checking up on Mila. However, after seeing the nature of the lesson, I wonder if my own skills might need sharpening.'

Her tone was playful, but the venom beneath it was not lost on Mila. She looked away, not wanting to watch the exchange.

'Your husband would have me fed to the dogs if he found out.'

Her smile grew. 'You are right. My husband is forgiving of most things, but not the use of weapons.'

Mila glanced over at Sabina, whose expression had not changed.

'Come now, Mila,' Prisca said, clapping her hands. 'Let us see all that you have learned these past weeks.'

Remus and Mila looked at one another, then away. As Remus bent to collect the swords, Prisca laughed.

'Goodness. Fetch the girl a *real* sword.'

Remus straightened and then gestured for Nero to fetch some weapons from the storeroom. The boy was desperate to be useful, always hanging on Remus's every word. Albaus went with him. Prisca and Sabina sat down again, waiting for the display to begin.

Nero burst back into the arena, hugging two swords to his chest.

'Thank you,' Mila said, taking one from him.

After giving the other to Remus, Nero collected the wooden swords from the ground and moved out of their way. Mila and Remus looked at one another, then down at the weapons in their hands. He waited for a signal that she was ready. She gave a small nod, her feet shuffling in the sand. She was so used to the feel of it, she was sure combat on a firm surface would completely throw her ability.

Remus struck first, a familiar sequence of blows—predictable, with nowhere near the force he used with the wooden swords. She responded with the techniques he had taught her, feeling strong and in control. It was easy when he was holding back.

'You are getting soft, Remus,' Prisca called. 'How is Mila to survive the arena if you go easy on her?'

Remus's jaw tightening was the only indication he had heard. Then came his attack, fast and relentless, each blow depleting Mila until she finally tired out, but she kept pushing on.

Clang, clash, clang.

Mila's sword flew from her hand and Remus's foot crashed into her chest, throwing her backwards into the sand. The cold tip of his sword was pressed against her neck. She tried to take in air, but nothing happened. He had winded her.

Another clap from Prisca.

'There he is,' she said, getting to her feet. 'Best way for her to learn. I can see the improvement, but she has some way to go.'

A shadow covered Mila, and she looked up to see Remus staring down at her. 'You good?'

She slowed her breathing and nodded. He offered his hand. She glanced at it before pushing herself up and stepping past him, coughing a few times, eyes on her feet. 'Do you want us to go again, Era?' she called to her domina. She felt Remus's gaze on her.

Prisca was silent, eyes on Remus.

'Think that's enough for today,' he said. 'You're tiring.'

'She does not look tired,' Prisca called.

'It's enough for today,' he said again.

Mila just nodded. 'Nero! Time to go.'

The boy jogged over to her, sand spraying up at Albaus, who trailed after him. She looked at Remus but did not say a word. There was something in his expression, something that made her look away.

'Usual time tomorrow,' he called after her.

CHAPTER 18

Remus looked at the sun to gauge the time, then glanced once more at the entrance. The afternoon was slipping away, and there was still no sign of Mila. He had a feeling something was off but hoped he was wrong. Prisca was a complicated woman, and not the first to be disappointed by his waning interest. He had ended the affair the moment he was freed, promising himself he would only bed women of his choosing, not those Brutus described as "good for business". It was not that she was unattractive, far from it, but that she was married, a fact that did not sit comfortably. She also happened to be demanding, and Remus did not have the time or patience for it. While she had eventually accepted the fact that their affair was over, she was jealous by nature. Mila's improved fighting skills had not been the only thing Prisca had witnessed the day prior. Nothing escaped that woman, and he doubted his facade had been enough.

'Has she given up already?' Fausta quipped as she passed him. Her left eye was swollen shut, and sand clung to her wet skin.

'Clean yourself up,' he called to her back.

Felix passed her from the other direction, wincing at the sight of her injury. He stopped next to Remus, who was pretending to watch the two men training in front of him while really watching the entrance behind them.

'Hope there is still an eyeball under that mess,' Felix said.

'She'll live.'

Felix looked around. 'Where are Mila and that big chatty fellow?'

'He's mute.'

'Ah, that explains a lot.'

Remus ran his hands through his untrimmed hair. 'Prisca came past yesterday. Now no Mila.'

Felix made a pained face. 'That woman is finely tuned to sexual tension.'

Remus glanced at him. 'Mila was showing her skills. Prisca said I was going easy on her.'

'Were you?'

Remus rested his hands on his hips. 'I'm training the girl, not defeating her. Woman insisted on real swords.'

A smile spread across Felix's face. 'So you *were* going easy on her. You like her, I get it. Prisca has never recovered from being rejected. Taking up with her slave is like salt to an open wound.'

Remus looked to the heavens for strength. 'I haven't taken up with her.'

Felix shrugged. 'Prisca does not know that. You should have remembered your gladiator face. Now she knows your secret.'

'My secret?'

'Not much of a secret, really. Fausta saw it the first time she saw the two of you together.'

'Saw what?'

Felix gestured between them as he struggled to find the word. 'Feelings.'

Remus shook his head and watched as one of the men plummeted face first into the sand before getting up onto his hands and knees, spitting.

'What are you worried about?' Felix asked. 'Prisca will send her elsewhere? There is no better training than here.'

'Don't know. We'll find out soon enough.'

Felix crossed his arms. 'Never seen you smitten with a girl.'

'Smitten?' He signalled for the men to begin again. 'She's attractive. Won't deny that.'

'What man would?'

'But nothing can happen.'

Felix frowned. 'Why not?'

Before he could answer, Mila walked in, eyes searching. When her gaze fixed on him, Remus took a step in her direction and then stopped when he saw her entourage: Albaus with Nero behind, Brutus in front, Titus at her side.

'This isn't good,' he breathed so only Felix could hear.

Mila eyes never left him as they approached. He knew he had to play it casual while he found out what was happening.

'You're late,' he said, as though it were any other day and the others were not standing with her.

Brutus spoke up, not one to waste time. 'The girl will be training with Titus for the remaining days.'

Remus listened, kept calm. 'Why?'

'Lady Prisca wants her pushed harder,' Titus chimed in.

Remus did not look at him, his eyes on Brutus. 'I'm pushing her as hard as I can without injuring her.'

The lanista's face was creased against the sun. 'The lady has her reasons.'

Of course she did.

Remus glanced at Mila, who was staring at her feet. 'Suppose her word is final, then?'

'Her coin, her rules,' Brutus said, clapping him on the back.

Remus nodded and laughed through his nose, a release of frustration. 'Her coin, her rules,' he repeated.

REMUS WAITED in the atrium for Prisca to join him. He could not keep still, pacing the length of the room, finding the atmosphere more overwhelming than luxurious.

'Remus. What a surprise,' Prisca sang, swanning into the room in a silk robe with not much beneath it. 'I must apologise for my appearance. Had I known you were coming, I would have worn something more appropriate for guests.'

Yet she had found time to put on jewels. Remus made a point of not looking down, where the outline of her nipples was visible through the sheer fabric.

'What brings you here?' she asked, closing the gap between them.

He exhaled. 'I think you know what brings me here.'

She touched a hand to her collarbone. 'That is rather forward. Enough to make a grown woman blush.'

He shook his head, his eyes never leaving her. 'Not that. Why'd you ask for Titus to train Mila?'

She gave a pretty laugh. 'Oh, is that why you are here? A battered ego?'

He studied her, trying to figure out her game. 'Thought you wanted her to win.'

She feigned surprise. 'I do.'

'I'm a better trainer than Titus and you know it.'

She was enjoying herself far too much. 'Come now, let us not turn this into a flexing of muscle. The fact of the matter is she needs to be pushed, and you are not the man to do it.'

'Titus will destroy her,' he said plainly.

'So will her opponent in a few weeks.'

He had to look away.

'Would you care to sit? Shall I organise some refreshments?' She glanced at the window. 'Is it too early for wine?'

He drew a breath. 'No refreshments.'

She looked up at him, the neckline on her robe widening every time she moved. 'Do not feel badly. You have done what you can with the girl. She has the skills. Now it is time to toughen her up.'

Perhaps Prisca was right. Just hearing her say those words made his entire body jolt. Yet the thought of Titus having free rein over her was worse. 'Titus is unpredictable, short-fused, and doesn't like women.'

She waved his words away. 'Mila is in no danger. Brutus is far too well paid to let anything serious happen to her.' Her eyes moved over his jaw, which was pulsing. A look of satisfaction settled on her face. 'I am doing you a favour.'

'How do you figure that?'

She lifted her chin. 'I saw your face yesterday when you disarmed her. It hurt you to do it, to strike her.' She took a step back from him. 'You have developed feelings for her. Remus Latinius, taken apart by a slave.' She looked around the room. 'I suppose that is what happens when you are forced to spend time with someone day after day.' She peered up at him. 'Just imagine if you had trained *me*.'

Remus did not like her being inside his head. 'Does your husband know about all this?'

Her expression did not falter. 'Of course. We have no secrets.'

'Does he know you intend to exploit her in his name?'

The smile fell away. 'Exploit her?' She stared at him. 'I am handing that girl everything. If she wins, she is free, and if she loses, she dies with all the glory a girl of her status could hope for.'

He froze, hoping he had misunderstood. 'Mila will not die.' He waited for her to confirm it. She just stared back at him. 'Will she?' he pushed, barely recognising his own voice. When Prisca did not reply, he stepped up to her so fast that he heard her intake of breath. 'Tell me you're not sending her into the arena to die.'

'No…' She swallowed and tried again. 'I am sending her in to win. Why do you think I am training her so hard?'

'Then you're sending her in to kill.' It came out as a whisper.

She shrugged and turned the cuff on her wrist. 'That is for the people to decide.' She arched one groomed brow at him. 'Now do you see why she needs a man like Titus? She will be fighting for her life. Best she gets used to it now.'

REMUS SAT in the tavern across the street from Ludus Magnus, the one he drank in most days, the one Mila passed on her walk home. He did not trust himself to be there while Mila trained.

He kept his eyes on the window, a drink in hand for appearances. The room smelled of sweat and ale, and so did the women who kept approaching him, legs and hips brushing his arm. He shook his head at them, gaze fixed on the street so as not to miss her.

Copa wandered over, her round cheeks flushed. 'Get you another?'

He spotted her then, walking slowly, an arm draped over Nero's shoulders. Albaus walked behind them, eyes on her feet, as though expecting her to fall down at any moment. She wiped blood from her nose. When she stumbled, Albaus reached forwards and grabbed her elbow, righting her.

Remus was out of his chair and through the door of the tavern in a few strides. He jogged across the street towards her. 'Mila.'

She looked up at the familiar voice, straightened, and withdrew her arm from Nero's shoulders. If she was trying to pretend she was fine, she was too late. He stopped in front of her, his anger already melting away despite the speech he had prepared on the way from Prisca's house. He did not like being lied to.

She looked past him to the tavern. 'Your home away from home, I assume?'

He nodded. 'Something like that.' Silence. 'Tough afternoon?'

Albaus grunted and everyone turned to look at him. He shook his head, not happy about something.

'Titus almost broke her leg,' Nero said, his face compressed and red.

Mila put a hand on his shoulder. 'It was not that bad. I am fine, just tired.'

Remus was going to have a word with Titus when he returned. 'How long have you known you'll be fighting to the death?'

Albaus shifted, and Nero looked up at her in surprise, no doubt waiting for her to deny the fact. She stared at the boy, looking suitably guilty. With a sigh, she said, 'From the beginning.'

Another grunt from Albaus. Nero's mouth hung open.

'You did not think to tell *me*?' Remus asked.

She looked too tired for the conversation.

'Would it have changed anything?'

Would it? He did not know.

'What if you die?' Nero asked, his voice coming out as a squeak.

She blinked. 'I plan to win. As soon as I can walk properly again,' she added, her smile weak.

Remus noticed it then, the swelling along her jaw. He reached up, tipping her chin, aware of the change in her breath when he touched her. 'That one is going to bruise.'

Looking up, she said, 'Nothing is broken. I can live with bruises.'

He released her face and they both resumed breathing. He realised he did not have room for anger; he was too broken by the prospect of losing her.

His hand dropped to his side. 'I'll walk you.'

They fell into step, Nero falling behind to walk with Albaus. Every alleyway they passed introduced a new smell: bread, offal, manure, flowers. The many scents of Rome. The streets were still warm beneath their feet. People had slowed down, their busy frowns fading with the sun, replaced with smiles as they went about making dinner plans.

'I am going to see my family tomorrow,' Mila said, filling the silence. 'Nerva has joined the senate, and Aquila is hosting a dinner party. Prisca said I could accompany her. A sweetener, perhaps.'

He rolled his eyes. 'That was big of her. A peace offering for the torture over the coming weeks.'

Mila was quiet for a moment.

'I think she actually cares in her own way.'

He released a breath. 'Thought I had her figured out once. I don't really understand her anymore.'

Mila's arms swung at her side, occasionally brushing his.

'I think she is lonely. A bit of a misfit in that world.'

'You forgot calculating and manipulative.' He glanced at Mila, who was watching him. 'What?'

'You liked her once.' Her eyes fell to his lips and then the street. 'Rather a lot, actually.'

He studied her. 'If I didn't know you better, I might say you're jealous.'

She lengthened her stride. 'Why do you gladiators always assume women are falling over themselves for you?'

He smiled. 'They usually are.'

'Well, beneath all that muscle, you are just ordinary men.'

'Tell me what you really think.'

She stepped in and shoved him lightly. 'You do not need me to fluff your ego.'

'No, but it'd be nice.'

She smiled at the street and they fell silent for a while, watching people move around them. It was the end of the workday, and many were returning home to rest before dinner.

'I was a slave then.' Once again, he did not need to explain himself, but he did anyway. 'She set her sights on me. I did what I'd done my whole life, whatever I was told.'

'I bet it was terrible,' she said, rolling her eyes.

'Awful,' he agreed. 'All the other gladiators were *very* sympathetic to my situation.'

She laughed, and when he looked at her, he saw a small dimple he had never noticed before. It was possibly his new favourite thing about her.

His arm brushed against hers. 'You mock me.'

'I *expose* you.'

She put some space between them, and he noticed her limp as she did so.

'How's the leg holding up?'

'Fine.'

She made an effort to keep her stride even. He looked away.

'Titus will train you harder than I ever could.'

A small laugh. 'I figured that out already.'

Two soldiers marched towards them with no intention

of changing course. Remus took Mila by the wrist and pulled her out of their way. He kept hold of her after the men had passed. She looked down at his hand, then up at him. Out of the corner of his eye, Remus saw Albaus grab Nero by the shoulder and pull him back. The little bodyguard was not pleased at being excluded from the conversation.

'I want you to win,' Remus said, realising how ridiculous he sounded.

She studied his eyes, his face, then gave a small nod. 'I know.'

A horse trotted towards them, its rider shouting at everyone in his way. Remus pulled Mila closer, and for a moment she was pressed against him, filling the grooves of his body as though the gods had made her to fit him. The moment the horse passed them, she stepped back. He let go of her wrist, and they resumed walking.

'What'll you do with your freedom?' he asked after a long silence. They had turned down a quiet alleyway.

'Whatever I need to do to earn enough coin to buy my family's freedom. Probably keep fighting. I have no other skills.'

They passed a man asleep in a doorway.

'And after that?'

She shook her head. 'I honestly do not know. Leave Rome, maybe.'

'And go where?'

She squinted up at him. 'I've never been out of the city. The country, perhaps.'

'And do what?'

She shrugged. 'Be free to choose, I suppose.' She thought for a moment. 'What about you? What holds you here? Family?'

'Does Felix count?'

'If you care for him like blood, then yes.'

A gush of water splattered the street in front of them. Mila pulled Remus back in time to avoid getting wet. She glared at the woman framed in a doorway, clutching the empty pail.

'Your reflexes have improved,' Remus said.

She turned to look at him, studying his expression. Perhaps she had expected him to shout and carry on, but he preferred to save his anger for things that mattered. They stepped over the dirty water and kept walking.

'I suppose you will take credit for that,' she said, picking up the conversation again.

He shrugged. 'If you want to put it down to one afternoon with Titus, go ahead.'

'Maybe I will.'

She smiled up at him, and there was light in her eyes. There was no denying her beauty in that moment, or his reaction to it.

'Admit it,' he said. 'You're in a lot of pain right now.'

She adjusted her stola. 'Honestly? Yes. Everything hurts.'

'That's what I thought.'

She turned to him again. 'Tell me about Felix. He is a civilian, is he not?'

'Yes.'

They turned down a narrow alleyway, that time ducking below hanging linen. Albaus was practically turned sideways to fit through the space.

'Where is his family?'

They passed a pair of soldiers, their gazes lingering on Mila. She seemed oblivious to the fact.

'His family doesn't exactly approve of his... life choices.'

She laughed and he wished he could see her face, but she walked in front, occasionally glancing back at him.

'I imagine his options were limited. Hardly seems fair to punish him for making the best of his situation.'

He noticed some welts on her right shoulder where she had been struck earlier. Nothing serious, yet he found himself keeping tally for when he next faced Titus in the arena.

They exited the alleyway, emerging a few streets from the Fadius household. Mila stopped on the corner, holding on to the stone wall for a moment. Remus noticed that her legs were shaking. He stepped closer.

'You all right?'

Nero stepped between them. 'I can carry you on my back, like Albaus did me when I was sick.'

She smiled at him, giving his arm a brief squeeze. 'What sort of gladiator would I be if I allowed such a thing?'

'When did you last eat?' Remus asked.

'This morning.'

'You need food.' He glanced down the street. 'Come.'

He took her hand, warm and small in his. Her skin was too soft, barely callused. They would need to toughen up before the fight. She did not pull away, letting him guide her along the street until they reached a shopfront where a baker was packing up for the day.

He turned to her. 'What do you want?'

'I will eat at the house. There is really no need.'

He pointed to the few remaining loaves and tarts. 'You mean after the rest of the household is fed? Eat now or you'll collapse.'

He saw her glance at the lemon tarts next to the bread, unsure what to do. He pulled out his coin pouch and nodded to the tarts. 'Two, please.'

'Bread is fine,' Mila protested. 'The cheaper one.'

Remus ignored her and paid the baker, thanking him before handing both Mila and Nero a tart.

'What about you?' Mila asked.

Nero did not hesitate, practically swallowing the thing

whole. 'Thanks,' he said, sending flakes of pastry flying as he spoke.

Remus nodded, knowing too well what a treat it was to eat those foods at that age. 'Already ate at the tavern,' he lied. 'And Albaus looks like he's cutting back. You go ahead.'

Mila glanced down at the tart and then lifted it to his mouth. 'At least taste it. Lemon is my favourite.'

Her face was all sweet and hopeful. How was he supposed to say no to her? He looked at the tart and then bent slightly, taking a bite. Citrus and sugar exploded in his mouth. He closed his eyes for a moment.

'Good?'

He nodded, opening his eyes and smiling. 'So good.'

Satisfied, she took a bite, groaning as she chewed. 'Maybe I will become a baker.' She wiped at the crumbs on her lips. 'Do they have bakers in the country?'

'You don't get to eat all the tarts. The idea is to sell a few.'

She laughed, and even though she brought a hand up to cover the food in her mouth, he witnessed her smile in all its brilliance: her brow smooth, her dimple deep, and her eyes creasing at the corners.

'Thank you,' she said.

He could have just stood there watching her eat, but he was aware of the passing time and did not want to get her into trouble. 'Best get you home. You all right to walk?'

She nodded. 'The miracle of sugar.'

They began their walk up the hill towards the house, their feet matched in pace while Nero bounded ahead, kicking a stone along the road.

'I'll leave you here,' Remus said, not wanting to be spotted by Prisca or any of her servants. He saw something resembling disappointment in Mila's eyes.

'Thank you for walking us,' she said. 'And for the tarts.'

He nodded. 'Be careful with Titus. He's…'

'Like most men?' she finished, brows raised and smiling.

His eyes went to her mouth. 'Just be careful.' He turned to leave.

'Remus,' she called.

He turned around.

'Where would *you* go? If not Rome, then where?'

Without thinking, he said, 'India.'

'*India?*' She mulled it over for a moment. 'Why India?'

He shrugged. 'I met a man once who travelled the world for a living.'

'Where did you meet him?'

'A tavern.'

She suppressed a smile. 'Ah, very reliable source, then.'

'He was sober for some of it.'

She studied him. 'How did this sober man make his living?'

'He was a spice trader.'

'Oh.' She seemed surprised by that.

'What?'

She shook her head. 'I think I was expecting you to say something less… honest.'

'Good to know you have such a high opinion of me.'

Another smile, as beautiful as the last.

'You know, the elephants in India are smaller than the ones in Africa.'

He frowned. 'How do you know that?'

She shrugged. 'My sister and I were tutored when we were young.'

His frown deepened. 'You were?'

She nodded. 'We might not have the Papias name, but Rufus did what he could.'

'That explains a lot about you.'

'It does? Like what?'

He checked their surroundings, worried someone would recognise them. 'Your snobbery, for one.'

'My snobbery?'

'I'm not finished. Your rebellious nature. The fancy way you talk. Your detachment from the real world.'

'I am still stuck on snobbery.'

He grinned. 'You think you're better than other slaves, that you deserve more.'

She shook her head. 'No, no, no. The only difference between me and other slaves is that I have figured a way out of this life.'

They fell silent for a moment.

'I have always wanted to see an elephant,' she said, 'but not watch it die in the arena.'

He studied her serious face. 'Maybe I'll take you to India one day.'

'You could go right now. What are you waiting for?'

He did not have a good answer. 'Felix isn't a fan of spicy foods.'

Mila glanced behind her to where Albaus and Nero stood waiting for her to catch up. He did not want to her go.

'Until tomorrow,' he said, turning away again.

She raised a hand. 'Good day, Remus Latinius.'

CHAPTER 19

Judging by the way Aquila had prepared the house, one might have thought Nerva had just become emperor rather than a mere senator.

Mila stood against the wall, still as the artwork framing her, going to great efforts not to look at Nerva for fear she would burst out laughing at the ridiculous fuss being made.

The guests gathered in the *triclinium,* lounging in comfort while admiring the food laid out before them. The furnishings had been reupholstered and were covered with colourful cushions made from the finest materials. The food was typical fare, but more of it than necessary for such a small party. Unsurprisingly, Aquila had skipped the inclusion of sow's udder, opting instead for a pheasant dish that also happened to be Germana's specialty.

'Let us drink to Nerva, and all that he will do for Rome,' Jovian said, raising his polished cup.

'My cup seems to be empty,' Aquila complained. A servant rushed forwards to fill it.

Mila's former domina had made a point of not looking at Mila the entire evening. Though slaves were generally invisible, Aquila had always ensured she felt it. This was her opportunity to remind Mila of her lowly status, in case she had somehow forgotten.

'We are a few slaves down at the moment,' Aquila explained. 'Many caught the fever that seems to have swept through the city.'

Prisca nodded. 'We were not unscathed. However, my sons remain well, thank heaven.'

'It is usually slaves who bring these diseases with them,' Aquila said, 'infecting the rest of the household.'

Mila risked a glance at Nerva, who was staring into his drink. By the looks of him, he had not even heard. He seemed positively miserable.

'Who made your cushions?' Prisca asked, running a hand over the luxurious fabric. 'The detail in them is to die for.'

Now it was Aquila's turn to stare into her cup.

'Our seamstress,' Rufus said, answering on behalf of his wife.

Prisca's eyes widened in feigned surprise. 'Really? Let us bring her out so I might ask her about them.'

Aquila looked up at that. 'Really, Prisca, they are just cushions. Any competent seamstress could whip them up for you.'

'We do not need more pillows about the place,' Jovian said, casting a knowing look at Rufus.

'If I am to endure a house stuffed with pillows, then so shall you,' Rufus replied. He turned to one of the servants. 'Ask Tertia to come here.'

Mila stiffened and Nerva sat a little straighter, glancing at his mother, then at Mila. The guests filled their cups and picked at the tray of cured meats.

Finally Tertia entered the room, stopping a safe distance from everyone. She glanced at Mila before addressing Rufus. 'You asked to see me, Erus?'

'Actually, *I* did,' Prisca said, propped up on one elbow. 'I have been admiring your work.' She ran a hand over one of the cushions. 'Your dominus tells me you created these yourself.'

The women chatted back and forth for a few moments while the men spoke among themselves. Aquila picked at the food on offer, eventually waving the servant holding the tray away.

'All right,' she said, losing patience. 'Let the woman return to her work. That is what she is here for.'

Tertia looked to Rufus, who nodded. She bowed her head and turned to leave.

'Mila,' Prisca said, looking over her shoulder. 'Would you like a few moments with your mother before we depart?'

Tertia slowly turned back around, her hopeful gaze returning to Rufus.

'Only if it is not an inconvenience to the household,' Mila said, ensuring she said all the right things.

'I am afraid it is,' Aquila said. 'Tertia has much work to do. The social gathering is for us, not those who serve us.'

Prisca's expression did not change, always smiling despite contrary thoughts.

'Mother,' Nerva said, leaning forwards. 'Surely they can have a moment together.'

Aquila pretended to look confused. 'The work will not do itself. Is that not right, Rufus?' She was practically holding her breath as she waited for his reply.

Rufus exhaled and took a long drink from his cup. All eyes were on him. He signalled for more wine. 'Perhaps the girl can speak with her mother while she is doing her work.' He kept his eyes on the servant pouring the wine.

The girl. Mila replayed the words in her head.

Aquila's face tightened, her mouth pinched in a way that made her look ten years past her forty years. She seemed to be waiting for Rufus to look at her, to heed her warning, but he would not raise his eyes from his cup. 'Be quick about it,' she said, turning to glare at Mila.

Prisca seemed to be enjoying the tension, winking at Mila as she followed her mother from the room.

The moment they were out of sight, Tertia hugged Mila to her. Neither of them spoke, simply enjoying the closeness they had missed over the past weeks. Eventually her mother pulled away and led Mila to the back of the house, to the familiar room she had shared with them her entire life. She found Dulcia lying on the bed, drawing with charcoal.

'Dulcia,' her mother said. 'Look who is here.'

Her sister turned, face lighting up. She scampered across the bed, leaping into Mila's arms. 'How long do you have?'

'Just a few moments,' Mila breathed. 'Aquila was not pleased.'

'Understandable,' Tertia said, enjoying the sight of her daughters together.

Mila looked at her. 'Why is that understandable?'

'Because she put a lot of work into the evening. It was supposed to be about her.'

'It was supposed to be about Nerva, and he hates these gatherings.'

Tertia smiled. 'She is a proud mother.'

Mila shook her head. 'She is a lot of things.'

Tertia tutted.

'I do not want you to go,' Dulcia said as Mila lowered her to the ground.

'I know, but Nerva might bring you to see me again soon.'

Tertia shook her head. 'I shall pretend I did not hear that.' The girls smiled at one another. 'How is Lady Prisca treating you?'

'Fine.'

Tertia studied her. 'Nerva told me about Ludus Magnus, that you are to fight at the Flavian Amphitheatre.'

Hopefully that was all Nerva had told her. 'It is one fight. If I win, Prisca has promised me freedom.'

Tertia appeared sceptical. 'Usually if it sounds too good to be true, it is.' She watched as Dulcia settled herself on the bed. 'What I would like to know is what does she get out of all this?'

'The thrill of my victory.' Seeing her mother's face, she added, 'She is not allowed to fight. I suppose this is the next best thing. A nobody becoming somebody, as she would have done had her father let her.'

'She is hardly a nobody. Her father is Celcus Heius.'

Mila rolled her eyes. 'Am I the only person who does not know who that man is?'

Tertia reached up to tidy Mila's hair. 'You have as much interest in politics as I do in gladiators.'

Dodging her mother's hand, Mila said, 'Well, Celcus Heius is a fool. I fought Prisca briefly, and she is excellent.'

'You *fought* against your domina?' Dulcia asked, eyes wide.

Tertia shook her head again. 'May the gods show mercy on you.'

Mila kissed her sister and mother. 'I should get back.'

Tertia hugged her. 'Tell me I have nothing to worry about.'

Mila let the familiar scent warm her. 'You have nothing to worry about.' She was glad her mother could not see her face or she might have recognised the lie as quickly as Nerva had. It occurred to her that it might be the last time she was in her mother's arms, and the thought made her tighten her grip for a moment.

'You are getting so strong,' Tertia said.

Mila released her and stepped back. 'I have a long way to go.'

'But you will win?' Dulcia said. 'Then come for us?'

Tertia stroked Dulcia's hair. 'Let Mila go. We do not want to get her into trouble.'

Mila heard the disapproval in her mother's voice. 'Of course I will come back for you.'

Dulcia looked relieved and her mother gave a tight smile.

'Go,' Tertia said, squeezing Mila's hand. 'And be careful.'

As Mila followed the smell of pastry and spices, she tried to shake the feeling that she was implementing a plan her mother wanted no part of.

CHAPTER 20

Each day, Titus trained her near to death, and Remus tried to stay away. The few times he paused to watch, he ended up losing his temper, one time punching Titus in the face when he caught him poking Mila with the training pole while she was vomiting. The following day, Titus got his own by pairing Mila with a slave twice her size, and Mila asked Remus on their walk home to never help her again.

It became their ritual. After training, they would meet near the tavern, he would spend a few moments examining her, cursing under his breath at every bruise and welt, and then he would walk her home. They would stop at the baker, and Remus would buy two lemon tarts. They would sit against the cool wall, sharing one pastry while watching Nero eat the other as though it were his last meal. Remus even offered to buy one for Albaus, but the bodyguard just grunted and looked away.

It was two weeks out from the fight when Mila entered the Fadius house and found Prisca waiting for her, a smile frozen on her face.

'You look very happy,' she said. 'Do I need to have a word with Titus?'

Mila glanced at Sabina, who was standing against the wall, not looking at her. Never a good sign.

'We must be doing something wrong if you are finishing the afternoon looking so… refreshed.'

There was something in Prisca's tone that warned Mila to consider her response carefully. Prisca kept going.

'Was it a pleasant afternoon at Ludus Magnus?'

Another glance at Sabina, hoping for a clue, but the body slave kept her gaze down. 'No, Era. Every day is harder than the last.'

Prisca moved closer, coming to a stop right in front of her. It was too close.

'Goodness.' She sniffed the air. 'What is that smell?'

Mila fought the urge to step back. 'I was on my way to bathe—'

Prisca held up a hand to silence her. 'It is not a bad odour, but rather divine—like lemons.'

Mila swallowed. Albaus shifted. Nero fidgeted. They all knew the explanation would not sit well with their domina. Prisca turned to the boy and clicked her fingers, signalling for him to step closer. He did as he was told. She bent to him, inhaling.

'Nero,' she said, remaining at his height. 'What have you been eating?'

'Nothing,' replied the boy, unflinching in his lie.

Mila closed her eyes. He was trying to protect her, but his lie would not end well for anyone.

'Nothing?' Prisca asked.

That time Nero looked up at Mila, unsure. She gave the slightest nod.

'Do not look at her, look at me,' Prisca said, the song leaving her voice. 'Why do you smell like pastries?'

Nero cleared his throat. 'Remus bought me one from

the baker. After training, Mila's legs shake. The food helps her.'

Satisfied, Prisca straightened and looked at Mila. 'There is no end to that man's chivalry. Does he think I do not feed you?'

'Of course not.'

Her eyes moved over Mila, as though looking for answers. 'Is there a reason Remus Latinius is accompanying you home every afternoon, walking all the way from Ludus Magnus, and spending his hard-earned coin buying you pastries?'

When Mila glanced at Sabina that time, the girl finally met her gaze. There was an apology in her eyes. She realised then that Prisca already had the answers, she simply wanted Mila to confess.

'He is a very generous man, and despite my objections, he seems to feel a sense of responsibility for my welfare.' All those things were true.

Prisca's smile returned. 'What a hero our Remus is, keeping Rome's slaves safe on the streets. I must remember to thank him.' She fixed the neckline of her garment, and then her gaze returned to Nero. 'Now is as good a time as any to let you know that you will be leaving us.'

Nero's eyes widened, and Sabina took a step towards them.

'What do you mean?' Mila asked, her hand going to Nero's shoulder.

'The boy is to be sold,' Prisca said, as though speaking of a horse.

'Please,' Sabina said, closing the distance between them. 'Do not punish him.'

Mila stared at her domina. 'Punish him for what? He has done nothing wrong.'

Nero stared at his hands.

'You know as well as I that I cannot keep a slave who lies to my face.'

Mila shook her head, trying to think of a way to salvage the situation. 'He did not want me to get in trouble, that is all.'

'That is all? Clearly you have lived a rather sheltered existence if you think you can finish that sentence with "that is all". The boy must go.'

'Over a pastry?' Sabina cried.

'Goodness, not you too. Do not upset yourself,' Prisca said, feigning surprise at her reaction. She turned to Albaus. 'And you are lucky you are mute. *You* are responsible for getting Mila safely to and from Ludus Magnus. If she cannot walk, you damn well carry her.'

Sabina pulled Nero to her. 'We don't even know if he's a slave. Turning him out is one thing, but to sell him?'

'That orphan became my property the moment I took him in.' She clicked her fingers and two men stepped into the room. 'Take the boy.'

Sabina stepped in front of him. 'No!'

Mila's chest hurt at the sight before her.

'Albaus, take Sabina out back,' Prisca said, remaining calm. 'She is to receive ten lashes for her insubordination. If she continues to carry on, double it.'

Mila felt her insides fall to the floor. 'She… she's in pain enough.'

Prisca turned to Mila. 'This is not the arena. You cannot win this fight.'

The boy was led away, knowing better than to struggle but unable to stop the tears falling down his young cheeks, a reminder that he was only a child. Albaus placed a giant hand on Sabina's shoulder. She left with him, resigned and too heartbroken to care about ten lashes. Mila's eyes met with the bodyguard's. His expression mirrored her own.

'Take her far enough so she does not disturb the household.'

Mila blinked. 'I will take the lashings on her behalf. The wrongdoing was mine.'

Prisca stared at her. 'I am well aware of your wrongdoings. While that is very noble of you, I need you able to fight. But be assured of this, Titus will work you extra hard tomorrow.'

Albaus led Sabina away and the room fell quiet for a moment. Mila felt as though she did not recognise the woman in front of her.

'Do not look at me like that,' Prisca said, smile long gone.

'Like what?'

'Like I am one of them. I saw you look at Aquila that way.'

Mila swallowed. She should have stayed quiet, said nothing. 'You act like one of them.'

Prisca flinched.

Mila braced. Surely she would be sent off for a good lashing now. Perhaps she would be starved or sold. Something. Instead, Prisca said, 'I should like to take a bath before dinner.'

She walked away then, leaving Mila no choice but to follow after her.

CHAPTER 21

Sabina had come to Mila after her lashings and collapsed in a heap of tears. Mila had soothed her and washed her back, surprised to find only superficial wounds. Albaus had done the task half-heartedly. He was not the violent man many assumed him to be. Sabina's tears were from the pain of losing Nero, not the beating. They learned he had been sold at the Graecostadium, likely stripped down on arrival, inspected, a placard placed around his neck detailing his origin and abilities. The idea made Mila sick to her stomach.

The following day, she returned to Ludus Magnus and searched for Remus. She caught sight of him across the sand, signalling to him. He took in her expression, then turned to the men in charge, giving them instructions before making his way over to her.

'What's wrong?' he asked, eyes moving over her, checking for something visible.

Titus watched them from the other side of the arena, so Mila wasted no time getting to the point. 'Prisca sent Nero to the Graecostadium yesterday to be sold.' She glanced at

Albaus, who pretended he was not listening. 'I do not know how to help him.'

Remus closed his eyes for a moment. 'Did something happen?'

'Prisca knows that you have been walking us home. She got angry about the tarts, practically sniffing the boy's breath. He lied at first, trying to protect me.'

He shook his head. 'This isn't about a tart or the lie.'

'No,' Mila agreed. 'She suspects something between us. I told her she was wrong, that you feel nothing but a sense of obligation towards me.'

He blinked. 'She's not stupid. She knows I don't walk you home out of obligation.'

They stared at each other for a moment until he finally looked away.

'I'll ask around later, see where the boy ended up. Check he's all right.'

Her entire body sank with relief. 'Thank you.'

He hesitated. 'I'm not making any promises.'

'I know.'

She went to move past him and he grabbed her wrist. She stopped and looked up at him. His eyes moved over her face.

'Probably best if I don't walk you home anymore.'

She felt winded in that moment. Remus had quickly become the best part of her day, besides the stolen moments with Nerva and Dulcia. 'I agree,' she said, gaze falling briefly to his lips before looking away.

He released his grip and she left with a feeling resembling grief pounding in her chest. It was the same feeling she had the day she had been sold.

Prisca kept her promise to have her worked extra hard that day. The moment she reached Titus, he thrust weapons into her hands and told her to 'Get ready to cry.'

He paired her with a young slave boy, no more than seventeen years old. Judging by his pale complexion and the ribs on display, he was a new recruit. They would fatten him up before he was sent to his death. She had the advantage of being nourished, but that was all. Wherever he had come from, he had been taught how to fight.

She put the weapons down and stripped to her tunic. Albaus cast her a wary look before he wandered off to his usual spot by the wall of the cavea. Out of the corner of her eye, she saw Remus collect weapons from the ground and leave the arena. He never watched. It was best for both of them.

'You will fight until I tell you to stop,' Titus called to them.

Hacking, he collected something from the back of his throat and spat it on the sand. Mila made a mental note to avoid that spot. Another glance at Albaus, whose eyebrows were drawn together with disapproval. She felt a little better knowing he was there.

She turned back to her opponent, eyes drawn to the raw skin on his wrists where shackles had been moments earlier. This was no time to feel sorry for him. He met her gaze, no doubt trying to gauge her reaction to what she saw. She kept her gladiator face on, a technique borrowed from Remus.

They held a wooden sword in each hand, staring at one another as they waited for Titus's signal. Enemies for no good reason. The boy's jaw was clenched, his eyes burning at her. All bravery left her in that moment, suspecting she was about to pay for his every suffering.

'Begin,' Titus shouted. He crossed his arms, making his biceps appear twice their actual size.

She was thankful for the low-hanging cloud offering relief from the heat. As they circled one another, she watched the boy carefully, noting every twitch of his body as a clue to how he might come at her. But while observing him, she noticed something odd. His attention was divided. Yes, he was watching her, but his eyes flickered in all directions, taking in the entire arena and the men around him.

What are you up to?

She decided to strike first, while he seemed distracted. Even though she had grown accustomed to using a shield, she enjoyed the novelty of two swords, something Remus had discouraged, probably because he wanted to repeatedly shout 'shield up' at her.

The boy was fast, skilled, even while distracted. She let her surging adrenaline drive her fight, faster and faster, until she felt invincible. Eventually she knocked one sword from his hand, a move that seemed to get his full attention. He narrowed his eyes and smiled. Or was it a snarl? She could not tell. She readied herself, heart pounding so hard her body seemed to rock with the motion of it.

He came at her quick and strong, striking her shoulder despite her best efforts to block him. Pain shot down her arm as the tip of his weapon struck. The sword dropped from her hand, despite her determination to keep hold of it. She cursed under her breath and raised her other weapon just in time to block the next blow. He swung low then, but she saw it coming and stopped him.

They moved like that for some time, a dance of sorts, the only problem being that no matter how much Mila tried, her left arm refused to rejoin the fight. Eventually the remaining sword flew from her hand, and the boy stopped, stood still, panting. He lowered his weapon and stepped back. He had beaten her.

'You fight until I tell you to stop,' Titus reminded them.

The boy turned to look at Titus. His face twisted, as though something were pulling at his insides.

Titus nodded towards Mila. 'It is not over until she is on the ground with your sword at her neck.'

The slave's gaze returned to Mila. The fight had changed. He took a few steps towards her, and ignoring the pain in her arm, she dropped into a crouch and used her foot to try to take his legs out from beneath him. But he must have anticipated the move, because he leapt over her leg and brought the hilt of his sword down on her head. It was not hard enough to lose consciousness, but enough to send light dancing across her vision. The problem with head injuries was they tended to bleed—a lot. Blood ran from the top of her scalp over her left ear and eye. Then her body betrayed her, tipping, despite her mind knowing better. She landed on her bad arm and cried out. The boy's wooden sword pressed into her neck.

She turned to look at him as he stood over her, blinking through the blood and blurry vision. His expression made her go still. It was not one of victory but of something much darker. He slipped a hand beneath his worn tunic, and the blade of a dagger flashed between them.

'For my family,' he whispered, his accent thick.

Mila shook her head, but before she could react, he spun and threw the knife, striking Titus through the throat. It was so fast she could barely comprehend what was happening. She turned, trying to focus on Titus who remained upright, clutching his throat with both hands while he choked. Every man in the arena stilled. A few trainers came running, with nothing but wooden swords.

At the same time, Albaus propelled himself off the wall, pulling a dagger from a hidden nook and throwing it with great force at the slave. It landed with a dull thud in boy's chest. He cried out, his legs giving way as he sank down, collapsing on top of her. She tried to push him off with her good arm, but all strength had left her. A growing warmth spread through her middle as he bled out. Turning her head, she watched as Titus finally collapsed to the ground, men shouting instructions around him but saying nothing that could help. The boy coughed on top of her, and she closed her eyes against the noise.

Finally he was lifted off and tossed onto the sand beside her. His wide eyes locked onto hers for a moment as air rushed into her lungs. Albaus reached down and scooped her up as though she weighed nothing at all, carrying her from the arena while she watched the scene over his arm.

What just happened?

Albaus stepped beneath the portico and marched towards the exit, not slowing for anything or anyone. She saw Brutus pass them as he ran to see what had happened. Both Titus and the boy would be dead by the time he arrived.

The gate opened and the noise from the street reached them. Mila turned to look through the opening. People passed by, going about their day, unaware of what had just taken place inside the walls of Ludus Magnus.

'It is all right,' she said to Albaus. 'I… I am fine. My legs are fine.' Though she did not really believe it. 'Put me down.'

As the gate swung shut behind them, Albaus lowered her to the ground, holding on to her while she got her balance. That was when she noticed the strange angle of her arm.

'Mila!'

She turned to see Remus slip between the gate just before it closed, his expression wild. He stopped in front of her, eyes moving over her and hands unsure. 'You're bleeding.'

She shook her head. 'Only my head. The rest is not mine.' The intensity of his concern made her look away.

'What happened?' He looked at Albaus, who could not give him any answers.

'Titus is dead,' she said, unsure how he would react. 'My opponent killed him.' She tried to move her left arm and winced. Perhaps it was broken. Perhaps she would not be able to fight. Prisca might sell her off as well. She kept a hold of Albaus's arm for balance while he stared off down the street, as though expecting to be attacked at any moment. 'Is… is my arm broken?' she asked Remus.

He stepped closer to examine it, and she tried not to cry as he gently felt along her shoulder and down her arm before attempting to move it.

She gasped and he let go.

'Shoulder's dislocated.' His eyes returned to her stomach. 'No chest or stomach wound, you say?'

She shook her head, her throat tight. His hand went to her head, examining the small cut.

'The head wound's not too bad. You'll have a headache though.'

What happened next was out of her control. A sob rose up, choking her, determined to humiliate her. She could not stop it. While she would never admit it to Remus, it was the first time she had seen men die that way. She had not been prepared for death up close.

Remus caught her as she sank down and lifted her off the ground. She felt like a child, her face buried against his chest to hide her embarrassment. She swallowed, determined not to make a further spectacle of herself.

'I can walk,' she said unconvincingly.

Remus ignored her and glanced across the street. 'We need to get that shoulder back in,' he said, carrying her towards the tavern. 'Best stay clear of Ludus Magnus until the mess is sorted.'

The three of them stepped inside the dank space that smelled of wine and stewed meat. Remus placed her down on a stool by the window and crouched in front of her, waiting for her to look at him.

'Do you trust me?' he asked.

She frowned and swallowed down the tears that had gathered in her throat. 'Not really.'

He smiled at that. 'I've done this enough times.'

Albaus shifted in her peripheral vision. 'Done what?'

'Popped a shoulder back in,' he said, tone casual.

She glanced at Albaus, who appeared just as wary. 'Surely the task requires a physician.'

Remus pulled up another stool and sat down at her left side. 'It's more common than you think. Easily fixed. Instant relief.' He turned to Albaus. 'Get something strong for her to drink.'

Albaus hesitated, grunted, and then walked off to fetch the tavern owner, who was busy shouting at two men who had brought dice into the establishment.

The moment Albaus was gone, Mila grabbed Remus's arm. 'Are you sure about this?'

He looked at her, his face close to hers. 'Prisca wants you toughened up.' A smile tugged at the corner of his mouth.

She released his arm. 'If you botch this, I am coming for you.'

'With one arm?'

'And one enormous sword.'

'No shield?'

She felt herself relax. 'Shields are for girls.'

They watched each other for a moment, the air still between them.

'What trouble have you brought in, then?' the owner said, arriving next to them.

Remus straightened, and Mila looked up at the round woman who stood scrutinising her.

'I've enough trouble keeping the gamblers out. Now you bring a slave girl in here looking like she's murdered her dominus.'

'Looking good, Copa,' Remus said, winking up at her.

She was obviously immune to his charms, slamming a cup on the table before filling it with wine. 'No water in it,' she said, placing the jug on the table next to the cup. She held out a hand, waiting for payment. The other wiped greying hair from her sweaty forehead.

Remus retrieved a few coins and dropped them into her hand. She made a point of checking them before her fingers curled around them and she walked away.

He looked at Mila and nodded after the woman. 'Another jealous lover.'

Mila suppressed a smile, glancing at the old woman whose wide hips swung away from them. 'You would be lucky to have her.'

A smile spread across Remus's face as he picked up the cup. 'Ready to get drunk?'

Mila looked down at the wine in his hand. 'Will Albaus have to carry me home?'

They both looked over at the bodyguard, who had seated himself at the table with the two men who had been accused of gambling. Clearly he did not have the stomach to watch.

'I'll carry you home if you make a mess of yourself,' Remus said, gaze returning to her.

It was foolish, but Mila felt invincible in his presence. She lifted the cup to her mouth and drank. Remus reached up, tipping it higher, forcing her to swallow the wine in large gulps. Once empty, she placed the cup on the table and felt the liquid warm her insides.

He reached up to wipe at her mouth with his thumb. 'Best have another to make sure.'

She held on to the table, her head already spinning. 'Make sure of what?'

'That you don't feel a thing.' He refilled the cup and handed it to her. 'Drink up.'

She hesitated, staring at it for a moment. He pushed it closer and she took it from him, emptying it before setting it down on the table.

'Ready?' he asked.

She blinked. 'Ready.'

CHAPTER 22

The sun was setting as the three of them strolled through the streets and alleyways of region four. Mila, wobbly from drink, was particularly slow, humming as she watched her feet move beneath her. Occasionally she would stumble and Albaus or Remus would grab hold of her, exchanging a knowing glance as they did so. Her attempts at appearing sober were wasted on Remus— he knew a drunk when he saw one. He had given her the first two drinks for the pain in her shoulder, the next two for all her other pain.

'Albaus,' Mila said, her voice higher than usual. 'What does your voice sound like if you actually try to speak?'

'Mila,' Remus said.

She held up a hand to silence him. 'No, no, no. Your days of telling me what to do are over.' She looked at Albaus. 'Obviously the words would not be clear, but we could get an idea of the tone of your voice.'

Albaus shook his head.

'Can you sing?' she went on.

Remus took her arm and pulled her away from the bodyguard, settling her on the other side of him. She leaned in to Remus and whispered loudly, 'Would it not be the funniest thing ever if he turned out to have an excellent singing voice?'

Albaus grunted.

'Hilarious,' Remus said, tone dry.

'Do you want to hear *me* sing?' she asked.

'Not particularly.'

She faced forwards. 'Lucky. I cannot sing to save myself. That would have been rather embarrassing.'

'We couldn't have you embarrassing yourself now, could we?' Remus said, glancing at Albaus.

She stumbled and he caught her without breaking stride. So light. She needed more muscle on her if she stood a real chance in the arena.

Mila laughed. 'Albaus, sing something.'

'All right,' Remus said, creating more distance between them. 'Let's not poke the large bodyguard.'

She tripped on his foot and his arm went around her, steadying her.

'Had no idea what an annoying drunk you'd be,' he said, shaking his head.

'Neither did I. I never drink.'

Remus glanced down at her. 'I see why.'

She leaned closer, mouth stretched into a wide smile. There was that dimple. 'Look how handsome you are close up, even with a beard.'

He reached up and ran his free hand over the trimmed growth on his face. 'What do you mean "even with a beard"?'

'No wonder women fall at your feet. You are a fine gladiator specimen, Remus Latinius.'

His eyes moved over her face. 'I'm going to remind you of this conversation when you're sober. Watch you squirm at your own words.'

The smile fell from her face, but she continued to look at him. 'If I were a lady, like Prisca—'

'Trust me, you're twice the lady.'

'Let me finish—'

'No more questions tonight.'

She frowned. 'There will not be another time.'

He studied her, missing her dimple already. 'What are you talking about?'

'What do you think Prisca is going to do when you bring me home drunk?' She tripped on her own foot that time, and his grip on her tightened.

'Leave Prisca to me,' he said.

Mila turned so she was walking backwards, and his arm fell away.

'That's not a good idea. You're struggling to walk forwards,' he pointed out.

She tilted her face up to him and his pulse quickened.

'And what is your plan, Remus Latinius? The only thing you have to bargain with is yourself. She wants to *be* a gladiator, and she wants to *bed* a gladiator.' Her body brushed against his. 'Which one will you give her?'

'Albaus,' Remus said. 'Turn right up ahead.'

The bodyguard raised an eyebrow in question.

'Trust me.'

Mila faced forwards again, shrugging and closing her eyes. 'It feels better. My shoulder. Almost like it never happened.'

'Open your eyes before you fall.' He was ready to catch her.

She watched her feet again. 'He must have known they would kill him, but he did it anyway.'

'They would've tortured him first,' Remus said. 'Albaus did him a favour.' He was growing to like the bodyguard more each day.

'That poor boy.'

'Is better off now,' Remus added, wanting her happy again. 'Stop at the fountain,' he said to Albaus.

He led Mila to the small fountain while Albaus wandered off to sit on the other side. 'Let's try to sober you up a bit.'

Mila nodded and knelt so her stomach wrapped the edge and her face was above the water. With the sun so far west, she could see her reflection.

'Oh' was all she said at the sight of herself.

Blood had dried over her face and hair. She looked as though she had just returned from war—one she had lost.

Remus began splashing water up at her face, and when that proved to be ineffective, he pushed her entire head into the water. 'Use your hands to wash it off.'

Instead, she punched him in the ribs and he released her. She came up gasping, red water dripping from her face.

'Are you trying to drown me?' she said, shoving him.

He laughed at her reaction. 'You'll know when I'm trying to drown you.'

She coughed and looked at him, her scowl eventually giving way to something resembling a smile. She let out her hair and then, closing her eyes, plunged her head back into the water.

He watched the water turn red around her. When she came up, hair clung to her face and neck. She sat next to him, brushing it with her fingers. He had never seen her with her hair out. He swallowed thickly. 'Better?'

'I imagine so.' She flicked some water at him. 'I suspect everything will hurt when I wake tomorrow.'

'Especially your head.'

She smiled and the dimple reappeared. 'I suspect Prisca might have gone easier on me if I had not washed away the afternoon.'

'Told you, let me worry about Prisca.'

Her smile faded. 'I cannot predict her reaction.'

'I've had a few more years' experience.'

Her eyes moved over his face. She was too close.

'I thought I had you all figured out. Perhaps I was wrong.'

'Don't overthink it. What you see is what you get.' He reached up to peel a few threads of hair off her cheek, and she closed her eyes as his fingertips brushed her skin.

'You have great hands.'

He suppressed a smile. 'Still drunk, then?'

'Mmm.'

His gaze fell to her wet lips, slightly parted and angled perfectly if he were to take advantage of the situation. He looked away and stood, pulling her up with him. Her eyes snapped open at the movement.

'Time to move,' he said.

She was quiet for the rest of the journey, visibly sobering with each step.

He kept glancing across at her. 'You all right?' he asked, watching the transformation on her face, the small creases in her brow returning.

She nodded and reached up to plait her hair.

When they arrived at the house, Remus told Albaus to take her inside and have Sabina help her clean up properly. The bodyguard grunted and waited for Mila to start walking. She drew a breath and looked at Remus.

'Thank you,' she said. 'For everything.'

'Tell Lady Prisca I'm waiting outside for her.'

She nodded before turning away, and he watched her walk inside. Even with a heavy bloodstain wrapping her middle, he could not help but admire the gentle slope of her hips. Her plait reached the middle of her back, leaving a wet trail all the way to her…

He looked away.

'MY HUSBAND WILL BE HOME SOON,' Prisca said, her arms crossed in front of her. She glanced past him down the street, as though she were genuinely concerned about the fact. 'He might assume I have taken you as a lover once again.'

'Titus is dead,' Remus said, skipping the games.

She tried to hide her shock. 'At whose hand?'

'A slave boy paired with Mila.'

'I suppose that explains her appearance.' She studied him. 'Not the fact that she smells of wine though.'

He shrugged. 'Her shoulder was dislocated. I put it back in. You're lucky it was her shield arm.'

'And that you were there—her saviour.'

He looked away tiredly. 'You should be thanking me.'

'For what? The girl is no longer your responsibility.'

He nodded. 'Yes, you made sure of that.' His gaze returned to her. 'You need to decide what you want.'

She frowned. 'Whatever do you mean?'

'It's time to put your pride aside and make smart decisions.' He paused to ensure she was following. 'You're an intelligent woman, and you know I want her to win. Who better to train her than someone who wants the same thing you do?'

She looked past him. 'You dare to come here and lecture me. Do not forget I knew you when you were nothing but a nameless slave.'

He exhaled. 'You sound like them.'

She lifted her chin. 'Like who?'

'The people you hate. The ones who told you no, you can't fight.'

She shifted. 'Oh, do you mean the ones who told me not to let a slave into my bed because it would not end well?'

His expression did not change. 'You're married. How'd you think it would end?'

She pressed her lips together. 'I thought we were having fun, but apparently *everyone* is against my happiness—even the slaves I lie with.'

'I thought you were above all that snobbery, thought you saw me as just a man.'

'I did.' She swallowed. 'And now you expect me to give my blessing as you take up with those who serve me.'

He looked at her. 'I haven't taken up with her.' It was the truth, and she knew him well enough to recognise it. 'Let me train Mila. You know I'm the best person to do it. Titus is dead, and if he hadn't died, he'd have likely killed her by accident.'

She appeared to be thinking the suggestion over.

'Do you want her to win?' he asked. 'Maybe the outcome's not important to you.'

She took a moment to form her reply. 'I want her to fight at her best, to mark people's memories with her skill and courage, have them tell her story to their children. I want her to be memorable. That is all that is important to me. Live or die—that is up to her.' Seeing his scepticism, she added, 'But if she wins, I will keep my word. I will free her.'

He was silent a moment. 'I'll make sure she fights well, that she's memorable. Just let me do my job.'

'Since we are being honest…' She watched him through painted lashes. 'Tell me one thing. Do you have feelings for the girl?'

It was a fair question. 'None that I've acted on.'

She nodded, and he watched the conflict play out on her face. It was easy for her to behave like the person with all the power, because she was. 'And can you put aside those feelings in order to train her properly?'

Could he? He took a moment to assess. 'Yes.'

A nod of resignation. Prisca's body language dissolved into something less upper-class and more human.

'You have two weeks. Fourteen days to transform her into a killer.' Prisca's eyes moved over him. 'That's if you want her to live.'

He glanced at the house. He needed her to live. And he wanted her freed. 'She's physically strong. Mentally… I'm not sure.'

Prisca nodded. 'She has been sheltered, despite what she might believe. You will need to break her before, or she will break in the arena.'

'I agree.'

They watched as two slave girls passed them on the street.

'My husband is unaware of the nature of this fight. He thinks she is my muse, my outlet, a way to pass time so I might behave.'

'Is he wrong?'

She stared down the road. 'Yes.'

He thought she seemed quite vulnerable in that moment. 'What is she, then?'

Her lips pressed together as she considered her answer. 'She is… an escape.'

He thought that was a strange reply. 'From your privileged life?'

She frowned at him. 'You mock me.'

'I wouldn't dare. Prefer you onside.'

She studied him for the longest moment. 'You had me onside once. We were quite a pair. Do you remember?'

He remembered. Though probably remembered it a little differently. He did not have the heart to say that. 'We had to grow up eventually.'

'I wish we could go back to that time.'

'And be a slave again? No thanks.'

She hugged herself as though the air was cold. 'I will send word to Brutus that you are to complete her training.'

He nodded. 'Have a pleasant evening, Lady Prisca.' He went to leave.

'Remus.'

He turned to look at her. She seemed torn about whether to speak.

'Do not let your feelings for the girl contribute to her death.'

There was a heart beating beneath all that expensive fabric after all.

'We both want her to fight her best fight.'

As he walked away, Prisca's gaze on his back, he knew she saw his overwhelming affection for Mila as clearly as he felt it. He was back in the arena, but this time defenceless. For the next two weeks, he would need to push down everything he felt, every tender thought, every urge.

Push them all the way down so he could keep her alive.

CHAPTER 23

When Mila arrived at Ludus Magnus the next day for training, she was surprised to see Fausta standing with Remus in the arena. Her head seemed to pound twofold in that moment. She stopped a safe distance away to remove her sandals and stola. As she handed them to Albaus, she tried to come up with a good reason not to go over there. She glanced back at the exit and saw a young boy enter the arena, arms loaded with weapons. Her heart pounded as she recognised him.

'Nero!' she called, breaking into a run.

The boy peeked around the side of the shields, a smile spreading on his face. He struggled to keep hold of the weapons as her arms wrapped around him.

'Thank the gods,' she whispered, planting a kiss on top of his head. 'Are you all right?' She pulled away to examine him.

'Remus bought me,' he said, eyes lit up. 'I'm going to live here, at Ludus Magnus.'

'Bought you to work,' Remus said, walking towards them. 'Take the weapons to Fausta.' His tone was gentle, despite the serious expression.

As the boy rushed off, Mila smiled up at Remus, her gratitude so overwhelming that she felt the urge to hug him. He stared back at her with indifference.

'A thousand thank yous to you, gladiator,' she said, stepping closer.

He turned his body away. 'No need. Got him cheap enough.'

She stayed where she was. 'How?'

'There was a rumour the boy was prone to fits.'

She studied him. 'And who started the rumour?'

'I did.'

She looked impressed. 'Very clever.'

He did not look at her. 'I knew he was a solid worker. Had some coin saved.'

She knew very well that was not the reason for the purchase. Clearing her throat, she asked, 'So you bought him for his strong work ethic?'

'Time to get to work.' He gestured for her to move. 'How's the shoulder?'

She fell into step beside him. 'A bit sore, like everything else.' She glanced up at him but he continued to stare ahead. She was beginning to think it was intentional.

Fausta was jumping up and down on the spot, swinging her arms, warming her muscles. Her bleached hair was braided to one side and her eyes were painted black, making her appear more fierce than usual.

'I am fighting Fausta today?'

Remus nodded. 'You'll be training with her right up until the games, working harder than before. You'll finish each day in pain, wake in pain, and do it again. You'll rest the day before your fight. Until then, I suggest you grow a thick skin.'

She took in his words, his body language, the lack of eye contact. She wondered what had changed overnight. 'What did you say to Prisca yesterday? To make her agree?'

Remus's jaw was tight and his attention focused on the weapons.

'Told her I'd make sure you win.'

She waited for him to look at her, to say more. 'I *will* win.' When he did not reply, she asked, 'Did you promise to be more like Titus? Is that what you are doing right now?'

Fausta let out a long whistle and stepped back from them.

Remus turned to Mila. 'I suggest you keep your energy for the long afternoon ahead. You can start with thirty laps.'

The coldness in his tone made her stomach tighten. 'Is Fausta also running thirty laps?'

'Now,' he said, taking a fast step towards her.

She stepped back, glancing at Albaus, who watched them with interest. Nero was next to him, speaking at a gallop, never pausing for breath. Fausta chuckled, shaking her head as Mila's cheeks burned.

MILA COLLAPSED on her hands and knees, retching water onto the sand. Her arms shook beneath her, and she was all too aware of everyone watching. She felt a small hand land on her back at the same time Nero's bare feet appeared next to her. He held out a waterskin and she took it from him, rolling into a sitting position and keeping her eyes on her knees. She rinsed her mouth and spat the water onto the sand, then took another drink before handing it back to him.

'Are we done, then?' Fausta called, breathless as she wiped at her nose. Blood smeared her hand.

Remus had not moved from the spot he had anchored himself to, a sand platform from which he barked instructions, shouted at her, pointed out every way in which she was lacking until she had nothing left.

'Mila,' he called. 'You done?'

She refused to look at him, desperately wanting to say, 'No, let's go again'. More than anything, she wished she could stand up like Fausta, with something left to give. 'I'm done,' she replied, her throat burning and voice hoarse. She let her forehead drop to her knees.

Remus walked over to her, and Nero scrambled out of his way.

'You sure?' he asked. 'You've nothing left?'

She leaned forwards, spitting blood onto the sand. A tear ran down her cheek, exhaustion gripping her. She reached down to scoop sand over the mess and then looked up at him, eyes struggling to focus. 'I have nothing left.'

She saw the briefest flash of pity, guilt perhaps, but it did not linger. He offered her his hand, and she wanted to slap it away. She would have if she had been able to get to her feet without help. He took hold of both arms and pulled her up, holding onto her for a moment until he was sure she could stand on her own. She was torn between pulling herself from his grip and the temptation to tip forwards and rest her head against him. The smell of him was so familiar now, the scent of sand and something uniquely him, something pleasant that lingered on her own skin after he touched her.

Remus signalled to Albaus to come and take her. Once the bodyguard was there, he let her go. 'Same time tomorrow.' He turned and walked away.

She watched him leave, nodding in response. No more walks through the city, their arms brushing. No more shared tarts. Now it was all turning away and indifferent glances.

'Nero, collect the weapons,' Remus called to the boy.

She gave Nero a weak smile before he ran off. He was the most resilient child she had ever met.

Her gaze went to Fausta, who seemed to be faring only slightly better than her: ghostly pale, with black paint streaking her cheeks.

'See you tomorrow,' Mila said to her.

The gladiator nodded, bending to lean on her knees. Mila discreetly took hold of Albaus's arm as she turned away. She needed to make it out of the arena without falling down.

THE FOLLOWING DAY, Fausta appeared well-slept and far too perky, a vast contrast to her own creaking bones and countless bruises. Mila began to wonder if she would survive the rest of her training.

As she was getting ready, Remus came over and handed her a bronze helmet.

'You want me to wear it now?'

'You'll wear it every day from now on. Get used to the weight and feel of it, any restrictions on your vision. Soon you'll forget you're wearing it at all.'

She pulled the cloth over her hair before slipping the helmet on. 'I doubt that.' She already felt claustrophobic.

Remus gave the helmet a few taps before walking away. Nero came running up to her, shield and sword in hand.

'Are you all right?' he whispered, handing the weapons to her.

Mila gave him a small smile. 'Just a bit sore.'

The boy glanced over his shoulder at the others. 'Don't be fooled by Fausta. Watched her struggle out of bed this morning.'

Mila's smile grew. 'I woke feeling as though I had been trampled.'

Nero stepped closer in a conspiratorial manner. 'He's not angry at you, he's sad.'

She shook her head, confused. 'Who is sad?'

Another glance to ensure no one was listening. 'I heard Remus tell Felix that he doesn't want you to die, that he'll do whatever it takes to save your life.' Nero paused. 'I want you to win too.'

Mila swallowed. 'I have no intention of dying.' She glanced at Remus. 'And when I win, you can come live with me. I am much nicer than he is.' She smiled to show she was joking.

Nero looked at his feet. 'Remus says you're not ready, not strong enough to win.'

Her lips pressed together as she tried not to let her reaction show. 'Well, he is wrong.' She ruffled the boy's hair with her free hand. 'I still have twelve days to prove it.'

He looked up, unsure.

'Shall we begin?' she called to the others with an edge to her tone. She tilted her head from side to side, trying to ease the tightness in her shoulders and neck.

Men shouted and weapons clashed around them. Fausta and Remus looked at one another while Albaus retreated to the wall.

'The slave girl's ready for more,' Fausta said, a smile flickering.

Remus studied Mila for a moment. 'Let's begin.'

CHAPTER 24

Twelve, eleven, ten, nine, eight, seven. The days slipped past in a blur of routine and hard work. She had shown up every afternoon, barely speaking a word to anyone other than Nero, bringing everything she could to each fight, and whenever Remus thought she was finished, she would try to give a little more. It was not uncommon for her to collapse or vomit during their session, but she made a point of getting up and getting on with it.

Prisca showed up six days out to watch, quietly taking a seat in the cavea without creating her usual scene. Her gaze rested briefly on Nero, but she did not mention the fact that he was there. Sabina had sat at her side, eyes on the boy she still missed, her face etched with worry, as though it were her who would soon be fighting for her life. Her domina did not speak or applaud, her expression serious as she observed Mila's technique, watching her feet, seemingly transfixed. Mila was surprised she had not come by more often. Perhaps she trusted Remus more than she let on.

Five, four, three. Three days to go.

Mila said no more than what was necessary to Remus in those sessions. She noticed a change in him also. He grew tenser with every passing day, his body more rigid, his stares more fierce. He watched her carefully, analysing every detail, like the angle of her knee or the position of her elbow. He was obsessed with precision, and she could barely do a thing right.

All too soon it was Mila's last day of training. Remus circled her like a hungry beast, shouting instructions from all directions.

'Shield up! Step into it! Right, left. Down!' His hands went into his hair. 'Harder! *Harder!*'

Despite proving herself a little more each day, it was not enough for him. Anger and resentment were beginning to boil over in Mila, fuelling her, pushing her past her limits. On that final day, she was determined to exceed his expectations, to prove him wrong.

When Fausta collapsed at her feet during their last session, unable to get up, Mila could hardly believe it. She had done it, beaten Rome's best female gladiator.

She turned to Remus, expecting to see satisfaction or pride. Instead, she saw the same indifferent expression he had worn every day for the past few weeks. Her body threatened to betray her, to fall down next to Fausta. To just stop. But she remained upright beneath Remus's cool gaze, breathless and nauseous.

What was the matter with him? That was what they had been working towards.

Do not fall down.

Remus walked over to her. 'Nero, fetch Felix. He can step in for Fausta.' He said it in the same tone he had used for weeks.

Mila blinked away the sweat pouring down her face. 'What?'

He glanced at her. 'You keep going until you are done. Same as any other day.'

She blinked again, not sure whether to cry or claw his face off.

He tilted his head in question. 'Are you done?'

He was waiting for her response, but not one of her thoughts was coherent.

'Am *I* done?' She repeated the question as though she did not understand it. Her insides heated. 'What more are you expecting?' A laugh escaped her, one she did not recognise. 'My opponent, the best female gladiator in Rome, is lying in the sand. I put her there!' New energy came from somewhere. 'When will it be enough for you?' His blank face pushed her closer to crazy.

'You done?' he said again. 'Yes or no?'

She lunged at him with closed fists.

At first he just stood there, arms by his side, while she pounded against his chest. Seeing that she was having no effect on him, she shoved him as hard as she could. Then he took hold of her arms and gently pushed her back, and it was like someone took a torch to her in that moment. She ran at him, her shoulder slamming into chest, desperate to knock him down, but his chest was like a stone wall and he barely stumbled, let alone fell.

'Enough,' he said, his voice still calm.

She pushed up onto her toes, trying to match him in height. 'Are you done?' she screamed at him, mimicking his voice. 'Is that all you have?'

He stared at her. 'What are you doing?'

She looked around for the training poles, finding them in the sand a few feet away. She marched over to them, picked them up and threw one at him. He caught it inches from his face.

'You want to finish me off, gladiator?' she screamed. 'Now's your chance!'

Everyone in the arena had stopped to watch.

'Stop it,' he said, now struggling to stay calm.

'Fausta is beat, but I have something left just for you.' She had come completely unhinged, and she did not care one bit. Out of the corner of her eye, she saw Albaus take a step towards her and she held up a hand. 'Don't you dare!' she warned the bodyguard.

Remus tossed the pole onto the sand between them and crossed his arms.

'Pick it up,' she demanded.

He watched her for a moment. 'Don't embarrass yourself any more than you have.'

She stepped up to the pole and kicked it so it landed by his foot.

Fausta pulled herself into a seated position. She looked between them, her eyes confused but also full of amusement.

Remus shook his head and bent to pick up the pole. Without warning, Mila went for him, striking as hard as she could. He raised his own pole just in time, the force of the blow making him stumble. She saw his face change, glimpsed anger for the first time. He stepped forwards and, with three swift moves, knocked the stick from her hands. It flew some distance through the air, landing a short distance from Albaus. She stared after it, her anger evaporating. All right, now she was done. She collapsed onto the sand, certain she would never get up again. Her hands went over her face and she cried into them.

Yes, she was definitely done. Utter humiliation had finished her.

Remus's familiar arms went around her. He scooped her up, his scent suffocating her. 'Back to work!' he called to the men who were still watching them.

'Put me down,' Mila said feebly. But she was like a sleeping child in those strong arms. Her limbs dangled uselessly as he carried her into the shade. The others had the good sense to stay back.

'Nero, help Fausta,' he called to the boy. When Nero hesitated, he added, 'I'll take care of Mila. Go on.'

The boy ran to help Fausta to her feet, walking slowly at her side across the sand. Albaus stayed where he was, ready if needed. Remus sat on the ground with Mila in his lap. Her eyes sank shut. Exhaustion had won.

'Mila, open your eyes,' he said.

The effort seemed too enormous. She felt him brush hair and sand off her face, then his warm lips pressed against the top of her head. Heat spread through her. She wanted to tip her head back, to offer her mouth to him. Her eyes remained closed.

'I'm sorry,' he whispered. 'I need you to win.'

That made her eyes open. She stared up at him, and a few tears escaped. 'Why?'

He did not reply right away. 'I want you to live.'

It was not enough. 'Why?' she pushed. She thought she knew the answer, thought she felt it, but she needed to hear it. When he did not reply, she realised she was asking too much of a gladiator. Her eyes moved over his face, studying every small scar, the ones only visible close up. 'How many men did you have to kill for your freedom?'

His eyes were as bright as the sky behind them. 'Too many.'

She blinked. 'I only have to do it once.'

His arms shifted beneath her. 'Can you do it?'

She smiled, feeling returning to her body. 'My sister will never forgive me if I lose.'

He propped her up against his knee and traced the curve of her throat with his free hand. She closed her eyes, savouring the sensation, praying she would feel the warmth of his lips on her again.

'Can you stand?' he asked.

She opened her eyes, disappointed. She did not want to stand. 'Do you want me to stand?'

His eyes went to her lips. He leaned closer, and she could feel his heart beating against her side. She thought he was going to kiss her, but he stopped himself. More disappointment.

'Go home. Rest.'

She stared up at him, not wanting to move, but he signalled to Albaus with his free hand and a few moments later she was lifted to her feet. She felt cold suddenly.

'I already told Prisca you need rest, plenty of food, some meat. And no work.'

She nodded. 'You will take me through the tunnel?' He was still close enough to smell.

'I'll take you through. Nice and early.'

She waited, just long enough in case he wanted to kiss her. She hoped she was not imagining the desire.

'See you at the tunnel,' he said, stepping back.

'HOW ARE you meant to fight in two days when you wince at my touch?' Sabina said, rubbing oil into Mila's skin.

The sun hung low in the sky, painting it pink and orange. Mila sat on a stool in a private part of the garden, watching the colours change, appreciating its beauty more than ever.

'It is amazing what one can do when the alternative is death.' She looked up at Sabina, expecting to see a smile. No smile. Another one who had grown more and more serious over the passing weeks, despite reassurances that Nero was happy and settled at Ludus Magnus. 'It was a joke. Remember when you used to laugh at things?' Still no reaction. 'Whatever is the matter?'

Sabina gave a strained smile as she picked up the *strigil*, running it over Mila's skin to remove the oil. 'Nothing. How's Nero?' she asked, changing the subject.

Mila faced forwards again. 'He will be lanista of Ludus Magnus in no time.'

Sabina actually smiled at that, then signalled for Mila to stand so she could do her legs. 'I'm pleased Remus treats him well. He deserves a father figure.'

'I am certain he misses his mother figure.'

Sabina sniffed. 'It's better this way.'

Mila observed for a moment. 'Remus will free the boy when he is old enough to care for himself. I do not doubt it for a moment.'

'Oh.' Sabina splashed on some more oil. 'That's kind of him.'

Mila frowned. 'Are you all right?'

Sabina straightened. 'Of course. Why wouldn't I be?'

They stared at one another for a moment.

'Perhaps you should take to the arena and earn your freedom. Then you could care for the boy yourself,' Mila said. Then, seeing her friend's expression, she added, 'That too was a joke.'

Sabina shook her head. 'There's no free life for me.' Her hand went over her mouth to stifle a sob.

Mila placed an oily hand on the woman's shoulder. 'Do not speak like that. You have as much right to freedom as I do. You probably deserve it more than I do given how much you have lost. It was no accident that you and Nero found one another.'

Sabina brushed tears away and reached for the cloth floating in the pail by her feet. 'I'm a body slave. My place is with my domina. In this life and the next.' She began to wash Mila's skin.

Exhaling, Mila replied, 'That is what they want you to

believe. They can buy anything they want, except immortality. They are afraid of being alone in death. Rather than facing that fear, they expect their slaves to keep them company, even in death.'

'I have served Lady Prisca most of my life. There's an expectation—'

'A ridiculous expectation.'

Sabina stepped behind her, running the cloth down her back. 'It's too late for me.'

Mila looked over your shoulder. 'Too late? What are you talking about?'

Before Sabina could reply, Prisca swanned into view, gaze sweeping down Mila's naked body, pausing at each bruise. Mila fought the urge to cover herself with her hands.

'You finally have some muscle on you.'

'And bruising every colour of the rainbow,' Sabina said.

Prisca only smiled. 'Every mark is something to be proud of. Do you not feel proud?'

Mila thought that was taking the gladiator's oath to an extreme, but nodded. 'Yes, Era.'

'As Remus is insisting you skip training tomorrow, I thought you might wish to see your sister and mother. I could try to arrange it if you like.'

Mila was speechless for a moment. 'I would very much appreciate that.'

Prisca waved the gratitude off.

Mila had come to know both sides of her domina—the side swept up in all the power and privilege, and the side that tried to rise above it all.

'The day will be yours. Do with it as you please. Ensure you eat, and you might want to pray.' Prisca glanced at Sabina. 'I need to get ready for dinner. Mila can finish up here.'

'Yes, Era,' Sabina said, walking around and handing Mila the cloth. Their eyes met briefly, and Mila saw something unfamiliar in them before her friend turned away. A light breeze blew in, bringing with it an uneasy feeling that wrapped her bare skin. She shivered despite the warm air.

CHAPTER 25

Prisca sent word to Nerva that Mila wished to see her mother and sister before her fight. They all knew Aquila would never agree to such a thing. She received word back that Nerva was not at home—or even in Rome. His father had taken him south to their villa in Antium, where he would remain until winter. Mila heard the news from the other side of the wall, where she had been ready to leave for some time. Only once the opportunity was snatched from her did she realise there was a very real chance she might never see her family again, and that realisation sat like a stone inside her chest.

'Oh' was all she said in response to the news.

'Maybe there's someone else you'd like to visit?' Sabina said. 'A friend?' She wrung her hands in front of her. 'You could visit some temples. If there was ever a time to pray…' She looked away.

Mila left the house with Albaus in tow. Prisca did not want to risk anything happening to her the day before the fight.

She made her way to a number of the city's temples, with nothing to offer the gods but her tearful pleas.

If I must pay with my life for my desire to be free, please give strength to my mother and sister, and to Remus, who is not to blame. Please guide him to the free life he fought for.

Exhausted from prayer, she sat on the steps of the temple of Hercules, trying to think past the fight, imagining her free life. What would it look like? Where would she go? She would be alone at first.

'I will miss you, Albaus,' she said, glancing at the bodyguard who was leaning against one of the pillars, arms crossed. 'It will be like losing my own shadow.'

He nodded, eyes on his feet.

For some reason she had not allowed herself to think beyond the next day. Now the fight loomed in front of her, and she could not harness the thoughts racing in her head. She glanced at the sun, noting it was a little after noon. She did not want to return to the house.

'Where shall we go now?' she asked her bodyguard.

He sniffed.

'Not sure if that is a good idea.'

A grunt.

'All right, you talked me into it.' She pushed off the step, manoeuvring around an old man, his live offering tucked under his arm as he made his way up the steps towards the temple.

Albaus caught up to her, and the two of them walked side by side past the shopfronts where flowers, honey, and entire pig carcasses were on display. They turned the corner, passing the shoemaker, stonecutter, and silversmith.

A few turns later and there it was, Ludus Magnus.

Mila stopped across the street. 'What am I supposed to say? I was in the area and thought I would pop in?'

Albaus watched the street around them.

'He will be working.' She bit down on her lip. 'I should leave him be. Give him space.' She went to leave and

Albaus reached out to stop her. Exhaling, she looked up at him. 'I hope you are not getting soft on me.'

He crossed the street and she ran to catch up with him. She had no idea how Remus would respond to her surprise visit, so she tried to come up with a reason, a message, a question. What would she say when he asked what she was doing there? Her mind came up blank. The man at the gate recognised her, but even if he did not, one look at Albaus had him opening the gate.

She stepped through first and headed straight for the arena where he would likely be. Perhaps they could sit in the cavea and pretend they had come to watch the men train. That was an entirely appropriate reason to be there.

The space was alive with men and horses. She stood beneath the portico, searching for Remus among dozens of men with the same sunburned skin. Perhaps he was not there. He might have gone drinking, or was with a woman, maybe right at that moment.

'He is not here,' she said, turning away.

Albaus grabbed her arm, spun her around and pointed. Her hand went to her brow. She spotted him then at the far end of the arena, a net in one hand and a trident in the other. He shouted something at one of the gladiators, then dropped the trident onto the sand so he could roll up the net. His form was so familiar to her now that her entire body reacted to the sight of him. She lowered her hand, unsure what to do. She felt ridiculous standing there. He glanced in her direction, and his eyes narrowed on her. Her heart beat faster.

Too late to leave now.

Remus walked over to one of the other trainers and said something. The man nodded. She had no choice but to stay where she was, trying one last time to come up with a clever story. But as Remus walked towards her, his toned arms swinging, his eyes fixed on her, her brain just gave up.

After a few painful moments filled with something resembling nausea, Remus stepped up onto the firm ground and stopped in front of her. She swallowed.

'What are you doing here?' His gaze swept over her. 'You all right?'

She nodded, unable to hide her nerves. He waited for her to answer, and when she did not, he repeated himself.

'What are doing here?'

Where was her intelligent answer? Her wit?

'Well, Prisca said the day was mine to do as I pleased. I wanted to see my family, but Nerva is away.' She replayed the words in her head, wondering if they answered the question.

He tucked his hands in his armpits. 'You are supposed to be resting. Have you eaten?'

She nodded. 'I...' She cleared her throat and tried again. 'I thought I might visit you.' She winced. 'To say thank you,' she added, trying to bring some logic to her explanation. 'And watch the men train.' She looked past him. 'And the horses... trot.'

Albaus coughed next to her.

Remus's amused gaze never left her. 'You came to watch the horses trot?'

She screwed her nose up. 'I did not know there would be horses, actually.' Gods, it was hot suddenly. Remus seemed taller as he continued to stare down at her, his eyes a little brighter as they searched her face. She willed her lungs to work.

'I should let you get back to it,' she said, stepping back and almost colliding with a passing slave.

He grabbed her hand, pulling her forwards again. She turned to apologise to the young boy before looking back at Remus.

He took hold of her arms. 'Why'd you come here?' His voice was softer that time.

She blinked. 'I don't know,' she blurted. It was honest.

Albaus began to wander off towards the cavea, and when she went to call after him, Remus tightened his grip on her. Her body softened beneath his touch. She was sure he could hear the pounding of her heart. He continued to stare at her, as though deciding on something.

'Come with me,' he said, taking her hand.

He pulled her along the walkway, setting a pace she could barely match. She snuck a look at his face, but his expression gave nothing away. She followed blindly, asking no questions.

They exited the portico through a doorway, stepping into shadows. Mila glanced both ways down the corridor with all its curtained-off rooms, her heart keeping time with Remus's steps. He stopped suddenly, spinning to face her, her body crashing against his. She did not step back that time.

'Why'd you come here?' he said again, bringing his face close to hers.

Gods, what answer did he want? 'To thank you,' she lied, noticing his breath was as shallow as her own.

He reached up, warm hands cupping her face.

'Why'd you come here? I need to hear it.'

She thought he was going to kiss her, but he hovered just out of reach, waiting for her reply. 'For you. To see you.' She swallowed. Was that enough for him?

'Did you come here just to see me?'

Slowly, she reached up and ran her fingers along his beard. 'And to touch you.'

Apparently that was the answer he had been waiting for, because his lips came crashing down against hers, his mouth open and ravenous. She felt it everywhere, in every limb and organ. She moaned into his open mouth, all control gone. Her arms wound around his neck, pulling him closer so she might taste him properly. His hands travelled down her back and slipped beneath her backside, lifting her off the ground. Her legs moved on instinct, wrapping him, muscle against muscle. Then her back pressed against the wall, and she thought the sensation might undo her. When his mouth went to her neck, her head rolled back, and she realised at that moment that she would need to return to the temple for another prayer on her way home.

Her back left the wall and Remus pushed through the curtain on the other side of the passageway, almost stumbling backwards into the small room. She opened her eyes to see two beds, one of them occupied by a rather surprised dwarf.

'Remus,' she said, pulling away from him.

He turned to look, not letting go of her.

Felix closed his mouth and pushed himself off the bed. 'I am guessing you would like me to leave.' He was already moving towards the door.

Remus all but shoved him. 'Take care of my men.'

Felix shook his head as he opened the curtain to step outside. 'Sure. All right. I will do your job for you,' he complained as he wandered off down the passageway. 'Unbelievable.'

Mila's back slammed onto the bed and Remus landed on top of her, his hands tugging and pulling at her clothes, his hot mouth on her bare skin making her eyes roll back.

This was one fight she was happy to lose.

'I HAVE TO GO,' Mila whispered, her fingers wound through his. Her eyes were closed, her face pressed into the curve of his neck. 'Brutus will come looking for you any moment, and I would rather him not find me here, like this.'

Remus opened one sleepy eye. 'I like you like this.'

She smiled against his skin. 'You have ruined me for tomorrow.'

'Don't say that.' He opened both eyes and slowly propped himself up on one elbow. 'Now you've every reason to win. I'll dangle myself at the gate.'

She took in his smug expression. 'Hmm.'

He traced a finger along her collarbone and between her breasts. 'When I first saw you arguing with Gallus, I told myself to keep walking, don't get involved.'

Her eyes travelled to his lips. 'Why did you change your mind?'

He bent to kiss her, long and deep, then pulled away. 'Had a feeling about you. Thought it was something to do with your fighting, your spark.'

'It was not about my fighting?'

He pressed his lips against her forehead this time. 'Wasn't *only* about your fighting.' His hand travelled along her back, making her eyes close. 'You were pleasant enough to look at.'

Her eyes snapped open. 'Now I know how you do so well with the ladies.'

'My way with words?'

'Mmm.'

His hand roamed farther south. 'Should've used the word beautiful instead?'

She caught his wrist. 'I would have settled for pretty, or smart.'

'Smart? Wouldn't go that far.'

Her smile grew. She felt utterly content in that moment.

She felt free.

'What'll you do tomorrow? After you win?' he asked.

'I was thinking about that today.'

'Just today? You don't have a plan?'

Her smile fell away. 'I have a long-term plan. I need to earn more coin.'

'That'll take some time. Where will you live? How will you pay for food?'

She rolled onto her back. 'I need to get through tomorrow first.'

'You should be talking like winning's a sure thing.'

She sat up and reached over the edge of the bed for her clothes.

'What are you doing?'

'Getting dressed.'

'Don't do that.'

She smiled. He watched her dress for a moment.

'Let me take care of you.'

She glanced at him. 'What?'

'You just have to win the fight. I'll handle everything after that.'

She paused with her arms through the sleeves of her tunic. 'That is very generous, but I will manage just fine.'

He swung his legs over the edge of the bed. 'How?'

'With whatever coin is thrown after I... defeat my Spanish opponent.'

Remus reluctantly reached for his own clothes. 'What if I want to take care of you?'

She laughed. 'The entire point of freedom is that you are independent.'

He stopped and looked at her. 'No, the point of freedom is that you're free to choose. You'll still need people in your life.'

'I know, it is just that I would prefer not to depend on someone else.' She slipped her stola on.

'I'm not anyone,' he said, taking her hand. 'If you want to keep fighting, you'll need to join a school.'

'I do not want to belong to a school. If I do that, I will never leave Rome. I will be stuck here, like…'

He stood up from the bed. 'Me?' When she did not reply, he said, 'I chose to stay here.'

She looked up at him. 'Because you are afraid. You do not know any other life. It is understandable.'

'You don't know what you're talking about.'

She closed the distance between them, pressing her hips against him. 'Let us not fight.'

He stared down at her. 'I think you should marry me,' he said, unflinching.

She stepped back. 'What?'

'You heard. Once you're free, we should get married and leave Rome.'

'And leave my sister?' She looked down, surprised at how excited the offer made her.

'Not forever. We'll earn the coin together, away from the arena, and come back for your family as soon as we have enough.'

Why was she even considering it? Maybe because she had done something very stupid—she had fallen in love. 'And go where?'

'We already decided on that,' he said, pulling her close again. 'India.'

She laughed. 'India.'

'To see the small elephants.' He bent to kiss her.

'Better go,' she said into his mouth. 'Albaus will be wondering where I am.'

'Albaus is mute, not stupid.'

She pulled away and began to fix her hair. It was usually up for training, so she left it half out. He kneaded the hair between his fingers as she secured the top part.

'What are you thinking?' he asked.

She shook her head. 'I think I am just in shock. A few

hours being ravaged by you and a marriage proposal is a lot to take in.'

'You came here for the ravaging.'

She smiled. 'I did.'

'But not the proposal.'

She watched him. 'That part was unexpected.' She laughed to herself.

'Don't laugh. Do I need to throw you down on that bed again?'

She shook her head. 'No.'

He tugged on her clothes and she slapped his hand away.

'All right,' he said, shrugging. 'Forget I asked.'

She suppressed a smile. 'Forget your marriage proposal?'

'And the elephants.'

She pushed herself up onto her toes and kissed him. If only she could stop time.

'I think that's why I couldn't keep walking that day.'

She frowned. 'What do you mean?'

'I knew, even then.'

Her eyes prickled and she looked away to prevent another embarrassing display. 'I am not entirely sure I deserve you.' She mentally patted herself on the back for keeping her emotion in check. 'I know you do not want to hear this, but what if I lose?'

'Don't even think it.'

She looked up at him. 'What if I lose?' she whispered.

He took a small step back. 'I taught you everything I know, every skill, every trick. Then I hand you my heart…' He shook his head. 'You can't lose. Your sister won't forgive you. I won't forgive you. Your only choice is to win.'

She closed the distance between them, wrapping her

arms around his middle, her head pressed against the steady beat of his heart. 'Will you promise me something?'

He kissed her head as his fingers combed her hair. 'Ask it first, and then I'll decide.'

She closed her eyes, enjoying the warmth and regretting her decision to dress. 'If anything should happen—'

'It won't.'

'Will you check in on my sister? Tell her whatever she needs to hear.'

He cupped her face and lifted it to him. 'Tell her yourself when you're free.'

'And Nero… will you free him? When he comes of age?'

His thumb moved over her cheek. 'He's already free. Took care of it the day I bought him.'

More pins to the eyes. She blinked against them and a tear escaped. 'You are the best man I know.'

'What about Nerva?'

She nodded. 'You are the second best man I know.'

He wiped the tear away with his thumb. 'If that's true, you should really get out more.'

'That is the plan.'

He slid his hands down her arms. 'And we should marry before you see what else is available to you.'

She raised her chin. 'Presumptuous. I have not accepted your offer yet.'

His smile was gone, but there was light in his eyes. 'Win your freedom, and marry me.'

She could hear the emotion in his tone and see it in his face. It was not just an impulsive question. He wanted to marry her, and she wanted that too.

'Make sure you are waiting at that gate.'

CHAPTER 26

A strange mood engulfed the Fadius household on the first morning of the games. Or perhaps Mila was viewing her world through a veil of tension. The other servants left as she entered the kitchen, leaving only the cook clanging pots on the stove, and Sabina staring into her porridge.

Mila took a seat beside her, and the body slave slid a pear across the bench towards her. 'You get this also.'

Mila picked the fruit up and smelled it. 'I will share it with you.'

Sabina shook her head. 'I'm not very hungry.'

The cook placed a bowl of porridge in front of Mila and trudged back to the stove.

'Thank you,' Mila said, her gaze remaining on Sabina. 'Is it just my imagination, or is everyone behaving as though I am already dead?

Sabina scraped up the last of her food, shoved it into her mouth, and stood, her stool screeching. 'I think you'll win.'

Mila stared up at her. 'Surely that is cause for happiness.'

A weak smile came to Sabina's pale face. 'I suppose we're all a bit nervous.'

Mila picked up a knife, cut a slice of pear, and held it out to her friend. Sabina hesitated before taking it.

'Perhaps I should try to buy your freedom. Just imagine the havoc we would cause.'

'Prisca would never agree to the sale.'

Mila shrugged. 'Then we shall have to make her an offer she cannot refuse.'

Sabina was silent and thoughtful for a moment. 'Will Remus continue to care for the boy, no matter what?'

Something in her tone made Mila go still. 'Of course he will.'

The cook placed a tray of food in front of Sabina. Breakfast for their mistress. She picked it up and left the kitchen without another word. Mila gulped down her porridge in a few mouthfuls and hurried after her.

Prisca was sitting up in bed when they arrived with the food. It was an ungodly hour for a woman who liked to sleep late. She was looking out the window, chewing a fingernail. Her eyes went to Mila as she entered the room, following her to the cupboard where she began sifting through dresses.

'What would you like to wear for the games, Era?' Mila asked.

Prisca picked up a boiled egg, then placed it back on the tray and pushed it away. Seeing that Sabina was busy, Mila stepped forwards to take it.

'Let Sabina take care of that,' Prisca told her. 'Go ready yourself. Albaus will escort you to Ludus Magnus in time for the procession. You will go in a litter to reserve your energy. I have even employed a crier for a little intrigue.'

Mila wondered what Jovian thought about the whole thing. There had been no hiding it from him once the matches had been announced, and yet she had barely heard a word spoken about it. Libertas and Hebe, a Spaniard no one had heard of. A fight to the death on the first day of the games. Unsurprisingly, few outside of the house cared that much; they preferred to speak about the men who would follow them.

'Are you ready?' Prisca asked, her intense gaze on Mila.

Was she? She thought for a moment. Sure, she had trained for weeks, was the fittest she had been in her life and had learned from one of the best gladiators in Rome. But was she ready to take the life of a stranger? To die at the hand of her opponent?

'Yes.'

What other answer was there?

'I shall see you later,' Prisca said, turning back to the window.

She did not say when, just later. An uneasy feeling continued to swell inside of Mila. She found her feet anchored in place.

'What is it?' Prisca asked tiredly.

'When I win… that will be enough? After that, I am free?'

'Enough?' Prisca's face softened. 'To be given such an opportunity, to fight at Rome's grandest venue, and give everything to that fight…' She shook her head. 'To have thousands of people watching, shouting your name. Is that enough?' Her shoulders fell. 'It is everything. Few women are remembered in history, but if you fight your best fight, you might be.'

'There is only glory for the victor.'

Prisca twisted a piece of hair. 'You are wrong. There is no more glorious way to die.'

Sabina bent to collect the tray. Everything rattled.

'If you win,' Prisca continued, 'you will have earned

your freedom.' She signalled to Sabina to put the tray back down. 'Perhaps I will eat after all.'

REMUS WAITED with Felix and Fausta at the entrance of the tunnel that ran from Ludus Magnus directly to the gate of life at the Flavian Amphitheatre. Remus was silent, mostly due to the fact that he could not follow even a simple conversation. He calmed his nerves by focusing on the idea that Mila would soon walk free. He thought about marrying her, what their life together might look like. He had never imagined that life with anyone—never let himself. Those thoughts helped thaw the parts frozen by visions of a sword at her neck and a hammer raised above her head, held in place by her oath.

'Stop bouncing your foot,' Felix said. He was leaning back with his eyes closed, the previous night's wine not sitting well based on his grimace.

Remus glanced down at his hands, which had not made a sound. 'How'd you know I was doing that?'

'I am the mighty Minui Spiculus, finely tuned to the sufferings of men.' He opened his eyes and lifted his head off the wall. 'And because that is what you always do when you are nervous.'

Remus wiped his hands on his tunic.

'You did everything you could outside of killing her opponent yourself,' Fausta said, pacing in front of them. She was not good at standing still either. 'She's as ready as she'll ever be.'

Remus saw Brutus coming towards them with their gladiators trailing behind. But no Mila. 'I'd feel a lot better if I knew something of this Spaniard. No one's heard of her.'

'She's a foreigner. No one cares,' Fausta said.

'And that is a good thing,' Felix reminded him. 'Better a nobody than a household name.'

Fausta stopped walking. 'I'm a household name.'

'Not for the reasons you might think,' Felix said, winking at the gladiator.

'Say that when I'm holding a sword,' Fausta replied, resuming her pacing.

Brutus came to a stop in front of Remus. 'Where's the girl?'

Before Remus could reply, Mila came jogging down the path towards them. 'Sorry,' she called. 'The entire city has come to a halt for the parade.'

Brutus said nothing, walking off into the tunnel. The others followed after him, and Remus and Mila fell to the back of the group.

'Here,' Remus said, handing her helmet over. 'Put it on.' His eyes ran over her, inspecting her beneath torchlight. 'Everything fit? You comfortable?'

She looked down at the breastplate and the manica on her arm. 'I think so.'

Remus tugged at her belt, checking it was secure.

'Do not get any ideas,' she whispered.

He released the belt. 'How are you making jokes right now?'

She shrugged. 'Better jokes than tears.'

They fell silent for a moment.

'Did you eat?' Remus asked suddenly, causing her to jump.

'Yes.'

He continued to stare at her. 'You focused?'

She turned, exasperated. 'I am trying.'

He nodded and faced forwards again, listening to the scuff of sandals on stone.

'You know, something seemed off in the household this morning,' she said, keeping her voice down.

His gaze returned to her. 'What do you mean?'

Shaking her head, she replied, 'I might be imagining things, but I feel as though everyone knows something I do not.'

Remus's arm brushed hers and she moved closer to him.

'Did you ask Sabina?'

'She has been acting strange for weeks. The confident woman I met all those weeks ago is gone. I keep waiting for her to fall apart at any moment. Just yesterday she was in tears, as though my death were a certainty.'

He tried not to let his concern show. 'Maybe she thinks it is. She's wrong.'

Keeping her eyes ahead, Mila slipped her warm hand into his and he gave it a squeeze. He felt a tightening in his throat. He could not lose her now.

When daylight began to fill the tunnel, he released her hand, knowing they were close to the gate where the other gladiators would be waiting. The fighters would join the end of the procession as it moved into the arena, paraded in front of hungry spectators.

There were four female fighters in total. Two were bestiarii—beast hunters. No helmets. No armour. Exotic costumes with breasts exposed. Silver scars on their backs and legs contrasted their dark skin. One of them had a nasty line reaching from her left armpit all the way to her nipple, likely from a razor-sharp claw. The pair would work together to kill whatever starved, provoked animals were released upon them.

The third woman was Mila's opponent, the Spaniard. She was lightly armoured, breasts partially covered and a helmet concealing her face. There was barely a scar or mark on her, which meant she was either inexperienced, or always won. Remus noticed Mila shifted next to him and he wished he could take her hand again, or least hand her a weapon to hold, to give her hands something to do. He caught her eye, cast in shadows from her helmet, and gave her a reassuring smile.

They waited on the side while the procession entered the arena. Emperor Septimius Severus led the way, standing in a chariot pulled by four black horses. There were tamed zebras pulling decorated floats; in them, young men and women held poses, telling stories of the gods. Other exotic animals followed, their handlers clutching chains and whips. Dancers swirled in front of them, showering rose petals that were quickly swallowed up by the sand. Musicians marched, instruments deafening as they passed. And finally the Vestal Virgins, modest in every sense of the word.

Mila turned to him, and he saw that her hands were shaking.

'If I don't make it out, tell my family—'

He shook his head. 'Shhh. Don't.' He leaned closer so she would hear over the music. 'Get out of your own head. I know what these final moments feel like, but it's part of your fight.' He tapped his head. 'So you need to keep your shield up. Hear me?'

She swallowed, nodding.

'Time to go,' Brutus called to his fighters. 'Grab your weapons. Join the back of the line.'

The Spaniard grabbed her sword and red shield, contrasting Mila's blue one. The bestiarii took up spears, the retiarius his net, dagger, and trident. The eques mounted his horse and Brutus passed weapons up to him.

Chink, clank.

Remus stepped back, joining Felix and Fausta, his eyes never leaving Mila. She looked like one of them, not like the first time she had entered the arena. She was carried out onto the sand by music, applause, and strong legs. Then she was gone.

'I hope the gods heard your prayers this morning,' Felix said.

Remus glanced down at him. 'Me too.'

CHAPTER 27

Uri, vinciri, verberari, ferroque necari patior. That was the oath she had made upon arriving at Ludus Magnus all those weeks earlier. *I will endure to be burned, to be bound, to be beaten, and to be killed by the sword.* Remus had shaken his head; after all, she was Prisca's plaything, protected by the Fadius name.

He was so very wrong.

As he settled into his seat at the top of the amphitheatre, almost touching the clouds, his gaze fell to Felix's hands, gripping the edge of his seat. 'Still afraid of heights, I see.'

Felix rolled his eyes. 'Yes, yes. We all know how amusing it is for you big people.'

Fausta, seated on the other side of him, leaned forwards. 'Do you remember the first time he climbed this high?'

Remus nodded. 'How could I forget? People were yelling at us to move the frozen dwarf out of everyone's way.'

Felix shook his head. 'Go on, get all the jokes out now before the games begin.'

Brutus cleared his throat and they all fell silent.

The gladiators had formed ranks in front of the emperor. Mila was lost amid men and horses. Raising their arms, they all shouted, '*Ave imperator morituri te salutant.*'

We who are about to die salute you.

Remus looked away. How was he supposed to remain in his seat and watch her die when the scent of her still lingered on his skin? Her smile flashed in his mind—and that dimple—the one he had consumed just hours earlier. She had sat on top of him, legs wrapping his waist, head thrown back. He recalled the feel of her hair on his bare skin, her breath hot against his chest, the way her thighs had squeezed when—

'Remus.'

He looked at Felix, who was staring at him as though he had lost his mind. 'Sorry, what?'

Felix shook his head. 'I was saying I thought Lady Prisca would be seated for her big moment.'

Remus's eyes went to the podium where the senators were gathered.

'I saw her slave earlier,' Fausta said. 'So she's here somewhere.'

Felix turned to her. 'Which slave?'

'The one who wipes her arse.'

'Ah,' Felix replied, nodding. 'I would just like to point out that when I was once part of a noble family, I wiped my own arse.' He turned to Remus. 'You have spent a lot of time with Prisca over the years. What say you on the subject?'

Remus was searching for Prisca amid the white togas. 'I didn't go to the latrine with her, if that's what you're asking.'

Music drifted up to them, organ and horn, building suspense for the performance that would soon begin. Remus leaned on his knees. 'I feel sick.'

'The woman you love is preparing to fight to the death,' Felix said. 'I would be rather surprised if you felt any other way.'

Remus searched for Mila in the arena, but she was no longer there. Men in ridiculous armour had replaced her, carrying weapons good for nothing but theatrics.

'It is an awful lot of time and coin to spend on a slave girl for one fight,' Felix said.

Fausta snorted. 'If I were her, I would buy fifteen such girls, a few for each games of the season. She's a bored noblewoman past her prime. What would you have her do, take up weaving?'

Remus turned to his friends. 'I'm going to marry Mila. Today. The moment she's free.'

Felix's jaw just about fell to his knees. He checked to see if Brutus was listening and found him talking to the man on the other side of him. Fausta leaned back, shaking her head. Felix closed his mouth.

'Well, you could do a lot worse.' He clapped Remus on the back. 'Congratulations. Ignore Fausta, she is upset because she does not get a lot of marriage proposals.'

'I get plenty of *other* proposals,' she replied, not looking at them.

Felix cast a knowing look at Remus. 'It is true. She is like honeycomb.'

They fell quiet, watching grown men roll about in the sand, their weapons ridiculous, their movements exaggerated. The crowd laughed around them.

Next came the trained animals, mounted zebras, lion cubs with cute antics that made everyone sigh and laugh simultaneously. A full-grown lion quietened the crowd with one mighty roar. It was set free in the arena with a crocodile so large there was a collective intake of breath, temporarily emptying the stadium of air. When the crocodile lay dead, the starved lion hissed at the noisy crowd.

Enter the bestiarii, drums alerting the crowd to their arrival. The animal put up a good fight, but it was the women who walked away, though not without injury. One woman's calf was torn open, leaving a trail of blood as she limped from the arena.

Afterwards, Emperor Septimius Severus ate food from silver trays while criminals were brought into the arena for execution. But not just any execution. The sentenced men were made to perform as stars of their own show—a tragedy ending with their inevitable death. Some were forced to fight one another. Never mind if they won, because the next man was sent in, and then the next, until exhaustion won and they became easy prey. When only one man remained, sweating, bloodied, and afraid, the ground opened up and a leopard emerged to finish the show.

Remus sat still as the crowd applauded around him. 'I need a walk.'

Felix looked up. 'Want me to come with you?'

He shook his head, stepping past them and making his way down the steps into the walkways below. It would be Mila's turn next, and he did not think he could sit still to watch. Instead, he wandered, the arena flashing in and out of view as he made his way along the passageways.

'Libertas.'

The word sounded throughout the amphitheatre.

Remus stopped in an archway to watch Mila enter the arena. The spectators were still making their way back to their seats after using the latrines and filling their bellies with food. There was no way he could sit. His leg bounced beneath him and he rubbed a hand over his beard. Even at that distance he could see she was afraid. Sixty-five thousand people witnessing your death did that to a person. Applause. Whistling. Calls for her to bare her breasts. No surprises there.

He closed his eyes a moment to gain control of himself. It did not help.

'And all the way from Spain, her first fight in Rome, Hebe!'

Remus watched the goddess of youth stride into the arena as though she had been born on the very sand she walked on.

Hebe. It was to be a fight between gods, then.

His heart sank at the sight of her. Her confidence suggested she was a much more experienced fighter, even if no one in Rome had heard of her. He wondered if he had done enough for Mila. She appeared to be wilting beneath the noise, weighed down by it.

The *summa rudis* spoke to them, reminding them of the rules. With a stick in his hand and a whip at his hip, the referee was there to ensure the fight was fair and entertaining. Mila stared blankly at the man while Hebe's gaze swept across the admiring crowd who cheered, impatient for action.

'Remus,' came a voice from behind.

He turned to see Prisca's body slave standing in the shadows, her face pale. 'Sabina.'

She remained there, staring at him. 'I need to talk to you.'

MILA NODDED AT THE REFEREE. Whatever he was saying, she had to agree to it—so she did. He waved his stick a final time and stepped back, giving them space to fight, to kill. The crowd quietened. Mila softened her knees, focusing only on the woman in front of her. What had Remus told her? *Imagine your sister is standing behind you, and your opponent wants her dead. Now go save your sister.*

She struck first, her polished sword reflecting the sun.

Hebe's body curved in order to avoid the weapon, her shield gliding gracefully overhead, as though it were a dance. Mila bent at the waist, striking at Hebe's left calf, but her feet left the ground and she sliced only air. She raised her shield, knowing what would follow. *Crash.* Swords screeched. Mila sprang sideways, blocking her opponent, finding her rhythm.

How easily it could all be over. Their weapons were not made of wood. The blades were not blunt.

Mila slammed her shield into Hebe's helmet, causing her to stumble. The spectators liked that, some jumping to their feet to show their approval. A gentle roar hummed around them. She felt slightly encouraged. Taking off at a run, she leapt, smashing aside the readied weapon with her shield while aiming her sword at the exposed shoulder above the breastplate. No such luck. Hebe's shield rammed into her stomach and she tumbled into the sand, curled up in pain as feet landed on the ground next to her. She sucked in a breath.

Shield up, Remus's voice screamed in her mind.

Up it went—just in time. She rolled once and scrambled to her feet, but her opponent's shield knocked her down again. She swung a foot, grunting with the force, and took Hebe's legs out from beneath her. The woman landed on her side in the sand. Mila sprang to her feet, heart pumping adrenaline through her. Hebe went to roll, but Mila brought her shield down on the woman's head before she had a chance, stunning her. Blood poured out from beneath the helmet. At that angle it was possible she had broken her nose.

Mila had a small window of opportunity, but she missed it, freezing for a moment. A foot smashed into her knee and Mila's leg buckled. She was down on one knee in the sand and Hebe was back on her feet, blood dripping from her chin, eyes blazing through the slit of the helmet.

Shield up.

Mila blocked the sword coming at her thigh, an injury that would have finished her, and staggered onto her feet, cursing as pain shot up her leg. *No, no, no.* She kept her eyes on Hebe as she limped around for a moment, fingers tightening around her weapon.

Her opponent lost patience and came at her again, and then again. Mila tried to focus, but her vision had blurred and Hebe's moves were too swift.

Shield up.

A sword grazed her arm and she felt the sting, then blood running. They were out of their seats again. Nothing like a little blood to get the crowd riled up.

A roar formed in Mila's stomach, travelling up her throat, like acid in her mouth until she opened up to release it.

REMUS WAS TORN between wanting to watch Mila fight and needing to know what Sabina had to say. 'Speak,' he said, walking over to her, his back to Mila.

Sabina glanced past him. 'If Mila should win, my domina has put her wishes on parchment. Everything is in the small chest beneath her bed.'

The crowd roared and Remus spun around in panic. He had studied Mila for weeks—every tremble in her hands, every flexing muscle in her legs and arms. He worried if he looked away for too long, she would come undone. *Get your goddamn shield up.*

He turned back to Sabina, trying to focus. 'Why are you telling me this?'

'So you know she kept her word.'

The crowd was on their feet, and Remus turned to see Mila down on one knee. He took a step towards the archway. *Get up.* She did. He turned back to Sabina, maintaining the distance, his mind struggling. What was she saying to him? She stared at him with the hollow expression of one defeated.

'I think she'll win.'

'Mila?'

'Yes.'

Her expression did not match the words coming from her mouth.

Remus's gaze returned to the arena. He watched as Mila transformed before his eyes, a fire lighting within her, looking every bit the gladiator.

'Where is your domina?' he asked, turning back. He saw it then, her hands wrapped around a dagger. It was not pointed up but down, as though to harm herself. His feet moved towards her while trying to pull together the fragments of thoughts clashing about in his head. She took a step back and held up one hand.

He stopped. 'What are you doing?' Searching her outstretched palm for an answer, he found only red skin from clutching a dagger for too long. He narrowed his eyes on her. 'Where is Lady Prisca?' It came out as a whisper, because the pieces were fitting together.

She blinked and some tears escaped. 'This is what she wanted, more than anything.'

His gaze fell to the dagger. The crowd cheered again, but that time he did not turn to look. 'What are you saying?'

The dagger shook. Sabina's free hand went over her mouth and she inhaled against it, looking past him to the arena. 'When she dies, I must follow her into the next life.'

Applause rang like an insistent bell behind him. He had to turn, had to check if she was still standing. She was—towering over Hebe, who lay panting at her feet, her sword and shield some distance from her. Mila was looking around, scared and unsure. Her shield fell to the ground, and both hands wrapped the hilt of her sword. She turned her head to the emperor.

'Lugula!' the people shouted. *Kill her.*

Remus felt cold suddenly. He blinked once and faced the wall, leaning against it for support. 'Hebe, the goddess of youth… She's not from Spain, is she?'

Sabina swallowed and shook her head. Blood pounded in his ears.

'Mila's about to kill her domina,' Sabina said, her voice breaking at the confession she had held inside for so long.

Remus knew Mila would never walk free. It would not matter what was written on parchment beneath Prisca's bed.

'Killing your domina is the worst form of crime. Mila will be put to death,' he said aloud, miserable, mind racing. 'And possibly every other slave in the household alongside her. It's the law.'

'Lugula!' they continued to shout.

Sabina shook her head. 'Lady Prisca wrote every detail down. It's all there. I saw it with my own eyes.'

Remus's fist collided with the wall. 'It won't matter!'

There was only one thing to be done.

He turned towards the arena—and ran.

SEVERUS STOOD at the edge of the podium, looking about and listening.

'Lugula!' the people shouted.

Mila watched Hebe's chest rise and fall, eyes struggling to remain open. She kept her sword steady, the tip pressed to Hebe's neck while she waited for the emperor to decide the woman's fate. He had one arm outstretched, observing the reaction of the crowd, wanting the people to feel heard. The entire amphitheatre vibrated.

Kill her.

The woman had fought well, but she was a Spaniard, and the people felt no attachment to her.

The emperor's thumb turned up, like the thrust of a sword. The crowd responded with cheers and clapping. Mila stared down at the woman, a fallen goddess at her feet. The sword shook in her hand, and she wondered if she would be able to finish what she had started—what she had promised.

She had tried to imagine the moment, every detail, playing the scene over and over in her mind more times than she cared to admit. She had sat in the kitchen and watched Germana slice through raw meat with a sharp knife, imagining the animal's heartbeat slowing, its lungs emptying.

She had thought she was ready.

She pulled Hebe up by the arm into a seated position. The woman slumped against Mila's leg and coughed, blood spraying from her open mouth. Her injuries were worse than Mila had realised. She recalled the dog she and Nerva had found as children, the one hit by a cart and left to die. Nerva had broken its neck and Mila had let him, knowing the animal was better off. Was this the same? Was she just putting an end to the pain?

'Mila!'

She blinked and the sword wavered. For a moment she thought she could hear Remus calling to her. What would he think of all this? Yes, he would be grateful that she had lived, but would he look at her differently? Treat her like a killer?

'Mila, stop!'

She shook her head, trying to focus on the task. Raising her sword, she stared at the throbbing spot on the woman's neck that she would pierce. Hebe's breaths shortened, the noise distracting her.

That was when she noticed the small scar above the woman's breastplate.

'No! Mila, put the sword down!'

She blinked, certain she was seeing and hearing things.

'Mila!'

She looked up then, wanting to prove to herself that Remus was not there. But to her surprise, he was, sprinting across the sand towards her.

'It is all right,' said the woman at her feet, her voice like splintered wood. 'Listen to that crowd. It is glorious.'

Mila released her grip and staggered back. Hebe collapsed onto the sand, coughing and gasping. She looked up at Remus, who was shaking his head at her.

Hebe's breathing turned to a wheeze as Remus skidded to a halt next to her, falling onto the sand and pulling the helmet from her head.

Mila's sword fell to the ground and her insides coiled like a snake. She looked down at her empty hands, unsure whose blood was on them.

The guards who had chased Remus across the sand arrived the same time as the referee. They all stared down at a blood-soaked Lady Prisca Fadius. She was dying.

'Someone get a physician!' Remus shouted. 'And find Jovian Fadius.'

The men turned and ran towards the podium where the emperor remained on his feet, watching.

Mila fell to her knees and crawled towards them, every movement an effort. 'I didn't know,' she said, almost pleading. Who was she speaking to?

When she reached Prisca, she lifted her domina's head

and cradled it in her lap. 'I didn't know,' she said again, shaking her head at her own stupidity. Now that she did know, she wondered how she had not seen it from the beginning. She had been a pawn in an elaborate suicide.

Prisca stared up at her. Her skin had turned grey. 'It was everything I imagined.' Her breathing softened. No more choking or coughing, no more gasping. Her chest went still. Mila stared at it, waiting for it to expand. She blinked and tears escaped, falling into her domina's hair. She looked up at Remus, but he was staring at the sand. He raised a fist and punched the ground.

'I didn't know. I swear it.' She needed him to look at her, needed to see he believed her.

He raised his eyes, his expression as broken as her own. 'I know. But they'll never believe you.'

The crowd had grown quiet, watching as Jovian Fadius marched across the sand towards his dead wife. Remus continued to stare at Mila.

'You'll be put to death for this,' he said, glancing at the sword laying behind Mila.

Mila turned to look at the weapon. 'No,' she said. 'Whatever you are thinking, stop.' She could see he was torn between good sense and his desire to protect her.

Before he could reply, Jovian Fadius came to a stop beside them. He did not bend to his wife, simply looked at her, his expression collapsing for a moment before he gained control again. Remus stood. Mila gently lay her domina's head on the sand and did the same.

'What is this?' Jovian said, trying to process the sight in front of him. 'What have you done to my wife?' His eyes went to Mila, filled with accusation.

Remus spoke up. 'She didn't know. Your wife's slave, Sabina, came to me just moments ago. As soon as I realised, I stopped the fight. I was too late.'

Jovian kept his blazing eyes on Mila. 'You killed my wife. The mother of my sons. Your own *domina*,' he hissed.

'She didn't know,' Remus repeated, louder that time. 'Sabina will tell you.'

Something in his tone made Mila doubt that. As if on cue, a guard arrived, whispering to Jovian. Sabina was already dead. The past few weeks, she had not been readying for Mila's death but her own.

It was all there now, in plain sight.

Jovian shook his head and looked at Mila. 'Arrest the girl.'

'No!' Remus said. 'Your wife wanted Mila freed if she won—and she won.'

Jovian turned to Remus, almost laughing. He pointed at Mila. 'That slave is my property, and she is not free unless I say so.'

Remus fought to calm himself. 'I swear before all the gods, she didn't know. Your wife kept the entire thing secret.'

Jovian glared at him, mouth trembling. 'I am well aware of my wife's secrets.'

Remus shook his head and stepped back. When the two guards stepped forwards to take Mila, he swooped to collect the sword behind him, fixing his gaze on Jovian.

'Remus,' she pleaded. She thought back to the hardest times in her life and could not remember ever having begged for anything. But she would beg for him.

The sound of her voice stopped him. He looked at her, ignoring the third guard who had drawn his sword, ready to protect Jovian if need be. She held his gaze until he eventually looked down at the weapon in his hand. He flipped it, catching it by the blade, and held it out for Jovian to take.

'Your wife's sword' was all he said.

The senator stared at it for a moment before reaching out and taking it from him.

As Mila was led away, she glanced back at Remus. All of their plans were dead on the sand between them.

'Remember your promise,' she called to him.

CHAPTER 28

Mila thought Jovian Fadius would place her under house arrest. She had seen the dungeon door near the stables, heard slaves being thrown in there when they needed reminding of their place.

But she did not return to the Fadius household. Instead, she was taken to Mamertine Prison inside the Comitium at the foot of Capitoline Hill, a dark dungeon twelve feet underground. Mila was dropped through the hole where she landed in a crouch, her legs exhausted. The smell of death and human waste made her cover her mouth. She peered around the dark space, her stomach heaving in protest. The iron grid was replaced above her, broken light painting the filthy floor.

There was a reason she had never met anyone who had spent time in Mamertine—they were never released. Any who died inside were simply thrown into the sewer that ran below the prison. She suspected some of the bodies scattered around would soon join them.

As her eyes adjusted, she saw a young girl in a filthy red toga. The other prisoners appeared to be men. One had been stripped naked, likely dead.

No noble person would be held in such a place.

The room was cold, and when night came and the adrenaline wore off, she would feel it. She suddenly remembered she was wearing nothing but a breastplate, loincloth and a layer of sand. Her armour had been taken from her.

'Do you have any food?'

Mila turned to the young girl crouched against the wall a short distance away, looking at her. She was frail, and her eyes reminded Mila of the hunting dogs she had seen as a girl—unhinged and hungry. She could not have been more than seventeen.

'No,' Mila replied, remaining where she was. She studied the girl in the dark, watched as her head fell back against the wall, staring back at her like a wary cat.

'You a gladiator?'

Mila nodded. What other answer was there? 'Yes.'

The girl pushed hair back from her face, and Mila noticed a tattoo on her forehead: *FUR*. Thief. A common punishment for slaves caught stealing.

'When was the last time you ate?'

The girl thought for a moment. 'Days, I think. It's always so dark. I can't tell.' Her eyes moved over Mila. 'Why you in here?'

The answer seemed ridiculous. 'I accidentally killed my domina.'

The girl gave a sharp laugh, life flashing momentarily on her hollow face. She drew her knees up and rested her chin on them. 'You'll die for that. Not quietly—they'll make a big show of it. Can't have slaves thinking they can get away with murder.'

Mila swallowed. 'What is your name?'

'Tacita.'

She nodded at the tattoo on her head. 'What did you steal?'

Tacita rolled her bare feet on the ground. 'I didn't steal, really. I was collecting from a customer who didn't want to pay.'

'Pay for what?'

A pause. 'Me.'

Mila's gaze fell. 'He raped you?'

Another laugh. 'It's not rape when you're a whore.' She gestured to the door above. 'That's what they say.'

'The guards?'

The girl shrugged. 'Everyone.'

'Not everyone.'

Tacita pointed to her forehead. 'This is what they did the first time. The next time they put me in here.'

Mila sat down, wrapping her arms about her knees. 'Have they sentenced you?'

The girl just stared. 'Sure feels like they have. Probably forgot I'm here. Who's going to remember the young whore with the hideous face?'

Mila would—for whatever time she had left. 'Do you have family?'

The girl chewed on a fingernail. 'It was just me and my brother. He was a legionnaire. Used to send money, and when the money stopped, I knew he was dead.'

'I am sorry.'

It was a common story. Young girls did what they could to get by. Once you registered with a brothel, you were a prostitute for the rest of your life, so many took to the streets alone, telling themselves it would just be for a little while, until they found other employment or a husband.

'You should try to sleep as much as possible,' Tacita said, lying down on the cold floor. 'It helps pass the time and stops the hunger.'

Mila buried her face in her knees. 'I am not hungry.'

The girl closed her eyes. 'Not yet.'

Aside from an occasional cough or groan from a person

she had assumed dead, the room was still. Mila stared up at the light above her, imagining her mother and sister learning the news. She had been the better fighter. She had worked so hard to ensure she had won. She had a plan, a promise, and she should have been free.

Prisca had used her to end the life she despised. A woman with wealth and influence, two healthy sons, and every comfort she could desire. But below all that was resentment, discontent, and a gladiator's heart. At some point in her life, she had chosen something different than the life laid out for her, the life everyone had told her was enough. As much as Mila wanted to hate her for it, she understood. They had both been fighting for something more, wanting to take charge of their own fates. And the price of rebellion was death.

'Mila.'

She opened her eyes, taking in her surroundings. The air did not seem so putrid after breathing it for hours. She moved, suddenly aware of her aching limbs, every muscle in her body complaining. Too much fighting, too much cold. A stone bed had not helped matters. Her eyes sank shut.

'Mila.'

Her eyes snapped open and she looked up, pale light streaking her face.

'Remus?' Her voice was hoarse. She focused on his worried face visible through the bars. *Remus*. She sat up, wincing as she straightened her neck. Scrambling to her feet, she noticed Nero crouched beside him. 'I cannot believe they let you through.'

'Albaus knows one of the guards. They didn't exactly ask questions.'

They stared at one another. Remus's eyes were enclosed by dark circles.

'Have you... spoken to my mother? To Dulcia?'

He shook his head. 'I called by the house but Nerva's still in Antium with his father. Aquila wouldn't see me.'

Mila fought back tears. 'Aquila would have heard the news by now. I doubt she will even send word.' She thought for a moment. 'It is better this way. The news will be hard on Nerva.' She found a smile for Nero. 'Are you all right?' she asked him.

His fingers wrapped the iron. 'Sabina's dead.'

Mila swallowed. 'You must be hurting a lot.'

He just stared at her for a moment. 'Will they hang you?'

Remus put a hand on Nero's shoulder. 'Go and wait with Albaus. I'll be there in a moment.'

The boy glanced once at Mila as he stood. She smiled at him, doing her best to appear brave.

When they were alone, Remus said, 'I've visited all the schools, trying to find out who trained Prisca. Someone did. She'd never have fought unprepared.'

'I see it all so differently now, all the signs, all the clues. Everything so blatant.'

'Whoever helped her isn't talking. They've been paid too well.'

'It does not matter now.'

'We could prove that she wanted it kept secret.'

'Jovian Fadius does not care. He already knows the truth.'

Remus began pulling items from secret pockets. 'Catch,' he said, pushing them between the gaps in the iron bars.

Food rained down on her. A few small loaves, an apple, some salted pork wrapped in wax paper. And a *palla*, stuffed through a gap a few inches at a time until it floated down to her. She wrapped it around her cold skin, keeping hold of the food as best she could. 'No lemon tart?' she asked, attempting a smile.

'We ate them on the way here.'

A genuine smile that time. He stared down at her, and his expression made her chest hurt.

'You have to go soon?'

He nodded, then retrieved a waterskin. It did not fit between the bars, so he emptied some water from it before sliding it through. Balancing everything in one arm, she caught it with her free hand.

'Make sure every man in there knows you're a gladiator. They might think twice about stealing your food.'

Mila glanced around. Tacita's starved eyes were indeed fixed on her. One man had sat up for the first time since her arrival, but he did not look strong enough to actually stand. The others remained asleep or dead.

'Don't drink the water they bring,' Remus continued. 'Use it to wash.'

He remained where he was. She wished she could reach up and touch his face, have his warm arms wrap her for just a moment.

Someone called his name and he looked away, nodded.

'Got to go,' he said.

She really did not want him to leave, but she did not want to make a show of the fact either. It would make things worse for both of them. 'Is there any word on sentencing?'

He shook his head. She shivered, and the apple fell from her hand and rolled a short distance before being snatched up by Tacita.

Remus cursed.

'What is the best outcome I can hope for?' Mila asked, not caring about the apple.

He shifted above her. 'Best? You walk free. If I can just get my hands on those papers—'

'Remus,' she said, cutting him off. 'What is the most realistic outcome I can hope for?'

He swallowed. 'A swift death, and the rest of the house pardoned.'

Her knees gave out and she collapsed, somehow managing to keep hold of the food.

'Mila,' he called, gripping the iron bars. 'There's still time—'

'It is bad enough that I will die due to my own stupidity, but to punish an entire household…'

He blinked. 'It's likely some of them knew.'

She looked up. 'So they should die?'

'No—'

She lowered her gaze. 'You should leave Rome, at least until this all passes. I cannot be responsible for your death too.' She spoke through her fingers, holding in tears. 'Promise me you will forget about the papers and stay away from Jovian Fadius.' Her face was wet now. 'Promise me!'

His fist collided with the iron grid, and she jumped. He cursed and shook his hand.

'What would you do?' he asked her, his voice breaking. 'If you were me, what would you do?'

Tacita had already finished the entire apple. She sat eyeing the bread. Mila lay her free hand flat on the ground, her nails pressing into the stone until pain shot up her fingers.

'Can you… can you just promise me that you will leave it alone, and get out of the city while you can?' She could not look at him.

'I already made you a promise—if you won, we'd marry. That's my oath.'

She looked up then, eyes shiny. 'The Romans love a tragedy. Perhaps they will write a play about us.'

He stood up, apparently in no mood for jokes.

'Eat all the food. You'll need your strength.'

She scrambled to her feet. 'What are you going to do?'

He pressed his palms into his eyes. 'I love you,' he said, looking down at her. 'I've never told you that before. Should have.' Before she could reply, he added, 'Remember you're a gladiator, and gladiators don't enter the arena waving a finger in surrender. They fight their best fight, every time. Then the people decide who lives and who dies.'

She shook her head again. 'The people may scream and shout, but at the end of it all, one man has all the power.'

A wheezy cough sounded behind her.

Remus sniffed and looked away. 'Eat.' With that, he left.

CHAPTER 29

'The gladiator known as Libertas, property of Jovian Fadius, is hereby sentenced to death in the arena for the murder of Lady Prisca Fadius. Sentencing will be carried out at the Flavian Amphitheatre on October 1.'

It was just a few lines, buried amid the other public announcements—the births, deaths, and marriages of Rome's elite. It was not a surprise, as Remus had known it was coming, yet hearing the words spoken aloud made his heart stop.

'At least I think that is what it says,' Felix said, balancing on tiptoes. 'Why must they place them so high up?'

'I could lift you,' Remus said, staring at the words. They were just marks on paper to him. He could not read.

'Touch me and I will take off your hand. It is humiliating enough being stood on.'

Remus continued to stare absently at the notice. 'Tomorrow, then.' He was surprised his voice sounded as even as it did, because his hands were trembling. 'I should go to that house, fight my way in. Get those papers.'

Felix snorted, his heels returning to the ground. 'Why?

It will not help. He will simply throw you to the lions also.' Remus flinched, and Felix shook his head. 'Sorry.'

Remus backed away from the board and turned, walking beneath the arches and descending the steps. 'They arrested Albaus last night.'

'I heard. Not surprising given he was with Mila every day of her training. Good thing Lady Prisca sold the boy off before he was implicated in this mess.' Felix's legs had to move at twice the speed to keep up. 'What are you going to do?'

'I'm going to Antium.'

Felix gave up on walking and broke into a jog. 'All right. Why?'

'Mila's brother's there.'

'I thought she only had a sister.'

Remus did not slow down. 'Half-brother.'

'Oh, that brother. What are you expecting Nerva to do?'

Remus breathed out. 'I don't know. Something. Anything.' Felix grabbed hold of Remus's arm and he spun around. 'What? I don't have time to debate the idea. Tomorrow she'll be dead.'

Felix ignored the tone. 'You lost your heart to the girl, but surely not your mind. You are expecting too much of a young senator with no real power.'

Remus tore his arm free. 'What will you have me do? Get a toga made for the event? Tell me what I should do instead.'

Felix looked around, ensuring no one was listening. 'First thing, calm yourself.' When he was satisfied no one was watching them, he continued. 'Will you even make it back in time?' What he did not say was 'in time to watch her die'.

'If I ride overnight.' Remus shook his head. 'Thank the gods Jovian saw sense not to punish the entire household.'

'Hardly seems fair to sentence the bodyguard. The man

has no tongue and cannot read. Even if he had known, how was he supposed to report the matter?'

'Unfair treatment of slaves—who would've thought?'

Felix threw him a disapproving glance. 'Want me to come with you?'

'No. Stay here, keep the boy out of trouble and an ear to the ground. With Albaus arrested, I've no chance of getting food or water to her.' He pinched the top of his nose. 'I'll return as soon as I can.'

Remus went to track down an eques he knew who owed him a favour. He borrowed a horse, left the city, and headed south to Antium.

Keeping a steady speed, he was careful not to overdo it. He had to stop a few times to rest his horse and check directions. After a long day in the saddle, using muscles he had forgotten he had, he finally reached the city at dusk, just as a pink sky stretched out over the ocean. He had visited the coast before, but never like this. It was one of those places that made him question why he remained in Rome.

The city was built amid rocky terrain that was alive with flora. Villas dotted the foreshore, opening out to the Tyrrhenian Sea. Many of their wealthy occupants only visited in the summer when the heat and smell of Rome became too much for them.

He stopped at the temple of Fortune, wondering where he should begin his search. Dismounting, he asked every man in a toga if they knew the whereabouts of the Papias's villa. Either they all did not know, or they did not trust him with the answer. He could not blame them; he looked every bit the plebeian with his coarse tunic and worn-out horse.

He was resting across the street from the forum, considering his next move, when Nerva found him.

'Remus?'

He turned, and the relief he felt at seeing the senator walking towards him was overwhelming. 'Thank the gods.'

Nerva extended an arm and Remus took a firm hold of it.

'One of my servants said they heard a man asking around for my father. The reason for your visit cannot be a good one. I am afraid to ask.'

Remus released his arm and looked around, unsure where to start.

'Why do I feel like you are delivering bad news?' Nerva asked, crossing his arms. 'Tell me she won.'

'She won.'

Nerva let out a long breath. 'Is she free?'

'Not exactly.'

'Is she alive?'

'For now.' Nerva shifted. 'She's to be put to death in the arena tomorrow for murder.'

Nerva laughed, but the fear was clear in his eyes. 'Murder? Who did she supposedly kill?'

If only it were supposedly. 'Lady Prisca Fadius died in the arena yesterday.' He blinked. 'At Mila's hand.'

Nerva took a few unsteady steps and grabbed hold of Remus's horse. The mare was too exhausted to object.

'I should have gone to Rome,' he whispered. 'I think my father was afraid of my reaction. And maybe his own.'

'It's not too late.'

Nerva looked up and drew a shaky breath. 'You are going to need to start at the beginning.'

CHAPTER 30

Mila woke curled in a ball with her limbs frozen in position. She did not immediately open her eyes. The last two days had altered her mind in such a way that consciousness needed to be done in stages. Since Remus's departure, she had let her inner child do as she pleased: denial, tears, anger, daydreams.

As she coaxed her mind away from sleep, back into the real world, she became aware of warmth beneath her head. How was that possible? With great effort, she forced her eyes open, discovering a pillow of legs belonging to Tacita. She sat up, turning apologetically to the young prostitute.

'Sorry,' she said, pushing herself back.

The girl shook her head. 'I used you as a blanket. Call it even.'

Mila laughed, a soft noise. She remembered the girl stroking her hair as she had sobbed, half-asleep. Suddenly remembering the food, she looked around for it. She had stupidly left it unguarded. All she could see were rat droppings. Her eyes went to Tacita, but she could not blame a starving girl for eating. But the girl surprised her by pulling the food items out of her toga. 'Sorry about the apple,' she said, handing the remaining food over.

'You could have blamed the rats,' Mila said, taking it from her.

Tacita smiled, revealing discoloured teeth. 'I'd eat the rats before I let them eat the food.'

Shaking her head, Mila tore the salted pork in half and offered one part to Tacita. She shook her head.

'Your friend's right. You need it.'

Mila did not move. Eventually, the temptation was too much for Tacita, and she snatched up the meat. Mila chewed her own piece, not tasting it, but knowing swallowing was the end goal. Then she did the same with the bread, tossing a loaf to her new friend before sharing the clean water Remus had brought her.

Just as they finished their feast, the iron grid above them scraped and clanged and a head appeared.

'All right, everybody up. Let's move.'

Mila stood swiftly, and Tacita's bones creaked as she struggled to her feet. They looked around at the others. One man coughed.

'Only three of us alive,' Tacita called up to him.

'Anyone who can walk gets to leave with me,' he replied, beckoning them with a hand. 'Move.'

Mila gestured for Tacita to go first. The guard took hold of her frail wrist and lifted her up as though she weighed nothing. She probably did weigh nothing after days without food or water.

'Can you get up?' she called to the coughing man. No reply.

'Leave him,' said the guard, waiting for her.

She hesitated before reaching up. He needed two hands for her, even emitting a grunt as he pulled her into the light. She blinked and drew greedy breaths of clean air, realising she would rather die out in the open than live in a hole.

Another guard came forwards to shackle their wrists. She turned to watch as two men put the iron grid back in place with a bang. Tacita jumped beside her.

'Will there be a trial?' Mila asked, already knowing the answer.

The guard shook the shackles to ensure they were secure. 'You are to die in the arena.'

She stared at him, waiting for more, but apparently that was all he owed her. She cleared her throat. 'And the rest of the Fadius household?' She tried to keep her voice even.

He ignored the question, giving her arm a tug to get her moving. She glanced up at the sun to gauge the time of day. It was still early.

They stepped out onto the street, heading east towards the Flavian Amphitheatre. Mila stumbled and the guard pulled her upright.

'So, not just any old execution, then? Something spectacular?' she said to him. 'Death via combat, perhaps?'

She was about to ask another question when she spotted Felix and Nero walking down the street towards her. Behind them, she glimpsed her sister and mother. Dulcia broke into a run at the sight of her, and there was a part of Mila that wanted to flee in the other direction, not face the tears, disappointment, and heartbreak. She could barely face her own. But the guard dragged her forwards, her bare feet scraping on the stone.

Dulcia was in tears by the time she reached Mila. The guard pushed her aside.

'Do not touch her,' Mila said, digging her elbow into the guard's side. He shoved her forwards but she kept her footing, turning her head to find her sister sobbing and panting as their mother reached her, arms going around her.

'It is all right,' Mila said, unable to provide comfort outside of words.

Tertia gripped the girl as though the guards might slap shackles on her and drag her away as well. She held Dulcia's head against her chest, watching her eldest daughter march to her death. They stared at one another for a moment.

'I am so sorry,' Mila called to her. And for the first time in her life, she meant it. She had done that to her sister. Everyone had tried to tell her that what she had was enough. Their life together suddenly seemed plenty. Where was all that discontent now? She had done this to herself—and to her family.

'Move aside,' shouted the guard.

Felix pulled Nero out of the way. The boy's face was hard-set, his eyes never leaving her. She had done this to him also. The sight of him combined with Dulcia's violent sobs behind her almost undid her.

'You promised me it would be all right!' Dulcia screamed, causing Mila to jump. 'You promised me!'

Mila looked around for Remus. Where was he? He too had made a promise. He was supposed to care for her sister. 'Where's Remus?' she called to Felix as they passed him.

He hesitated before answering. 'He left the city yesterday. He—'

Arms wrapped Mila's middle, holding so tightly the air left her for a moment. Dulcia had broken free from her mother's grip. The guard raised a hand to strike her, and Mila pulled her arm free and blocked him. He would have to kill her in the street before she let him lay a hand on her sister. Felix ran forwards to pull Dulcia back just as the guard's hand came down across Mila's head. Her feet remained planted but her ear rang. Remus had built her tougher than that, but he was not there to witness it.

'Take them home,' she said to Felix, eyes pleading with him. 'I do not want them to see.'

Felix looked apologetic. He had meant well bringing them to see her, she was sure of it. But there was no easy way to say goodbye to one another in a situation like that. There was only pain.

The guard shoved Mila once more. Distracted, she fell, scraping her elbow before being pulled once again to her feet.

'Easy,' Felix called to the guard.

'*Futue te ipsum*,' the guard swore at him.

Felix raised a calming hand.

People on the street had stopped to watch the girls pass, their expressions blank. Mila glanced across at Tacita, who just stared down at the road. Then she searched the faces lining the street, foolishly looking for Remus among them. She had told him to leave, to flee the city, but a selfish part of her wanted to lay eyes on him before her death, draw strength from him in those final moments.

Another shove from the guard. She was not moving fast enough for him.

'Murderer,' shouted a man, spitting in her direction. She turned to look at him, not connecting with the word. *Shut up,* she wanted to shout back, or better still, throw him in the arena with her so she could watch his bravado dissolve into the bloodied sand.

She faced forwards again, done feeling sorry for herself. The problem was, with the self-pity gone, it made room for anger.

THE WORST PART about waiting for death was the time available to reflect. She thought about all the things she would do differently, but none of those things led her to

Remus, so she could not wish it all away. Their time together was so fleeting, but for a moment she had felt everything she had been chasing—hope, happiness, a quiet inside her, a peacefulness she had never known was possible. She prayed he had felt it too, saw what his life could be if he just broke free of his invisible chains. He had finally fled the city, but she could not ignore the crushing feeling of abandonment. She should have known he could never watch her die.

She waited at the gate with her guard, hands still shackled. Tacita stood on the other side of the passageway, jumping every time the crowd cheered. Mila tried not to think about what thrilled them so, what animal lay dead, which man had lost a limb and was bleeding out on the sand. Instead, she wondered if she would be given a weapon, if she would have to kill again, if she would have to do it over and over until her own wounds betrayed her.

Footsteps made her look up. It was Albaus. Her gaze fell to the shackles around his wrists and the guard at either side of him. As they stared at one another, a heavy feeling settled in her stomach. A sobbing woman stood behind him. It was Vita, another one of Prisca's servants. She had often run errands and delivered messages on behalf of her domina. Guilty by default.

'Open up,' a guard said.

A man with sunburned skin and grey hair pulled a rope and the gate lifted in front of them.

'What about the whore?' Tacita's guard asked.

'She can go in too.'

Tacita looked at Mila, her vacant stare replaced with blazing fear.

Albaus was first to step out onto the sand, casting a shadow over the three women who followed behind. The crowd grew noisy again, not cheering but shouting for blood.

They were marched out into the middle of the arena, the sun directly above them. The emperor picked through a tray of food while chatting with the empress. He looked up briefly before returning to his conversation. The people before him were nobodies: slaves and whores, light entertainment, something to appease spectators until the main fights.

Albaus's dark eyes scanned the arena, his face hard. The guards removed all of the prisoners' shackles before forming a line and marching back in the direction they had come. Mila's hands felt light and empty. Silence fell over the crowd and the four of them moved closer together, Albaus crouching slightly, prepared for whatever came next.

Gods, give me strength.

A gate opened and a horse galloped into the arena. Vita began to pray aloud, and Tacita cowered behind Albaus. Mila watched the horse, trying to block out the noise and fear. She was trained to fight with bare hands if that was all she had, and she had every intention of fighting.

Albaus must have had the same instincts, because he took a few steps towards the horse, stopping when it came to a halt halfway between them and the gate. The rider dropped a sword onto the sand, then another, and another, and another, before turning and galloping from the arena. Four swords, one for each condemned person.

Mila shook her head. There was no way she was going to kill the others. If the emperor wanted them dead, he would have to find another way.

Albaus straightened, clearly thinking the same thing, but when they heard the crank of a gate opening behind them, they looked at one another. Whatever came through that gate was coming for them. The people would get their show.

'The swords,' Mila said at the same time Albaus took off

at a run in that direction. She sprinted after him, but before they could reach the weapons, the sand shifted in front of them. They skidded to a stop, watching as a trapdoor opened like a gaping mouth. A large spotted leopard jumped out from the underground tunnel, growling and disorientated. Mila staggered back, and the cat fixed its gaze on her.

'Get the swords!' she shouted at Albaus, knowing he was the only one who stood a chance at reaching them.

He darted around the closing door and dove into the sand, grabbing the closest sword. The crowd drew a collective breath and Vita screamed behind her as the animal flattened itself against the sand before pouncing at Mila. She rolled forwards, tucking her body tightly and tumbling beneath the animal. It landed where she had just stood, immediately swinging around, searching for her. Mila was already on her feet, just a few paces from a sword, when she heard the leopard behind her. One more stride and razor claws would take her down. She dove for the weapon at the same time the leopard's feet left the ground. Her fingers brushed the hilt of the sword, unable to grasp it.

Albaus threw his weapon over her head, piercing the cat through the chest. A pained growl rippled across the sand. Mila rolled out of the way just as the animal landed with a thud next to her. Its wide eyes stared into hers as life drained away. It pawed feebly at the sand before going still. Without pausing to process the horror, she reached for the sword and tore it from the animal's chest before getting to her feet. The crowd cheered then, as though they had forgotten she was there to die.

As long as the people were entertained.

Her eyes went to the other end of the arena, to the open gate, then along the perimeter where a tiger stalked, watching Vita and Tacita as they huddled together—like bait. Mila snatched up the second sword and took off at a run towards them, checking to ensure Albaus had the other weapons. He did. They would die eventually, every one of them, but she would fight while there was life inside of her. Remus would never forgive her if she gave up.

As the pair reached the women, another trapdoor began to lift behind them, sand cascading like a waterfall as it rose.

Mila turned to Tacita. 'Can you use a sword?' she asked, holding one out.

The girl shook her head and stepped back from it. 'Not against a *tiger*.'

Vita stared at the weapon as though it were a venomous snake.

'Stay behind us,' Mila shouted as a second tiger leapt from the tunnel. Vita went behind Albaus, and Tacita moved behind Mila. She looked at Albaus, who signalled he would take the animal to their left. Nodding, she locked eyes with the other cat who continued to hunt them. It hissed at the crowd as they cheered, fear fighting hunger. It was common knowledge that the animals were starved to make them more aggressive.

'I hope *you* know how to use that thing,' Tacita whispered behind her.

The tiger's gaze shifted to Vita, who had collapsed to her knees in prayer. Mila knew Albaus would not stand a chance against both of them.

'Here!' she shouted, waving her arms to recapture its attention. It turned to her with a roar.

'What are you doing?' Tacita pleaded behind her.

The swords slipped in Mila's sweaty palms. She reminded herself that she was armed and fast.

The tiger came for her at the same time Mila heard another trapdoor lifting. It would not stop until all four of them lay dead—that was how it worked.

She swung her sword, shouting, her own version of a

roar, hoping to make the tiger think twice. To her left, she saw Albaus fighting back giant paws, claws extended for him. She heard the air leave his lungs with the effort of each swing. She knew with certainty he would tire before the beast did.

Mila stabbed at the tiger, narrowly missing each time.

Tacita screamed, and Mila glanced over her shoulder to see a third cat with its sights on them. She hoped Vita's prayers were being heard. She focused on the closest tiger, sword swinging as the big cat pulled up short and hissed in response.

A razor-like scream made her turn. She watched in horror as the other animal pinned Tacita to the ground, its jaws locking onto her shoulder. Mila moved to kill the animal, but a sting of claws lashed at her side. She swung instinctively, and by luck the tiger came down on top of her sword, howling and twisting. Gripping her other weapon tightly, she drove it through the stomach of the animal, blood running down her hands and arms as she struggled against the weight. It was too much and she toppled backwards, the beast collapsing on top of her, pinning her to the ground. She turned her head to see Tacita being dragged away. She had stopped screaming.

Panic surged through her and she turned the other way, looking for Albaus, glimpsing him as he ducked about, swords still swinging, trying to stay alive. Vita had curled up in a ball on the sand with her hands over her head, rocking and shaking. Mila shoved at the dead animal on top of her, trying to free herself. She pushed and grunted, finally freeing one leg and using it to push herself off the sand.

Albaus yelled as the tiger clawed one of his arms. The sword fell from his hand. If she could just get herself free.

After much effort, she wriggled out, pulling her swords from the dead beast as she scrambled to her feet. She threw one of the swords at the crouching cat about to leap at Albaus, piercing its side. It roared and collapsed to the ground. Albaus cut its throat and retrieved Mila's second sword, tossing it to her. She searched for Tacita and saw by the bloody-faced animal that she was too late. Mila's face contorted as she struggled to contain her emotion.

The enthralled crowd clapped and cheered. It seemed no one had been expecting them to live that long. Vita's sobs grew louder.

'Quiet!' Mila said, turning to her. 'I'm trying to keep you alive.'

Albaus collected his other sword and went to kill the remaining beast. The unsuspecting animal, lost in its hunger, never stood a chance against him. Mila probably would have let it live, because she did not want to see what it had done to her new friend. She knew when it was dead because the spectators erupted into cheers.

She pulled a sobbing Vita to her feet and looked around the arena, ready. She did not have to wait long, the sound of a gate opening making her go still. Her eyes went to Albaus as he made his way back towards her. He stopped walking, turning to the gate. His face told her everything she needed to know—they were about to die.

Two men entered the arena. No, not men, giants. A head taller than Albaus and twice the width. Their arms looked as though they were carved from stone, and their shoulders rose to the base of their skulls. These were the men sent to finish the job. A shield in one hand and a spiked mace in the other, they stomped out into the arena, leaving a cloud of sand behind them. They wore nothing but a loincloth and a helmet that served to intimidate rather than protect. Vita fell to her knees once again, praying and sobbing. Albaus glanced at Mila, no fear, just a practical question poised on his face.

'I will take the one on the left,' she breathed.

The men were more than twice her size and at least three times her weight. She would be crushed in moments. Her eyes went to the crowd, watching their reaction. Again she found herself searching for Remus, but he was not among them. What would he think of the men coming to kill her? What would he tell her to do? There were no shields available to her, only swords and a fierce heart.

Her gaze returned to Albaus and he nodded towards Vita.

'Get behind Albaus,' Mila instructed, shoving her in his direction. When the woman closed her eyes, she added, 'Now, if you want to live!'

She crawled across the sand, still murmuring her prayers.

Dark eyes peered out from beneath a helmet, fixed on her. Fingers tightened around his mace, and muscles flexed and shifted, seemingly growing in size.

All she had was speed.

He was still walking when he swung his mace. She ducked, her sword colliding with his shield. One blow from that man would be enough to kill her. Twisting her body, she moved closer, her sword slicing his leg. He roared as she tumbled out of the way of his weapon, which slammed into the sand beside her. All she could do was keep out of his way, but the crowd continued to cheer. Every moment she lived exceeded their expectation.

Mila allowed herself one glance at Albaus. He had certainly met his match. The pair battled between two dead beasts, her bodyguard dwarfed by his opponent. She tumbled, avoiding another blow. A trail of blood followed him as they shuffled through the sand towards her, but the injury did not slow him. Mace and wood came at her from both sides, and she had to remember how to fight with two swords. Remus had erased everything she thought she knew about fighting. What would he shout at her now?

A loud bang rang in her ear as the shield hit the right side of her head, knocking her into the sand. Her hand went over her ear. It was her first big mistake. She had let go of her sword.

She tried to focus. Where was he? Above her? She rolled onto her back and raised her weapon just in time. Sand was kicked up into her eyes and she blinked against it, momentarily blinded. She reached around for the other sword while kicking out instinctively, hoping to hit his knee.

The crowd was out of their seats, calling her name, telling her to fight back. If only she could. Giving up on the sword, she rolled again, unsure if it would be enough to save her. She hit something hard and looked up, expecting to see the giant. Perhaps she had misjudged where he was. By that time the crowd was deafening, competing with the persistent ringing in her ear.

What she was not expecting to see was Remus.

CHAPTER 31

Remus snatched up the bloodied sword he had seen fall from her hand and stood over her, a leg on either side of her body. If the man with the mace wanted her dead, he would need to get through Remus first. He shoved the giant back with his weapon. The guards who had given chase when he leapt into the arena were now stopped some distance away, looking to the emperor to see what they should do about the intruder. Severus was a smart man, and the excited reaction of the crowd made it almost impossible for him to have the retired gladiator removed. He waved the guards away and straightened to watch. They had his full attention now.

Remus stepped over Mila, pushing her opponent farther back, as best one could when said opponent was the size of a large oak. 'On your feet,' he called to her, resisting the urge to look, to check her injuries, inspect every inch of her. There was no time to watch her obsessively and mentally tally every knock and bruise.

Mila did as she was told, rolling onto her stomach and pushing herself up onto her feet. She ran at the giant, sliding beneath his shield and driving her sword into his side. He roared and dropped to his knees. Remus cut his throat with one clean swipe of his sword. It was not personal, it was survival. Someone had to die to satisfy the people's hunger.

Mila staggered back, horror flashing on her face. The arena had not desensitised her yet. He stepped up and grabbed hold of her. When she did not look at him, he shook her. As long as she was alive, they would keep coming, and he intended to kill every man and beast until there was no one left to send.

The feel of warm blood beneath his hand made him look down. She was bleeding. He had arrived too late. Cutting a piece of fabric from his tunic, he tied it around the bleeding limb, eyes going to Albaus who was clutching his left side, staggering around, barely fending off his opponent. Mila went to move and he caught her arm.

'Stay with the girl.'

She nodded, and he ran off to help Albaus.

The crowd sang with excitement. He was a hero returning to the arena to help the underdog. A retired gladiator was the ultimate treat, and having him appear unannounced, mid-execution, was beyond their wildest dreams.

Up went the gates—both ends that time. Remus cursed and looked around. Two sagittarius gladiators galloped into the arena, bows poised. They circled, more dangerous than any beast.

He turned to Mila. 'Get the shield.'

She took off at a run, prying it from the dead man's hand.

One kill at a time. It was all he could do.

He walked straight into the middle of Albaus's fight and knocked the mace from the giant's hand. Catching the edge of his shield, he drove his sword through the gladiator's stomach. He did not stand around to watch him die; he knew the wound was fatal, even if it took some time. As the man fell to his knees, Remus pulled the shield from his hand and tossed it to Albaus.

'Eyes on the archers!' he called to the others.

As if on cue, an arrow swept past his shoulder.

'We need to knock them off their horses,' he said to Albaus, who was leaning on the shield, clutching his bloodied side.

The bodyguard straightened and looked around, nodding.

The pained scream of a woman made him turn. Vita writhed at Mila's feet, an arrow protruding from her back. Mila covered them with the shield and tried to remove the arrow. The woman screamed again. The other archer took aim at Mila. The shield could only protect so much of them. When the second rider appeared on the other side of them, Remus almost fell over with shock when she caught the arrow and dropped it on the ground. He hurled his weapon at the rider as he galloped past, knocking him from his horse. The crowd ate it up, bursting from their seats, turning to one another with excitement. Albaus limped towards the fallen rider, sword in hand.

Another scream.

Remus turned and watched as Mila let go of the shield and tried to stop the blood pouring from a wound in the woman's neck.

'Pick up the shield!' he called to her.

She reluctantly let the limp body collapse against the sand and grabbed the shield. Remus narrowed his eyes on the second rider. He needed a weapon.

Hiss.

He dodged the arrow and took off at a run for the closest sword, skidding across the sand and snatching it up.

Hiss.

Remus swung the weapon, skilfully stopping an arrow from hitting him before chasing after the horse. The crowd erupted.

Hiss.

Albaus came running from the other direction.

Hiss. Hiss.

The horse was cut off, rearing as Albaus blocked its path. Remus pulled the rider from the saddle by his leg, driving his sword through the man's chest. He collected the bow and remaining arrows and turned to face Albaus, who was pale and close to collapse. He glanced down at the oozing wound. There was not much fight left in the bodyguard.

Mila was running around collecting weapons from the dead, the crowd cheering the fact that she was still alive. Remus met her in the middle of the arena and the pair looked around at their battlefield, a sea of blood and corpses. She dropped the weapons between them, keeping hold of one sword.

'You should not have come,' she said to him, close to tears. 'Now we will both die.'

He stepped over the weapons and pulled her against him with his free arm. 'Keep your shield up,' he whispered. 'We're not done yet.'

The hum of gates sounded behind them and they both turned to watch gladiators file into the arena, laden with swords, shields, spears, nets and daggers. They just kept coming, around fifty men, forming a circle around the three of them.

Mila's breathing slowed. Her sword went limp in her hand.

'They might still let you leave,' she said, looking at the men surrounding them.

He reached for a bow and arrows. 'We'll use the bows while we have the distance, then switch to swords.'

She stared up at him. 'You never taught me how to use a bow.'

Albaus limped over to them and held out his hand. Remus handed him the other bow. The emperor stood and walked over to the barrier, gripping it with both hands, his eyes moving past them to the gate of life, which was being raised.

What now?

Felix and Fausta walked onto the sand, stepping between the formation of gladiators who looked between each other, confused. The pair made their way over to where the others stood.

'What are you doing?' Mila asked as they selected weapons from the pile at her feet.

'Improving your odds,' Felix said, giving Remus a pat as he stepped past him.

Remus looked at Fausta. 'Did he talk you into this?'

'No one can talk me into anything I don't want to do.' She glanced about. 'Five against fifty isn't so bad.' Then, looking at Felix, 'Four and a half.'

'No,' Mila said. 'I cannot let you do this. You should all leave before it is too late.'

Fausta swung her mace and looked around at the gladiators waiting to kill them. 'I'm not one for watching.'

The spectators, having figured out that the gladiators had entered the arena of their own accord, began to cheer and whistle. Severus took in their reaction and everyone waited for his signal. He could have shut the whole thing down and simply cut the throats of the convicted.

But the game had changed.

MILA FELT SICK. She looked around at the people about to die alongside her and swallowed down her guilt. Why had

Remus come back? She had been somewhat prepared for her own death. To die fighting with a sword in her hand would have been enough.

Albaus looked ready to fall over. Too much blood loss. She caught his eye and he confirmed what she already knew—he would not survive the next fight. He was done.

The emperor raised his hands to quieten the crowd. He was about to say something when Nerva appeared on the podium, pushing past the guards who stood in his way. Severus turned to see what was happening.

'*Ave domine*,' Nerva said, greeting the emperor. He leapt over the barrier of the podium and dropped down onto the sand. There was a scroll in his hand, which he held up as he turned to address the people.

Mila glanced at Remus, who appeared relieved. She knew then that he had done this. He had not fled the city for himself. He had gone to find Nerva—to find help.

'What is the meaning of this?' Severus asked.

Mila felt a surge of panic. How many lives would be destroyed trying to save hers? 'Nerva,' she called. He turned. 'Don't.'

'Mila,' Remus said, taking a step towards her.

She held up a hand, and he fell silent. Looking at the emperor, she said, 'I will die in whatever way pleases you, but please let everyone else exit the arena safely.'

Her voice was washed away by the crowd, and judging by Severus's expression, he was not interested in hearing from her.

'The only person in the household who knew anything of Lady Prisca's decision to enter the arena was her body slave, who killed herself immediately after the event,' Nerva began.

'This is not a trial,' the emperor said.

'My understanding is that there was no trial, despite

evidence and a confession from Lady Prisca's slave before her death.'

Jovian Fadius, who was seated among the senators, stood, pointing a finger in accusation. 'That is hearsay,' he shouted.

'Except that it is not,' Nerva replied, shaking the scroll in his hand. 'This is a letter written by Lady Prisca before her death. A confession, one that clearly states Mila Salvius —or as you know her, Libertas—was unaware of the true identity of her opponent.'

There was murmur through the crowd.

'She intentionally kept it a secret, knowing her slave would never agree to the match. She also intended for Mila to be freed if she won. And she did win.'

Jovian's hand fell to his side. 'Where did you get that?'

'From the exact spot where Lady Prisca's body slave said it would be.'

More murmurs, louder that time. The emperor waved a hand to silence the people. Nerva took advantage of the lull.

'This morning I returned to Rome to learn that the woman who served loyally in my household for nineteen years had been sentenced to death for murder. Mila Salvius is many things—hardworking, loyal, stubborn.' A whisper of laughter from the crowd. 'But a murderer is not one of them.'

'My wife is dead,' Jovian said, stepping forwards. 'And the slave you are defending is responsible for her death.'

Remus took a few steps towards the podium. 'The moment Mila learned who her opponent was, she lay down her weapons. Lady Prisca died of her injuries. And every Roman there was a witness to the fact.'

Severus turned to Jovian, waiting for his reply.

'If you are trying to tell me that girl did not know, you are wasting your breath,' Jovian said.

Without missing a beat, Nerva said, 'You are her *husband*, and you did not know.'

Applause broke out.

'And what is your interest here, Senator?' Jovian asked, his face hardening. 'If you insist on defending my slave, you must tell the people *why*.'

Rufus Papias appeared at the edge of the podium. He stilled to listen. Nerva locked eyes with his father while everyone waited for his answer. Mila took a few steps towards him, and Remus reached out and stopped her.

'Mila Salvius is not just a slave,' Nerva said. 'She is my sister.' He gave the crowd time to react. 'I taught her to fight when she was just a girl. I never expected her to be this good.' Laughter. 'She is slaveborn, but that is not a crime, it is a cycle—one she hoped to break. One I too hoped she would break.'

Mila swallowed, feeling as though her chest were being torn in two.

'She is my sister,' he said, louder that time. 'And she was a pawn in a dangerous game she did not know she was playing.' Nerva held up the scroll. 'Prisca Fadius went into the arena to die,' he shouted, looking at Jovian. The senator's face was tight and red. 'She was not unlike my sister, trapped in a life she did not want, trying to fight her way out. She bought my sister because she was a worthy opponent, and she turned her into a killer.' The crowd was silent, everyone straining to listen. 'No slave in their right mind would kill their domina in front of Rome. If she wanted to kill her, she could have done it at any time, without sixty-five thousand witnesses.'

Jovian Fadius's shoulders fell and the people clapped.

'I will tell you one more thing,' Nerva said, waiting for silence. 'I will not stand by while she is fed to starved animals and forced to battle men three times her size. That is not the Rome I serve.'

Applause erupted, and Mila jumped at the reaction. Remus's arms wrapped her and she turned into them, trembling against him.

'Mitte! Mitte!' shouted the crowd. *Let her go.*

'What is happening?' she whispered into his chest.

Remus looked around. 'Justice.'

The crowd drank up the sight before them: the slave girl who had won Remus Latinius's heart, the gladiator prepared to die for her, and a senator of Rome speaking up for the vulnerable, speaking truths most in power preferred hidden.

Rufus Papias moved past the guards and approached the emperor, speaking to him in a low voice. When he stepped back, Severus raised a hand to silence everyone. It took some time to gain control of the spectators.

'Mitte!' they continued to shout. The word rumbling like trapped thunder.

Mila turned and looked at Severus, her heart beating against Remus's arm. She still held the sword, prepared to fight, to die.

'Senator Rufus Papias has asked that the slave girl before us, Mila Salvius, be permitted to return to serve in his household. I hereby call an end to the spectacle.' He waved his hand. 'Clear the arena.'

Applause broke out. The gate was raised again, and the gladiators began to file out.

Mila should have been relieved. Her life had been spared, and she had just been told that she would return to the household she had grown up in, to live again with her sister and mother—and her brother. She should have been happy. Instead, she was numb. Her life had just gone full circle. She was no better off than she had been a year ago.

Remus's arms fell away and her skin grew instantly cold. Looking up at him, she saw her own disappointment reflected back at her. She realised in that moment that it was not the freedom she mourned—it was Remus.

He tried to smile at her. She was alive, after all; happiness was the logical response. She knew more than anything that he wanted her safe. Better to be apart than dead, he would say. Then what? She would return to the Papias household, her safe place, her work, her smiling sister watching over her, ensuring she was never again out of sight. Her muscles would decay, and the fire would burn out—the one Remus had breathed life into.

'Mila!'

Nerva jogged forwards and crashed into her, laughing and thanking the gods. She watched Remus over Nerva's shoulder, her arms limp at her sides.

The corpses around her were dragged away on hooks. She should have been among them. Instead, she would walk away. There would be no more fighting now. No more Remus.

He turned away from them, and she watched as he walked over to Albaus, pulling an arm around his shoulder and helping him from the arena. Nerva kept hold of her, practically dragging her towards the gate. Her legs moved of their own accord across the sand. Felix and Fausta walked ahead in silence, alive, handing their weapons over to the men waiting at the gate.

'What is the matter?' Nerva asked, looking at her. 'Not the glorious ending you were hoping for?'

No, it was not the glorious ending she had been hoping for. Remus had already disappeared from sight.

Nerva hugged her closer. 'You are in shock. I am taking you home to your sister and mother. Just keep walking.'

Her hands went over her ears to block the noise. 'Where is Remus?'

'Safe.'

Where is Remus?

CHAPTER 32

Ludus Magnus began to feel like a prison, the routine suffocating. Remus tired of the sight of men in shackles being marched to and from the arena. He tired of shouting at them, pushing them, beating them when they did not perform. As he sat with Felix on the steps of the cavea, watching two new recruits hit one another with wooden swords, he found himself turning away.

'Run some laps,' he called to them, wanting the noise to stop.

The sun had lost its bite, offering warm light instead of heat. He liked that time of the year, before the cold arrived.

'Where did you disappear to this morning?' Felix asked.

'Nowhere.' He hesitated, weighing up the lie. 'The market.'

Felix kept his eyes ahead. 'I see. And was she there?'

Remus stared at the running men. 'No. Haven't seen her since… that day.' The day he had gone to fight with her, die with her. The day he had realised his life without her was not really a life at all. Had it really been weeks since he had laid eyes on her?

'You are lucky you are Brutus's favourite around here. He lets you do as you please.'

'Because I work hard.'

Felix leaned forwards. 'Yes, when you are here.'

Remus knew he had it better than most. Brutus was aware that as a free man, Remus could choose a life anywhere, and yet he stayed. Sure, he was paid a fair wage, but that was not what kept him at Ludus Magnus—it was habit, and maybe fear. He knew nothing else, no other life.

He almost had.

'This might not be my business—'

'Best leave it, then.'

Felix turned, ignoring him. 'However, Mila is a slave. Offer to buy her, then free her yourself. I know you have some denarii hidden away.'

'*Had* some denarii.' He gestured to Nero, who was crouched in the shade running a stick through the sand. When he realised Remus was looking at him, he stood, ready to do whatever was asked. Remus shook his head, and the boy sank back down.

'Well, let that be a lesson to you,' Felix said.

'What lesson's that? Only free slaves I want to marry?'

Felix tilted his head and nodded. 'That works.'

'I'll be sure to keep it in mind for next time.'

Felix watched Nero for a moment. 'I will admit, there are worse things to waste your wealth on. He has grown on me, despite my initial objections to him sharing our room.'

'I thought you hated all children with no exceptions.'

'Not children, babies. Only because of their helpless state. It frightens me.'

Remus suppressed a smile. 'Only helpless babies. I see.' He saw the gladiators had slowed considerably. 'Move it!' he called to them. They immediately lengthened their stride.

'I cannot believe I am suggesting this, but why not

return to the arena? You saw how the crowd responded. The emperor would pay you whatever you wanted. Then you could buy her freedom.'

Remus shook his head. 'It wouldn't matter how much coin I had. Rufus Papias isn't going to sell his daughter to a gladiator.'

'Aquila Papias might.'

'Her family just got her back. They're not going to let her go anywhere.'

Felix frowned. 'Goodness. So heavy with woe. That is it, then? We shall feel sorry for ourselves and never speak of her again?'

'I'm not feeling sorry for myself.'

'Hmm.'

'I'm being realistic. No point in getting people's hopes up.'

'People's or yours?' Silence. 'Perhaps it is time you stopped thinking like a slave. You have been free for some years now, and yet you insist on carrying your shackles around with you.'

Remus rolled his eyes. 'I feel a poem coming on.'

'I am simply saying do not give up the fight the first time you drop your weapon. Mila's mother seems like a reasonable woman. She is not going to deny her daughter a chance at happiness. Nerva will likely show his support, assuming of course his feelings are those of a sibling and nothing more sinister.'

Remus shoved him lightly with his shoulder. 'Get your mind out of the gutter. It's his sister.'

Straightening, Felix brushed off his hands. 'I was part of that world once. It is not as uncommon as you might think.' He thought for a moment. 'There is one obstacle I may have overlooked.'

Remus narrowed his eyes. 'What's that?'

'Perhaps she is content where she is, back inside her

safe bubble. It is amazing the new perspective a near-death experience brings.'

Remus shook his head. 'She's not like that. She's not one for bubbles. She wants to leave Rome.'

'I swear to the gods, if you mention India—'

'She wants to go to India,' he said, smirking. He leaned his elbows on his knees. 'We've both had enough of this city.'

'So go to the country. That is what normal people do.'

Remus's face turned serious. The possibility of a future together had only existed briefly. A few comments thrown around while caught up in the excitement of new love and the prospect of freedom. Yes, it had been brief, but he had felt it to his core, meant every word he had spoken. It was not the first time the subject of marriage had been raised after lying with a woman, but it was definitely the first time *he* had raised it.

His mind went back to that afternoon in the barracks, Mila nestled against him, his hands in her hair. She had been the most exquisite thing he had ever held, and he had thought of nothing else since. Of course he had to marry her. What other life was there? The first time he had seen her standing before Gallus Minidius, dressed in rags, carrying expensive swords, it had all been over.

'Honestly,' he said, returning to the conversation, 'it wouldn't matter where we went. I'd be happy any place if she was there and I got to call her my wife.'

A look of horror struck Felix's face. 'Can you hear yourself? Let us pray no one else heard. People will think you have lost your edge, and if I had not witnessed your heroic display in the arena some weeks back for myself, I might be inclined to agree.'

'That'll do,' Remus called to the men, standing up. They collapsed on the sand, white-faced and panting.

'Where are you going?' Felix asked, then held up a hand. 'Never mind.'

'If Brutus asks, tell him—'

'Yes, yes. Off you go.'

Remus ruffled the dwarf's hair, and Felix swatted his hand.

'You know I hate to be petted.'

'I know.' Remus broke into a jog.

HE WAS ALMOST at the house when he spotted Mila walking towards him, a basket swinging in her hand, her head bent so she could hear her sister. Dulcia was telling a story, gesturing wildly, a smile on her face. He stopped walking, content to go unnoticed for a while longer. Mila smiled, her dimple flickering and fading again. She swapped the basket to her other hand. Dulcia asked if she was all right, bringing a hand up to Mila's shoulder, only to be shooed away. Remus watched the exchange, noting how Dulcia's eyes moved over her sister and how Mila dismissed her concern.

'Leave me,' he thought she said. 'I am fine.'

Why would she not be fine? He walked towards them, drinking in the sight of her. She spotted him then, and he saw her hesitate, as though actually considering turning around and walking in the other direction. For a moment, he questioned if he had done the right thing in coming. Perhaps she did not want to see him, was trying to move on. But then he remembered her face the moment the emperor had spared her life, enslaving her once more. He had seen it, the same disappointment that had crushed him.

Dulcia spotted him and took her sister's hand, tugging it.

'It is all right,' Mila reassured her, glancing at the house that loomed between them. She gestured for Remus to cross the street, obviously not keen on having their conversation overheard by someone inside.

She stopped a few feet from him as though she did not trust having him closer. Dulcia watched him cautiously, keeping hold of her sister's hand, ready to drag her off at any moment.

'Good morning,' Mila said, looking up at him.

His eyes moved over her face, looking for clues, wanting to see what was in her mind. Maybe he needed reassurance that nothing was lost between them. 'Morning.'

She glanced nervously at the house. 'What are you doing here?'

His gaze fell to the angry red line on her arm where a claw had caught her. 'I'm hoping to speak with Nerva.'

'About what?'

He caught something in her tone that made him turn back. She wore that hopeful expression that Nero did whenever he announced he was going somewhere. 'About you.'

'Oh.'

'Why else would I be here?' He had not come to play games.

Mila studied him for a moment, her expression cautious. He did not like it when she was guarded around him.

'They have gone south again,' Dulcia said, speaking up. 'Waiting for the gossip to die down.'

Remus's eyes never left Mila's. 'Whose idea was that? Your father's?'

Mila wrapped her free hand around her sister. 'You should not call him that.'

He understood then. Rufus Papias may have saved her

life, but nothing had changed. Now he was dealing with the fallout, including, no doubt, one very unhappy wife.

'You should go,' Dulcia went on, seeming much braver than the last time he had seen her. 'One foot out of place and our domina will have Mila lashed. Those were her words.'

Remus eyes darkened. He remembered Aquila from the dinner party. She made no secret of the fact that she did not like Mila. Her son's confession in front of the entire city would not have helped matters. 'Has she lashed you?'

Mila tightened her grip on her sister. 'She wanted to make a point. And she made it.'

His jaw tightened. 'What point's that?'

Rolling her eyes, Mila replied, 'Let us not make a thing of it. It hurt less than the average training session with you.'

It was one thing to see her hurt in the arena while she was armed and able to defend herself, and quite another to imagine her tied up and flogged.

He stepped around her, and she turned with him.

'What are you doing?' she asked, panic in her voice.

'Checking your back.'

'No.'

'Stay still.'

She sighed and stopped moving. He pulled down the neck of her tunic, aware of Dulcia's glare on him. The tips of his fingers ran down her skin, taking him back to a time when they had ventured where they pleased. A ridge of skin made him stop. Pulling on the fabric, he saw the first red line. His hand continued down, slipping lower, counting the bumps, seven, eight, nine. He withdrew his hand as though he had been met with fire in the middle of her back.

'Mother says they will not even scar,' she said casually, turning to him with a vague smile.

He did not reply immediately, his rage palpitating inside of him. His hands went into his hair and he saw Mila take a step back, shielding her sister. 'I'm buying your freedom,' he said, trying to remain calm.

Mila stared at him, confused. 'What?'

He took a step back, not wanting to be close to her when his hands were curled into fists. 'I'm getting you out of there!' He pointed to the house. 'No more of this.'

She handed the basket to her sister and crossed her arms. 'And how do you plan on raising the coin?'

'In the arena.'

She was speechless for a moment. 'No,' she said, shaking her head. 'You are not fighting. You already risked your life once for me.'

'And I'll do it again.'

She closed her eyes. 'You do not understand. I cannot leave now.'

Remus stepped closer. Dulcia pressed against Mila, who did not move a muscle. 'This was *your* plan.' He pointed a finger in her face. 'You wanted to buy your freedom, and then your sister's and your mother's—'

'That was before I almost died. And before this.' She gestured between them. 'Before I knew better.'

'Mila, they will hear you,' her sister whispered.

'Let them hear,' Remus hissed.

'Lower your voice,' Mila said, straightening.

Remus ignored her. 'Just let Aquila try to lash you when I'm around.'

Mila glanced at the house and shook her head. 'I was wrong about everything.' Her hands fell to her sides. 'I could have returned here with enough denarii to sink a ship, and Rufus probably would have said no.' She looked down. 'He saved my life for my mother. He brought me back here, knowing what people would say, knowing what his own wife would say. I cannot turn my back on them now.'

He stared at her. 'You want to stay a slave for your mother?'

'You do not understand.'

'I understand. You're giving up.'

'She just got me back.'

Remus took hold of her arms, but the terrified look on Dulcia's face made him let go. 'What are you saying? You're choosing this life now? Really?'

'I do not expect you to understand. How could you?' She went to reach for him and stopped herself. 'I am sorry.'

He stared at the road.

'It would not work. I cannot live free while my mother and sister remain slaves, glimpse them from across the street, follow them to the market to steal a few fleeting moments with them.'

He understood. She was choosing her family. He had been expecting too much. One look at Dulcia hiding behind her sister confirmed it.

Stepping back, he let out a heavy breath. 'What do you want me to do, then? Leave you alone?'

She glanced at the house before answering. 'I want you to live the life you had planned for us. Stop living as though you are still a slave.'

Of all the answers he was expecting, it had not been that one. 'What?'

'You are no longer Brutus's property. You earned your freedom, and you owe that man nothing.'

He took another step back. 'I know that.'

'Do you?' She stared at him. 'What would you think if my dominus handed me my freedom and I chose to stay here in this household?'

He sucked in a breath. 'You *are* choosing to stay.'

'For my family. *You* are like a dog raised in a cage,

choosing to remain in the cage long after the door has been opened.'

He shook his head and began to pace, watching her as he did so. 'I'll ask you one more time. What do you want me to do?'

She pressed her lips together and blinked back tears. 'Leave.' Her hands were limp at her sides. 'Go live a free life for both of us.'

He stopped pacing and they stared at one another.

'Mila, the door,' Dulcia said, pulling her sister away.

They both looked across the street to where Aquila Papias stood on the step, barking instructions at her slave as she prepared to leave the house.

'I have to go,' Mila said, ushering her sister across the street.

He watched her cross, saw her take back the basket from her sister. She stopped at the bottom step, eyes on her feet, waiting for her domina to pass before entering the house. Only when Aquila had disappeared into a waiting litter did she turn at the door to look at him.

There was a part of him that wanted to cross the street, to go to her. But then what? She had made her wishes very clear.

He turned and walked away.

CHAPTER 33

Nerva remained at their villa in Antium with his father, away from the city's wagging tongues, submerged in political discussions and offers of marriage from families seeking a foot up on the social ladder.

Mila spent the majority of her time trying to avoid Aquila, which was not easy in the same house. It seemed whenever her domina attended a social gathering, she returned in a foul mood, no doubt reminded by one of the guests about her husband's illegitimate daughters. Each time, she would have Mila brought before her and vent her feelings on the subject. Mila did not mind. If anything, she was enjoying Aquila's public humiliation.

What she did not enjoy was the way her mother could not look her in the eye afterwards, and the way her sister clung to her silently for the rest of the day. It was a constant reminder that she was a slave and had no control over her life. It chipped away at hope until there was nothing left. She could have become despondent or bitter, but instead she chose to be grateful. She was with her mother, her sister; she was alive, fed, safe. That was what she told herself, because otherwise she might have to admit the truth—she was numb.

Her best coping mechanism was to fill every waking moment. She helped in the kitchen, the laundry, ran errands, mended, cleaned, swept, scrubbed. Anything to keep her mind occupied and hands busy. It was all fine during the day, but then at night sleep failed her. She would lie awake with all her thoughts. While the rest of the household slept, she would sneak out into the garden and sit by the wall, listening to people pass, talking to one another, imagining their lives. Occasionally she thought she heard Remus, and she would stand, palms on the wall, her pulse racing. But there was no reason for him to visit her region anymore. She would sink back down to the ground and sit with her disappointment. Often she nodded off mid-thought of him and felt the vibration of his voice, his breath on her neck, against her ear.

One morning she woke in the garden to someone shaking her. For a moment she forgot where she was, what point of time she was existing in. She snatched up the hand and pulled hard, eyes snapping open. For a moment, she was a gladiator, feeling for her sword.

Tertia's sharp intake of breath pulled her back to the present, and she looked down to see her mother slumped on her hands and knees, surprise frozen on her face. Mila leapt to her feet, helping her up.

'I am sorry,' she whispered.

Tertia sat down on the ground, her back against the wall. Mila sat beside her, leaning her head on her mother's shoulder, her hands like ice as she rubbed them together.

'This has to stop,' Tertia said, pressing her lips to Mila's hair.

'I fell asleep again.'

'I am not talking about the sneaking out. I am talking about the pining.'

Mila sat up. 'I am not pining. I am adjusting.'

Tertia looked sceptical. 'Adjusting to what? This has been your life forever. Everything is the same.'

It had not been her life forever. There had been Remus once. They had planned a very different life.

Her mother sighed. 'Tell me about Remus.'

Mila was not prepared to hear his name aloud. She jumped at the sound of it. 'He was my trainer.' Gods, he was so much more.

'And you fell in love with him.'

She shivered. 'Yes.'

Tertia smiled. 'Well, you are not the first girl to fall in love with a gladiator—'

'Stop.'

'And you will not be the last.'

Mila stood, brushing debris off the back of her garment. She would not have everything she felt reduced to a childish fling. 'You do not know what you are talking about.'

Tertia tilted her head. 'I understand love.'

'You know nothing about love.' The words came out blunt and cruel. She stilled, looking down at her mother. 'What I mean is loving a child is different.'

Tertia stood also, looking around the garden before speaking. 'If you think I know nothing about loving a man, you are wrong.'

Mila struggled to look at her mother. 'I only meant that—'

'I know what you meant.' They watched one another for a moment. 'Do you think I have never loved a man? That I have not been loved in return?'

Mila studied her. 'All right, tell me, then, who have you loved?'

Tertia shrugged. 'There have been other men over the years, but nothing that could survive this life.'

This life. Mila was not sure if she could survive this life either. 'You said "other men". Other than who?'

Tertia frowned. 'Other than Rufus, of course.'

Mila wrapped her arms around herself, shielding her skin from the cool air, and the words of her mother. 'You have never loved Rufus. He is your dominus, not your lover.' This was what she had known, had believed her whole life.

'He gave me you two girls and this life.'

'So? That does not equate to love.'

Tertia blinked. 'I have grown to love him over the years.'

'That is not love.' She stepped back. 'That is obligation.'

'Mila—'

'Keeping a roof over your head and inviting you to his bed does not equate to love.'

Tertia raised her chin. 'Rufus has his faults, but he has proven himself to be very loyal.'

'Not to his wife.'

Tertia drew a shaky breath. 'I am not pretending our relationship is not without complications.'

She wanted to block her ears. 'It is not a relationship! He bought you as a fetish, impregnated you and then denied us a father.'

'He was married to another woman. What would you have him do?'

Mila made an exasperated noise. 'Be faithful to his wife?'

Tertia exhaled and looked up at the pink sky. For a moment it seemed as though she had given up on the conversation.

'He married who his father told him to marry, but his heart was elsewhere.' Her gaze returned to Mila. 'I was not a fetish. I thought being older now, you would understand.'

Mila swallowed, her mouth dry. 'And yet you do not understand,' she whispered. 'Remus loved me.'

Tertia stepped closer. 'What he did for you during the execution is remarkable. I will forever be grateful to him for keeping you alive until Nerva arrived.'

'I feel a "but" coming.'

Tertia brushed loose hair from her daughter's face. 'Aquila is waiting for you to make a mistake, waiting for an excuse to be rid of you again. You must let go of that life.'

'I did let go. I sent him away. He came here, prepared to do whatever it took to see me free, and I sent him away.' Her words choked her. 'It will never be enough for Aquila.'

'If you work hard and—'

'I have never worked harder in my life, and still that woman beats me.'

Tertia flinched. 'As soon as Rufus returns—'

Mila threw her hands up. 'Ah, yes, the protective father. A true role model for the young men of Rome.'

'Mila—'

'What?'

Tertia took a calming breath. 'This might be difficult for you to hear, but this arrangement is best for all of us. Here we are together. Here we are safe, protected by his name. Out there…' She paused. 'Out there you would just be the gladiator's whore.'

The words hurt more than any beating from Aquila. 'Remus is not like that.'

'He is a gladiator.'

As if that summed up everything about him.

'You do not even know him.'

Tertia reached for her arm. 'Even if I am wrong, one thing is for certain. You are safest here with your family.'

Pulling her arm free, Mila hissed, 'Here I am a slave!' She leaned closer to her mother. 'Here I am powerless—like you.'

Here I am without Remus.

Tertia stood wide-eyed. 'Do you think I do not feel every beating you receive? She does not hurt you out of hatred, but out of her own pain.' Silence. 'When Rufus returns, things will return to normal.'

Mila winced. 'I am not sure if you remember, but normal did not work out very well for me.'

'Things are different now. You are different now.'

She wondered if that was true, and if it was a good thing.

Lowering her voice, Tertia said, 'Everybody needs someone looking out for them. Your sister has you, I have Rufus, and I am here to watch out for you.'

Mila's shoulders fell. Remus had looked out for her once. He would never have sat idle while she was beaten. He had come to her prepared to do anything, still looking out for her. And she had pushed him away.

Mila's eyebrows drew together. 'If you asked for your freedom, would Rufus give it?'

For a moment her mother was speechless. 'It is a much harder life out there.'

'That was not the question.'

Tertia's mouth opened and closed as she struggled to find words. 'If it was what I truly wanted, I believe so.'

Mila closed her eyes. All this time she had assumed they wanted the same thing. 'Then you are choosing this life. Worse than that, you are choosing it for me, and for Dulcia.' She took another step back, her legs suddenly unsteady.

'Here you are safe,' Tertia said again, her eyes welling up. 'Look what happened out there. You took a woman's life. You were sentenced to *death*. Rufus saved you, and still you cannot see.'

'No,' Mila said, holding up a hand. 'Remus saved my life. He fought for me. He wanted me to be free.' She drew a breath. 'Rufus took everything I had worked for, months of training, months of hoping, months of loving, and put the shackles back on.' She shook her head, missing Remus more in that moment than she could ever have thought possible.

A few tears ran down Tertia's cheeks. 'You are chasing things you do not understand. Freedom, love. You cannot comprehend how these things work in the real world. You are a dreamer.'

Was a dreamer. Now she was nothing.

Mila pressed her palms into her eyes. 'I know I love him. I know that. I understand how I feel with him, how I feel without him. I may as well have died in that arena.' Her breathing shortened, her thoughts pulling together with such clarity. 'You are right about one thing. When I went in search of freedom, I did not understand what that life would look like, but I know now.' Tears ran down her cheeks and she brushed them aside. 'We had a chance at a real life. No ridiculous expectations, conditions, concerns about political advantage or wealth. No crushing others along the way. Just two people choosing a life together.'

The soft clink of pots drifted out into the garden. The day had begun.

'Go eat,' Tertia said, her voice flat. 'Be thankful that every morning begins with food, that you are not left wondering if your father has gambled everything away.' She paused. 'Including his only daughter.'

Mila's gaze fell to her feet.

'And wake your sister, so she might linger in the kitchen, licking honey-covered spoons, free to be a child for as long as she wishes.' She shook her head. 'Instead of looking at everything you are missing, spend a few moments appreciating what we have. Be thankful that Dulcia is not expected to open her legs every time her dominus taps her on the shoulder, that she is not stuck in a mine doing hard labour, or in a cheap brothel like many her age.'

Mila swallowed down her shame and left to wake her sister.

THE CLAPPING OF wooden swords had come to sound like the clapping of hands next to Remus's ear. Each day his agitation grew and his fuse shortened. No one worked hard enough, or progressed fast enough. No one had Mila's spark, her determination, her stubbornness to push past the nausea and pain. Not one man wanted that chance at freedom like she had.

But that girl was gone.

Whenever he tried to reconcile those images, the ones of her training to the point of collapse in the arena with the girl he had seen returning from the market the previous month, they did not fit together. The light had gone out, or perhaps she had smothered it, desperate to be the person her family wanted—meek, humble, grateful.

'Get up!' he shouted at the men wrestling in the sand, their weapons now out of reach. 'You're gladiators, not children. Pick up your weapons!' The slaves scurried to retrieve their swords. Frustrated, he glanced over at the portico where he found Brutus watching him, arms crossed over his chest, feet apart to balance his large frame.

'Again,' Remus said, turning away. His voice was quieter this time.

The weeks slipped by. Nothing really changed except the weather. The sun disappeared behind a bleak, grey sky, his breath visible as he stood in the cold, confronted with another day. He pushed everything unrelated to training from his mind—including Mila. At least he tried to. If he let her in, he found he did not have room for anything else.

And yet every ninth day he found himself at the nundinae, wandering aimlessly between vendors, both afraid to see her and desperate for a glimpse. He was curious how she would react to him, what he would discover in her face, or what was missing. He told himself that if he saw her happy, healthy, her toned frame replaced by soft curves, her callused hands softened by laundry and house duties, her back healed, he would be able to let her go. Then he could go back to that time in his life when he wanted for nothing because he did not desire anything. In many ways she had ruined him, woken something within him that might never sleep again.

In other words, she had brought him to life.

In the evenings, Felix and Fausta invited him to the tavern to drink with them. At first he said yes, going along, losing himself to noise and drink, consuming more than he should in order to numb his mind for just a few hours. Then one evening Felix told him his brooding silence was repelling the women who normally gathered at their table, which meant he was forced to visit brothels instead.

Remus stopped going to the tavern.

It was the middle of December when he spotted her at the forum. She was standing in front of the public notice board, her long hair braided down her back, her arms leaner than the last time he had laid eyes on her. He did not need to see her face to know it was her. He had spent enough time studying every inch of that body, the way it moved, responded, glistened. He would know her anywhere.

He crossed the street, eyes never leaving her, afraid she would disappear if he looked away. She stood holding one arm behind her back as she read, her head tilted slightly. He wished he could read, if only to understand her mind better.

She turned before he reached her, freezing at the sight

of him. He stopped also, unsure if he should approach. Last time she had told him to leave—and she had meant it. But she smiled at him, her dimple on display, her body relaxing. She was even more beautiful than he remembered. Everything looked softer, from the colour of her skin to the roundness in her cheeks.

'Good day, Remus Latinius.' The smile held.

He took a few steps to close the gap between them. What to say? 'Thought it was you.' He looked past her to the notice board. 'Anything interesting?'

Her shoulders rose and fell in the sweetest shrug.

'I suppose that depends on your political interests.'

'Didn't know you followed politics.'

Her smile widened. 'I follow Nerva. Does that count?'

He breathed out a laugh. 'I hear his name everywhere nowadays.'

She looked past him. 'Ever since his heroic display at the Flavian Amphitheatre, his popularity seems to have grown. The people adore him.'

'He has you to thank for that.'

'And I shall remind him of the fact when he returns.'

Silence.

'What about you?' he asked. 'How are you?'

She crossed her arms. 'Keeping out of trouble.'

'Sounds boring.' She uncrossed her arms and pulled her palla tighter around her. He fought the urge to warm her with his hands. 'And your family?'

'Good.' She chewed her lip for a moment. 'How is Nero?'

'Following Felix about the place. I've been busy of late.'

'New recruits?'

He nodded.

She gave a strained smile. 'Any with my level of talent?'

'No.' Disappointment stopped him from smiling back. He had hoped to find her happy. While she did seem more… balanced, the light had gone out in her eyes. 'Heard Nerva bought Albaus from Jovian Fadius.'

A small laugh. 'Jovian charged an amount bordering on extortion. Never mind the fact that he was half-dead at the time of the sale.'

'Course he did.' He cleared his throat. 'That was a decent thing for Nerva to do though.'

She looked away. 'Yes, I owe him a lot.' She was quiet a moment. 'I thought you might have run off to India by now.'

He shook his head. 'Someone has to keep the new recruits alive.'

'Yes.' She studied him. 'Someone does. But must it be you?'

It seemed his disappointment was mutual. 'We all do what we have to.'

'Slaves do what they have to. Last I heard, you were free.'

There was no mistaking the longing in her tone. Gods, he really wanted to touch her. 'We dogs and our cages,' he said, suppressing a smile.

She reddened and looked down. 'A little harsh of me, perhaps.'

Unable to stop himself any longer, he reached a finger under her chin, raising her face to him. 'You seem different.'

'Well, I can guarantee you that if you asked me to run to the end of the street, I would not make the distance.'

He did not smile. His thumb travelled along her jaw. 'You've given up.'

Her eyes closed for a moment and she turned into his hand, inhaling. 'So have you,' she whispered, opening her eyes again.

'Mila,' called a woman behind them.

His hand fell away and he turned to see Mila's mother

waiting with rolls of fabric beneath one arm. She stared at him.

'It was good to see you,' Mila said, stepping past him.

He grabbed hold of her arm and she turned, looking up at him. What was he supposed to say?

I miss you. I love you. Stay.

'Keep well.' He released her arm, and she glanced down at the spot where his hand had been.

'And you, Remus Latinius.'

He watched her walk away, eyes down, over to her mother. She was a different person to the fierce girl he had first seen outside a shaky arena all those months back.

Tertia watched Mila pass her and then turned to look again at Remus. She wore the same guarded expression Mila usually did. He preferred it to the blank one she wore now. He raised a hand, a greeting. She nodded once before following after her broken daughter, back to the safety of tall walls.

He turned and did the same.

CHAPTER 34

Remus was stretched out on his bed, trying to find the motivation to visit the *thermae* for a bath, when Felix walked in.

'Brutus wants to see you,' Felix said, climbing onto the bed on the other side of the room.

Remus had an arm draped over his eyes to block out the light. 'Right now?'

'Is there any other time than right now with him?'

Removing his arm from his face, Remus turned to look at his friend. 'Do you know what he wants?'

Felix reached down to remove his sandals. 'Perhaps he is tiring of your bad mood.'

Remus groaned as he sat up. The simple act drained him of his remaining energy. 'What bad mood?'

Felix laughed and shook his head. 'I hope you are joking. How much longer do you intend to brood?'

'I'm not brooding,' he replied, throwing his belt at the dwarf. 'I'm tired. Some of us work, you know.'

Felix caught the belt and tossed it back, hitting Remus in the face. 'I am going for a bath, and then I am going for a drink. Come find me when you are done getting in trouble.'

'Thought you wanted me to stay away from the tavern.'

'You know I am also curious by nature. I want to know what he says.'

'Nosey, you mean?'

Felix slipped a clean pair of sandals onto his feet. 'Concerned, actually. If he kicks you out, I will be forced to follow you.'

'You'll be forced to do no such thing,' Remus replied, pushing off the bed and wrapping the belt around his waist.

Felix dropped onto the ground. 'No, but we both know I will anyway. Loyalty and all that.'

Remus exhaled, looking at him. 'You're a good friend. Perhaps one I don't deserve.'

'Shut up.' The dwarf grinned. 'He is waiting in the arena.'

Remus nodded and left the room.

The arena was empty except for Nero and another boy, who were sweeping the sand. Brutus stood beneath the portico, leaning against one of the pillars, watching them.

'You sent for me?' Remus said, coming to stand next to him.

The lanista straightened, waving him closer. Nodding towards Nero, he said, 'You've a good eye. The boy works hard. You'll make a tidy profit from him one day.'

Remus watched the boy for a moment. The fact that Brutus was referring to him as a good investment did not sit well. 'The boy's not a slave. He'll never be sold again.'

Brutus sniffed and glanced at him. 'Very generous. You don't owe him anything.'

'Not his fault he was orphaned.'

The lanista nodded. 'You're a good man, Remus—better than most. You're also my hardest-working trainer. You've proven to be loyal to the school, despite the many other offers you no doubt get.'

Remus crossed his arms. 'Thanks.' He knew Brutus had not sent for him just to pay him a compliment. He waited.

Brutus's gaze returned to Nero. 'I've seen a change in you of late. You've a way of getting the best from the men you train. You push them hard, know their limits.'

He pushed them hard because they would die in the arena during their first fight if he did not. He pushed them even harder of late because he needed to push something or everything building inside him would break him apart.

'Ludus Magnus has a reputation to uphold' was all he said.

Brutus nodded in agreement, running a hand over his receding hairline. 'I'm glad you feel that way.' He rested one shoulder against the pillar again. 'I can't be lanista forever, and as I've no sons to groom for the role, I think it's time we started getting you ready.'

'Ready for what?'

'To be the next lanista of Ludus Magnus.' He looked rather pleased with himself, no doubt expecting to see the same reaction in Remus.

Aware that some form of a response was necessary, Remus said, 'I don't know what to say. I'm honoured you'd consider me.'

Brutus frowned. 'Thought you'd be a bit happier.'

He hesitated. 'I'm happy, just not sure I'm the right person for the job.'

The lanista laughed. 'I'll admit, I've had moments of doubt myself. When you jumped into that arena to save the slave girl'—he shook his head—'I questioned everything I thought I knew about you. At the same, it was a reminder that fighting's in your blood. There's a reason you've never walked away from it. I've no doubt any future sons of yours will one day take to the sand too.'

Was that the reason he had never walked away? He turned to look at Nero, the closest thing he had to a son. There was no way he would let that boy fight in the arena. Brutus was wrong. 'I've not tried any other life but this one, so I can't tell you if that's true.'

'And why would you? You were born into this life.' Brutus stretched his neck. 'It was in Lady Prisca's blood too. Couldn't cleanse herself of it. Fighting is a disease. In the end, it killed her.'

The mention of Prisca took him by surprise. Before he could reply, Brutus whistled and Nero looked up. The lanista gestured to a patch of sand he had missed. Remus looked down. Whistling was for dogs.

'When Lady Prisca came to me, I thought she was crazy.'

Remus looked up. 'What do you mean, when she came to you?' A pause. 'When did she come to you?'

Brutus met his gaze and shrugged. 'Someone had to train her.'

Everything went still for a moment. 'Someone had to train her,' Remus repeated. The world moved again. '*You* trained her?'

Brutus picked at his teeth. 'She was out of shape. We had to be careful, of course. Discreet.'

'*You* trained her?' Remus asked again, hoping he had heard wrong.

Brutus frowned. 'Is that so surprising? Have you forgotten what I did before I became lanista? I trained your father up until his last fight.'

Remus had visited every school in the city looking for Prisca's trainer. It had never occurred to him that Brutus would keep a secret like that, would betray him in that way.

'Don't tell me you were still attached to the woman. That was years ago.'

Remus continued to stare. 'You didn't think to tell me about that?'

A smile flickered on Brutus's face. 'You mustn't understand the term *discreet*.'

'Mila was sentenced to death for her *murder*.'

Brutus rolled the name around in his head, trying to figure out who he was talking about. 'Ah, we're back to the slave girl.'

Remus's hands went into his hair. 'Yes, the slave girl. This information might have saved her life.'

'*You* saved her life. Now she'll forever be in your debt,' he replied, giving Remus a knowing look.

'If you'd told Jovian Fadius that his wife kept her identity a secret—'

'He'd have thrown me into the arena too! I'm beginning to regret mentioning the fact at all.'

Nero had stopped raking the sand and was standing watching them. The boy was finely tuned to conflict.

'Do you want to stand here arguing about this, or do you want to focus on becoming the next lanista of Ludus Magnus?'

Remus took a moment to picture himself as lanista. His father would have jumped at the opportunity, not because it was the only life he knew, but because it was the only life he wanted. Remus was different. He had once imagined another life. Perhaps he still did. He imagined telling Mila the news, the disappointment in her eyes, accompanied by a weak smile. At that moment, he had everything she wanted—the freedom to choose.

'Your silence is making me rethink my decision,' Brutus said. 'I suggest you get yourself together before I change my mind.'

Remus took a few steps back and looked over at Nero. There was that look again, ready to go, to do whatever was needed. The boy would follow him anywhere. Even to India. 'No thanks,' he said, turning back to Brutus. 'Never planned on staying here as long as I did. I should've left years ago. I'll not waste your time by giving my word when I can't keep it.'

Brutus's face hardened. 'Leave? What are you talking about? Ludus Magnus has been your home since you could crawl.'

He nodded. 'It has. But now I'm free to pick another home.'

Brutus's eyes were slits, his jaw clenched. 'Don't be foolish, boy. This is a one-time offer.'

'Sorry to disappoint you.' Remus glanced at the barracks. 'What about Felix? He has a good mind for business.'

The lanista's eyes widened. '*Felix*? You want me to leave the greatest gladiator school in Rome in the hands of a dwarf?' He emitted a cruel laugh. 'He's half a man, hired out to wealthy families and sent into the arena to give people a good laugh.'

Remus's fingers curled into fists. 'He's proven himself a good trainer.'

'He's a joke. People tolerate him for your benefit. He's like the three-legged dog at Ludus Dacicus that has outlived most of the men trained there.'

He could not listen anymore. He turned and called to Nero, 'We're leaving.'

The boy dropped the rake and came at a run. 'Where are we going?' he asked, stopping in front of them.

'To get our stuff and get out of here.'

Brutus took a menacing step towards him. 'I'm warning you, if you leave, there's no coming back.'

Nero stepped in front of Remus, his narrow chest pushed out the way he had seen older men do. Remus placed a hand on his shoulder.

'Let's go,' he said, giving the boy a push to start him walking. He felt Brutus's gaze scalding his back.

'You don't come back. Hear me?'

He heard. Nero went to turn, and Remus gave him another shove. 'You need to pick your battles more carefully,' he said, suppressing a smile.

CHAPTER 35

When Nerva returned for the Kalends festival at the end of December, Mila felt a flicker of life return to her. The house felt warmer with him in it, and her domina more bearable.

As he stood in the atrium, before the household's gods, kissing his mother's cheeks and pretending all was well between them, Mila lingered in the triclinium, peering in. She knew she would have to wait until he escaped his obligations later in the evening. Still, he looked around for her, catching her eye in the shadows and winking as a slave fussed around him. She needed tacky jokes, pointless discussions, laughter, and dare she admit it, a sparring partner. If she could just hold a sword again, maybe it would all be enough.

'You seem different,' he told her that evening.

Remus had said the same thing.

They were leaning against the wall in the garden, her refuge spot, playing bocce with stones.

'I have grown up. I thought you would be relieved.'

He picked up the cup sitting between them and took a

large gulp of wine before passing it to Mila. She finished what was left and placed it down again.

'I might be if you still resembled yourself.'

She shrugged. 'You cannot have everything.'

He studied her for a moment. 'You are not… no.'

'What?'

'Impossible.'

'What?' she asked again, shoving him. 'I am not what?'

A mischievous smile. 'You are not *lovesick*?' When she did not immediately deny it, he burst out in laughter. 'You are! You are pining for your gladiator!'

'Shhh.' She wished there was more wine. 'Do you want your mother to come out here and beat me?'

'Even in the dark, I can see your cheeks burning. I cannot say I blame you. He is handsome in that rugged, bearded sort of way.'

She pulled her knees up. 'He also jumped into the arena during my execution, so it is not all about the beard.'

'I too jumped into the arena.'

'With a scroll.'

'As a senator of Rome, I do not make a habit of carrying a sword around with me.'

She rested her wrist on top of her knees. 'How did you get into the Fadius household to retrieve that scroll unarmed?'

He shrugged. 'Like any civilised man, I bluffed my way with words once I was certain Jovian was not at home.'

'Well, it worked, so I suppose I should stop teasing you and start thanking you.'

'I should be thanking *you*. I have never received so many dinner invitations from Rome's elite.'

'You hate dining with Rome's elite.'

'True, but I enjoy knowing they want to dine with me.'

Mila rested her head on the wall, looking up at the sky.

Not one star was visible behind the thick cloud cover. 'He wanted to marry me.'

Nerva breathed out, watching the puff of steamy air leave his mouth. He glanced at the house where everyone had retired to their beds. 'He said that? Actually spoke the words "I want to marry you"?'

She rolled her head to look at him. 'Is that so hard to believe, that someone might want to marry me?'

'Of course not. You have a sort of boyish charm about you that might attract a particular type of lower-class man.'

'Goodness, do not make me blush again.'

He turned to face her. 'So what did you say? When he asked you to marry him?'

She stared at her knees. 'I was one day from freedom when he just spat it out. I should have said no.'

'But you didn't.'

'No.'

'Why not? Because you love him?'

She looked at him, a warmth spreading through her. 'More than that. I trust him with my life.'

Nerva whistled. 'That is rather a big deal for you.'

'There is not a person alive who cares about my happiness more than he did.'

Nerva went to object and then reconsidered. 'That might actually be true. The rest of us are just trying to stop you from killing yourself. Your happiness is secondary.' He winked at her, then asked, 'You do actually miss him, then?'

She nodded. 'Yes.'

'Have you seen him since you sent him marching?'

Another nod. 'Once.'

'How did that go?'

'Good, actually.' Her body warmed at the memory. 'For a moment, I felt like I could breathe again.'

Nerva stared at her in the dark. 'Well, it certainly sounds like love, but what would I know?'

She picked up a stone and tossed it. 'No seaside love affair for you, then?'

'Nothing like yours.' He picked up the cup, saw it was empty and put it back down. 'I am curious about something.'

'What's that?'

Nerva glanced across at her. 'All you wanted was your freedom. You have whined about it for years. Then in rides your heroic gladiator—'

'Walks.'

'In walks your heroic gladiator, prepared to return to the arena in order to buy your freedom, and you decline.' He shook his head, trying to understand. 'Why? Were you afraid he would get killed?'

She blinked, her eyes growing heavy. 'No. I was afraid of what it would do to Mother and Dulcia. I cannot leave them a second time.'

He nodded. 'The ultimate sacrifice. Your own happiness for theirs.' He frowned. 'I almost feel sorry for you.'

'Do not do that. Your pity would be unbearable,' she said, smiling.

He picked up a stone. 'If it makes you feel any better, my mother will likely have final say over who I marry, so I might reserve all my pity for myself.'

'That definitely helps,' she said, laughing. It felt good. 'At least she will be wealthy and fertile. What more could a young Roman senator ask for?'

'Would it be too greedy to ask for nice? Too shallow to ask for pretty?'

'Yes.'

'Then I shall settle for wealthy and fertile.'

Mila stifled a yawn. 'Still, I cannot be too sympathetic.'

'Of course not. Father is the same. Perhaps you get your stilted emotional capacity from him.'

It was the first time Nerva had ever mentioned the

blood connection, and she had no idea how to respond. She stared at him, fighting discomfort.

'What?' He leaned back as though she might sneeze on him.

She shook her head. 'Nothing. It is just that he has always been *your* father.'

Nerva threw the stone, his worst throw for the evening. 'Actually, he has always been our father, but you know, propriety and all that.'

'Now is not the time to do away with propriety, Senator.'

He smiled. 'As always, our conversations remain between us.'

'I cannot afford to have you banished too often.' Another yawn. 'I need to go to bed.' She patted his leg and stood. As she went to leave, he slid a foot out to trip her. She jumped over it, glaring at him over her shoulder. 'Child.'

'Prude.'

THE FOLLOWING MORNING, Mila helped Germana prepare *cena* in the kitchen. She placed chicken pieces into a pot with honey, oil, and herbs from the garden. Dulcia was kneading dough, a dusting of flour on her arms and chin where she had scratched her face moments earlier. She hummed a tune, making it up as she went along, unaware that she was being watched. Mila's chest squeezed at the sight. Her sister grew more beautiful by the day, and yet remained so frighteningly naive. In a few weeks she would be thirteen, and Mila suspected men were about to take notice of her budding sibling.

Dulcia looked up and caught her staring. 'What is the matter?' Her face was suddenly serious.

Always assuming the worst. 'You have flour on your chin.'

Dulcia wiped at it, only adding to the mess. 'Better?'

Mila kept her face blank. 'Much.' She looked down, placing the lid on the pot, enjoying the aromas wafting up at her. She slid it towards Germana, who took it without thanks. 'You are very welcome.'

A smile formed on Dulcia's face but she did not look up, probably too scared to be caught by the cook.

'Mila,' came her mother's voice behind her.

She turned, eyebrows raised in question.

'A word, please.'

Mila glanced at Dulcia, smiling reassuringly, before following her mother to the back of the house where the servants slept. She stepped inside the small room they shared and looked around. Tertia pulled the curtain shut behind them, the closest thing they could get to privacy.

'Goodness, what is with all the secrecy?' Mila asked, keeping her tone light. When her mother turned, Mila could see she was close to tears. 'What on earth is going on?'

Tertia tried to compose herself, drawing a deep breath before speaking. 'Last night I went looking for you in the garden. I heard you talking with Nerva.'

Mila tried to remember what they had said. The answer was usually nothing of any substance, but they had covered a few topics that were not for the ears of others. 'You should not take anything I say to Nerva too seriously.'

Her mother sniffed, looking at her with such tenderness that Mila felt panicked.

'All right, you need to tell me what has you so upset. What did I say? There was wine involved and every chance I might not remember.'

'It was nothing you said, more what you did not say.'

Mila shook her head, confused. 'What are you talking

about? Surely I cannot be in trouble for things I did *not* say.'

Tertia glanced at the curtain. 'And how you sounded—resigned and hopeless.'

Mila let out a relieved breath. 'Goodness, is that all? I have been that way for years.' She tried to smile. 'Why the tears now?'

Tertia's expression did not change. 'I have always thought you restless, quite spoiled. I think I really believed that after all this, you would see your situation differently.'

'I do.' Mila watched as her mother wiped a tear from her cheek, still unsure what was happening. 'Why are you crying? You were right. It is enough.' She gestured around the room. 'This is enough. It just took me a little longer to figure that out.'

'But it is not enough for a woman like you.' Tertia took a moment to select her words. 'I have spent your entire life trying to contain that fire in you. After you… after the incident in the arena—'

'My failed execution?'

Her mother recoiled at the words. 'I thought we could resume our life together, without the threat of being burned—'

'I am not being painted in a very positive light right now.'

'I never imagined that fire would be completely extinguished. It is not easy for a mother to see such a deep change in her child.' Tertia stared at her, eyes shiny. 'The truth is I did not know how to handle you. You see, I am more like Dulcia, and she is happy here. This *is* enough for her.'

'What? Dulcia wanted freedom as much as I did.'

Her mother shook her head. 'No, she wants to be with you. You want another life, and she wants to follow.'

As hard as that was for Mila to hear, she knew it was

probably true. 'So you brought me in here to tell me you have just figured out that I am a lost cause?'

Tertia shook her head and wiped her nose with her hand. 'I brought you here to give you this.' She pulled a small scroll from an inside pocket and held it out.

Mila just stared. 'What is it?'

Her mother glanced down at the waxy paper. 'Your freedom.'

Mila felt blood rush to her head. She did not move. Her hands remained where they were, the scroll between them. 'What?'

'In all the years I have lived here, in his house, I can honestly say I have rarely asked Rufus for anything. I am not one for expensive gifts. I have everything I need. But last night when he sent for me, I asked that he free you and your sister—and he agreed.'

Mila shook her head. 'I do not understand.'

'He is announcing it to the rest of the household as we speak. When he is able, he will register you both as citizens.'

Mila's hands tingled. 'He… he just said yes?'

'He listened to what I had to say, and he agreed to it.' Tertia took Mila's hand and closed her fingers around the papers. 'I realise now that I should have asked for this some time ago, and for that I am sorry.' She studied her daughter. 'I was afraid. I thought I was doing what was best for you.' When Mila did not say anything, she continued. 'Of course, Dulcia will stay here with me, at least for now.'

Mila struggled to process everything. 'So I am to leave?' she asked, feeling strangely exiled.

'You can stay if you wish, continue as you have been, food and bed in exchange for work, but we both know that is not what you want.'

No, that was not what she wanted. For the first time in

her life she was allowed to leave, go wherever she chose, and the decision was paralysing her.

Tertia pulled her close, gripping her tightly. 'It is all right,' she whispered. 'We will be fine without you.'

Tears spilled down Mila's cheeks. 'How can I leave when he keeps you a slave?' Her voice broke.

Tertia breathed into Mila's hair, her shoulders collapsing. 'Look at all he has done for me. My girls are free.'

'Is that really enough for you?'

Her mother pulled away, a wide smile on her face. 'Is that enough? Mila, what more could I want? Besides, this is my home. Where would I go that is better than here?'

Where would she go? 'I do not think I can leave.'

Tertia gripped her harder, tears falling. 'It is natural to feel afraid. It is a lot at once.'

'Dulcia—'

'Will be fine. This is not goodbye. You are not being separated.' She wiped at another tear. 'It is time for you to live the life you fought so hard for.' She rubbed Mila's arms. 'Go to Remus. Go to your gladiator. If he loves you as I suspect he does, then go to him. That is what you want, is it not?'

She nodded, something shifting within her. Her fear giving way to hope.

'I am free to leave? Right now, if I choose?'

Her mother's face collapsed for a moment. 'Right now. If that is what you truly want.' She leaned forwards and kissed Mila's face. 'You are *free*.'

CHAPTER 36

Dulcia surprised Mila by not crying when she heard the news. Instead, she helped her sister gather the few belongings she owned, including a coin pouch Nerva had handed her when he came to see her after the announcement. No one made a fuss, despite all of them feeling the change.

'I would feel a lot better if you cried and carried on for a bit,' Mila said as she hugged her sister goodbye.

'After months of watching Aquila hurt you, I feel only relief. Remus will take care of you. He loves you. I saw it that day he came to the house.'

It was possible that her sister was finally growing up. Mila stared down at her sister. *Remus*. Hearing his name was like opening floodgates. What would he say of the news? Perhaps he had moved on from the whole thing. She could not blame him for that. 'You do not feel abandoned?'

'Not if you promise to come back, promise not to disappear forever.'

She hugged her sister close. 'Give me some time, and I promise I will come back to you.'

As she walked through the atrium, the front door in

sight and her heart drumming inside her chest, she glanced inside the tablinum. Rufus sat behind the large table, quill in hand. She stopped walking and waited for him to look up. They stared at one another for a moment, and then she did something she had never done in her life: she bowed, all the way to the ground. She looked at him as she straightened, trying to read his expression. He gave nothing away, nodding once in her direction before returning to his work.

She turned away and kept walking, exiting the atrium, striding through the vestibulum until she reached the door. Her hand hovered near the handle for a moment, and she wondered if she might change her mind. Shaking her head, she pulled the door wide open and stepped through it. That first gulp of outside air was like a cool drink on a hot day. She drank greedily, choking up at all she was feeling. She stood on the top step for a moment, eyes closed and hands shaking. The cold air made her feel alive.

When she finally opened her eyes, she saw a large man sitting on a tall horse waiting at the bottom of the steps. It was Albaus. She immediately broke into a run, taking the steps two at a time, falling against his thick leg when she reached the bottom.

'Did Nerva tell you the news?' she asked, looking up at him.

There was light in his eyes as he handed her a note. She took it from him and unrolled it.

Mila,

You did not think I would let you out into the world without a trusted bodyguard, did you?

Before you scold me for giving you a slave, he comes to you a freed man. He serves you not by law, but out of loyalty. He told me so himself.

All right, bad joke.

Make sure you feed the poor man.

YOUR BROTHER,

Nerva

MILA FOUGHT the urge to run back inside and hug him, but the thought of running into Aquila, who had managed to remain hidden for the morning, stopped her.

She looked up at Albaus. 'Only come with me if you want to.'

He nodded and leaned down, extending a hand twice the size of her own. She slipped the note into the canvas bag filled with her belongings and took hold of his hand, pulling herself up behind the saddle. Albaus turned his head, waiting for instructions. She pulled her palla over her head and hugged the bag to her chest.

The thought of showing up at Ludus Magnus after all this time made her hands damp. What if Remus had moved on? Erased her? Fallen in love with someone… easier? But *she* had not moved on. Nothing had changed for her. She had no choice but to go to him, and no desire to go anywhere else.

'What are your thoughts on visiting Remus?'

A grunt, and the horse walked forwards.

She turned to watch the Papias household shrink behind her, her family, her entire world, disappearing. A stiff wind blew. She used Albaus's back as a shield against it, brushing aside tears before they froze on her cheeks.

REMUS RENTED a room in the city, explaining to the owner that they would only need it for a few nights while they finalised their travel plans. The three of them had sat in the small room, bewildered. Felix had remained surprisingly calm despite the fact that he would soon board a ship to Myos Hormos in Egypt. Nero had done nothing but bounce around, hungry for adventure, until Felix shouted at him to be still and stop that incessant smiling.

On their final day in Rome, Remus paced, feeling guilty at having uprooted all their lives. He was having second thoughts but was too proud to admit it. He needed to go. There was no logical reason for him to remain in the city.

'Ever been seasick?' Felix asked Nero. 'You will wish yourself dead.'

'I've never even been on a boat,' replied the boy, his excitement infectious.

'Gods help us.' Felix looked up at Remus. 'Let us go. The horses will be waiting to take us to the port.'

Remus nodded and looked around the room, feeling as though he had left something behind.

'What's wrong?' Nero asked, reading his mind.

He gave the boy a shove towards the door. 'Nothing. Time to go.'

Outside, two slaves waited with two mares.

'I hate horses,' Felix said, stepping past Remus.

'I got the shortest ones I could find,' Remus called to his back, suppressing a smile.

As they were loading the mares with supplies, Felix made it clear that he would not share his horse for fear the boy would cause him to fall. Remus was only half listening while trying to ignore the growing feeling in his chest, the one that told him not to go. His mind went to Mila, like it always did, and he realised it was not fear keeping him anchored to the city—it was her. He wondered if he should send word that he was leaving, that he had done it, walked away from the gladiator life and the city that had imprisoned him for so long. He could send the message to Nerva. Perhaps she would not care to hear it.

He turned away from the horse and looked off down the street that would lead them west to Ostia Antica, the harbour where their ship waited. That was when he saw her, standing in the middle of the road, a still figure amid chaos, watching him.

Mila.

The palla slipped down her head, coming to rest on her shoulders. Pieces of hair blew about her face, and she made no effort to tidy them. They continued to look at one another. For a moment he thought he might be hallucinating as people stepped past her, moving as though she were not standing in their way. She looked every bit a goddess—a stark contrast to the sunburned sweat-soaked girl he had trained months earlier, but every bit as beautiful.

She disappeared beneath a long shadow. *Albaus*. He stood beside Mila as he had in the arena, holding the reins of a tall horse. If it were not for the shock, and perhaps his pride, he might have run to her, or at least smiled. Instead, he crossed his arms, leaning his weight on one foot. She made the first move, walking over to him, taking in the scene behind him—loaded horses, Felix, and an incessantly talking Nero who had not drawn a breath all day.

She stopped in front of him, and when he did not greet her, she said, 'Where are you going?'

He turned to the horses, as though he needed to check the answer for himself. That was when Nero noticed her, his face lighting up. He tried to go to her but Felix caught hold of his arm, pulling him back. The boy looked between them and gave up the fight.

'First stop, Egypt,' Remus replied, turning back to her.

She nodded, looking past him again. She seemed

nervous. He had seen her that way before, but this was different.

'You are actually doing it, going to India.'

'Assuming the ship doesn't sink and there's no plague outbreak, yes.'

She looked really proud of him in that moment. His hands fell to his sides.

She glanced around for a moment before asking, 'Is there room for two more?' She gestured behind her. 'We have our own horse.'

He could not stop the reaction inside him. There was nothing he wanted more. That was why the question was so cruel. She was not his to take anywhere. 'Guards would stop us before we reached the city's wall. They'd kill us both.'

She opened the bag she had been carrying over her shoulder and pulled out a small scroll. 'Would this help?'

He stared at it for a moment before speaking. 'That depends. What is it?'

She swallowed. There were those nerves again.

'Papers.' Her voice cracked and she cleared her throat. 'Signed by Rufus Papias this morning.'

He crushed the hope rising in his chest because he knew the disappointment would be too much. 'What do they say?'

'That… that I am free.'

She said the words as though she barely believed them herself.

He looked down, scratching his nose, sure that if he looked directly up at her he would weep like a baby. What had she just said? He knew what he had heard, but what had she actually said? 'You're… free?'

'Yes.' It was barely a whisper.

His hands began to tremble, and he looked behind him at the others to gauge their reaction before allowing himself to feel anything. They seemed equally shocked by the announcement.

'I went straight to Ludus Magnus,' she said, filling the gaping silence. 'Fausta told me you had left a few days ago.' Another clearing of the throat. 'When she told me of your plans, I realised that I might not survive the disappointment of losing you a second time.' She paused. 'You see, I am very much in love with you. I thought it might go away with time, but apparently it does not work that way.'

He definitely could not look at her. Even still, his legs carried him forwards and his hands reached for her, taking handfuls of soft, clean hair, something else that was new about her. His lips crashed against hers. She was not shy, pushing up on her toes, her hands winding around his neck. She smelled like honey and herbs, and tasted like butter and cinnamon. He pulled her closer, really hoping he had heard correctly, because by that stage he was prepared to leave the city with her anyway—fight his way out if need be.

Felix coughed and Mila pulled away, smiling. He would punch that dwarf later. His head tipped forwards, resting against hers; whatever he was feeling, he was dizzy with it. A strange laugh escaped him, probably a release of the fear he had been stifling for months. He could not stop smiling.

'So that is a yes, then?' she asked, closing her eyes and rubbing her face against his beard.

He straightened, threading his fingers through hers in case she tried to flee. 'Only if you agree to be my wife.'

She stepped back from him, but he did not let go of her. 'That depends. What would it be like to be married to Remus Latinius, one of Rome's most notorious gladiators?'

He glanced down at her hands, trapped inside his. 'A lot like this, I imagine.'

She pretended to think on the subject. 'Will I need a shield?'

He pulled her back to him, hating the distance between them. 'No shield,' he murmured into her smiling mouth.

She wrapped her arms around his neck again and jumped up, legs wrapping him. He caught her with an *oomph*.

'You've really let yourself go,' he teased.

Her mouth went over his again, silencing him.

Albaus led the horse past them, settling himself among the travelling party, ruffling Nero's hair as the boy beamed up at him. Felix nodded a greeting and patted his giant arm.

'Excellent. Now people are going to think we are a travelling circus act.'

Albaus groaned, turning to look at Remus and Mila, who remained in the middle of the narrow street in the heart of Rome.

'Let's move!' Felix called.

Remus placed Mila on the ground and went to smack her backside. She sidestepped and he missed.

'Now who has let themselves go?' she called over her shoulder.

He gave chase and she broke into a run, reaching the horses well ahead of his half effort. Nero hugged her before pulling away to tell her about all the amazing things they were going to see.

'Are you excited to see the pyramids?' he asked, his face bright.

She draped an arm around his shoulders. 'The pyramids and elephants are the only reason I am joining this circus.'

'What about the tigers?' Nero asked.

'No,' Mila and Remus said at the same time, glancing at one another.

'Can I ride with Albaus?' Nero asked.

'Suits me,' Felix said. 'Now, who can help me mount this beast without laughing?'

'I've never laughed at you mounting a horse,' Remus said, stepping forwards and linking his hands to make a stirrup.

Felix raised a foot. 'What about that time you raised me with too much force?'

A laugh escaped Remus. 'That *was* funny. But to be fair, I'd have laughed at any man flying over the top of a horse.'

Felix cursed as he settled himself in the saddle.

'Who should I ride with?' Mila asked.

Remus took her bag and handed it to Felix before scooping her up in his arms. 'You'll ride with me.' He walked over to his horse and stopped. 'But before I carry you into our marital home, making our union official—'

'The horse is our marital home?' she laughed.

He continued as though she had not spoken. 'You must consent.'

'I have already consented.'

'No you haven't. A few bad jokes do not a marriage make.'

She kissed his cheek. 'Do you not want to hear the details of my dowry first?'

'Not really. Right now I just want your consent. If you turn out to be wealthy, that'll be a nice bonus.'

'Fair enough. I consent to marry you.'

He kissed her, deeply, and then placed her on top of the horse. 'Done. See? Wasn't so hard.'

'We have only been wed a few moments. Ask me in a year.'

He used the stirrup to pull himself up behind her. His arms wrapped her as he took up the reins. 'Who's ready to leave this godforsaken city?'

'Thought you would never ask,' Felix said, kicking his horse into a walk.

Remus turned to Nero, eyebrows raised in question.

'Me,' said the boy, turning to the bodyguard. 'You ready, Albaus?'

Albaus pushed the horse forwards.

Remus's lips hovered near Mila's ear. 'Ready?' he whispered.

She glanced over her shoulder at the busy street behind them. 'Ready.'

EPILOGUE

May 17, 204AD

The hut was made from baked bricks and wood Remus had cut with his own hands. He loved to work with wood, and Mila would sit in the chair he had made for her, watching him work barefoot beneath the large silk-cotton tree. Its bulging roots provided a steady work surface.

She pulled her feet up and gazed out over the coarse grass that gave way to soft sand and calm water. There, wading in the shallows, was their daughter, her small hand wrapped by Nero's much larger one.

Upon arriving in Muziris four years earlier, they had made their way to the city of Barace, where Remus had set up contacts for the trade of pepper. A few months later they had found a pocket of land south of the city. The owner had agreed to let them build on it for a cut of the profits. A year on, Asha had arrived, her small hands clenched into fists and her lungs in perfect working order.

'Look at her,' Remus had said to an exhausted Mila. 'She looks ready for the arena.'

Mila had laughed, watching as the baby was passed from Nero, to Felix, and finally to Albaus, who immediately handed her back to Remus, visibly terrified by the size of the small infant in his large hands.

'I can't stop looking at her,' Remus had said.

Mila had smiled, blinking away exhaustion. 'Look at what we made. And she is free.'

He had teared up at that.

Her gaze returned to him, his form familiar and as beautiful as the first time she had seen him. 'You should go for a swim, cool off,' she called to him.

He laid down his tools and wiped the sweat from his brow. 'Good idea.'

She watched as he peeled off the tunic she had made for him, then walked over to her.

'What are you doing?' she asked, instantly wary.

He bent, scooping her off the chair and throwing her over his shoulder. She squealed, pounding his back with her fists. 'Now I am covered in your sweat.'

'Yes you are.'

Nero looked up as they approached, pointing to them so Asha turned to see. Laughter erupted from the three-year-old.

'I swear to the gods, if you throw me in with my clothes on…'

Remus strode across the sand and into the water, past Nero and his daughter until he was waist deep in the sea. Mila clung to him, trying to keep her sari out of the water.

'Take me to the sand right now!'

Remus looked at Nero. 'What do you think?'

A smile grew on his face. 'I say throw her in.'

Mila tried to turn her head. 'I will remember that later when you ask for a second serving of dinner.'

Remus ignored her. 'What about you, Asha? Should we throw your mother in?'

With both hands gripping Nero's, the girl nodded mischievously.

'Remus!' Mila said. 'The moment we are on dry land—'

Before she could finish her sentence, Remus held her by her waist and threw her into the water. She came to the surface, gasping for air and wiping at the hair clinging to her face.

Remus smiled down at her. 'Refreshing?' he teased.

Without warning, she leapt up and tackled him into the water, holding his head under for good measure. 'See for yourself.'

'Mila, stop drowning your husband.' Felix's voice carried across the water. She turned to see him smirking at her.

She released Remus and he emerged laughing. Once he had found his feet, she shoved him backwards again before wading back to the shore where Felix waited with the wooden swords and shields.

'Nero,' Mila called, 'you want to train with me?'

In his fifteenth year, Nero was growing up and out, eating anything that was not tied down. He waited for Remus to take Asha before joining Mila on the beach. Felix tossed him one of the swords and a shield, and he spent a moment adjusting his grip.

'My hands are wet,' he said.

Mila shrugged. 'I am afraid you will not be able to request ideal fighting conditions when the time comes.' She hoped it never would.

They fought, Mila giving the boy as much as he could handle and occasionally a little more.

'Step into it,' Felix called to Nero. They all wanted him ready for whatever the gods had in store for him.

Out of the corner of her eye, Mila saw Remus step out of the water and place Asha down onto the sand.

'Sword!' Asha cried, picking up a long stick and running towards them.

'Shields up!' Remus called.

Mila suppressed a smile, feeling her husband's laughing eyes on her. Nero turned to Asha, crouching to her height as she came crashing in, waving her stick and squealing with laughter. After a moment, Nero collapsed on the sand with a theatrical groan, and Felix declared Asha the victor.

The life they had built was by no means a privileged one, but it was happier than most. It was more than enough.

Albaus strode down the grass slope towards them, too large for the shifting sand beneath him. He went straight to Mila, handing her a scroll.

'A letter?' she asked.

He nodded. A ship had docked in Muziris the day before, bringing gold and jewels to pay for the pepper it would take back to Rome. She glanced at Remus, his playful expression gone, and unrolled it. She recognised Nerva's handwriting. Her eyes moved over the words, absorbing the information and names of the people she had left behind.

Nero picked up Asha and carried her off in the direction of the hut. He had always been good at reading tense situations, and he protected Asha like a brother.

'Emperor Severus is forming a new legion. He has asked Nerva to lead it.'

Remus walked over and took the letter from her, scanning its contents. Mila had taught him to read during their first year together. Like most things, he had picked it up fast.

'That's quite a step up given he's only been a centurion for a few years,' he said, handing the letter back to her.

'Yes, but he has always been a leader.' She looked out at the water, questions rising in her mind like mountains.

Remus brushed a hunk of sand-covered hair off her face. 'What are you thinking?'

She shook her head. 'Dulcia will be alone when he leaves.'

'Dulcia's not a child anymore.' His tone was gentle.

She swallowed. 'I know. It's just… I promised her I would come back. We had only planned to be away for a year or two.'

He nodded. 'Then Asha came along. We agreed the journey was too risky for an infant.'

Her gaze went to the hut and then to Albaus. She knew he would follow her anywhere, even if he had never spoken the words. Looking at Felix, she asked, 'How do you feel about returning to Rome?'

'I never wanted to leave.' There was humour in his tone.

It took a surprising amount of strength to look at Remus. 'What about you, husband? This is the life you wanted,' she said, looking around. 'Can you see yourself walking away from it? Returning to the city where we lived as slaves?'

His gaze swept their surroundings. 'Who says we can't come back?'

She wrapped her arms around his middle.

'The only life I want is one with you,' he murmured.

'Walking away,' Felix said, pointing to the hut. 'You can fill me in on the details later.' He turned and left, Albaus following after him.

Remus kissed the top of Mila's head. 'I mean it. If you need to go to Rome, we go to Rome.'

She pushed herself up on her toes so she could kiss him. 'You will trade all of this for filthy city streets?'

'For you, yes. Everything's set up here. There are men I trust to take over.'

A flock of storm petrels flew overhead, casting flickering shadows across the sand.

Mila turned her head at the sound of Asha playing outside the hut. 'She needs to see the city we came from, meet the small family she has outside of the one we made.'

The smell of fish guts and turned oil was already returning to her. She tipped her face up to read Remus's expression. He brushed sand off her forehead and kissed it.

'To Rome?'

She closed her eyes against the sun. 'To Rome.'

In 200AD, Emperor Septimius Severus banned female gladiators when he issued a decree banning single combat by women in the arena for "recrudescence among some upper-class women, and the raillery this provoked among the audience".

—*Cassius Dio, Roman History*

AUTHOR'S NOTE

There are a few things I wanted to mention about the writing of this book, the first being that all the characters are fictional, with the exception of Emperor Septimius Severus. Not only was Severus the emperor at the time in which the story is set, but he was also the man responsible for the banning of female gladiators, so I felt his inclusion important.

It's worth pointing out that I have used some modern phrases in instances where I felt the reader would not understand some words in a particular context. The last thing I wanted was readers coming out of the story to google terminology. You might also have noticed that the dialogue is not a true representation of that period, and that's intentional. I wanted the story to be accessible to a wide audience.

Historians cannot agree on what the sponsor's thumb signals represented. It was tempting to follow Hollywood interpretations, which suggest a thumbs up means let them live, but after much research, I concluded that no one knows for sure. The next best thing is an educated guess. I tend to lean towards the theory that a thumbs up signifies an upwards thrust of a sword through the heart. In other words, kill. A thumbs down, then, would signify laying down/dropping the weapon.

Finally, there is not a great deal recorded on female gladiators. While evidence points to female gladiators first appearing under Augustus, Augustan authors don't make reference to them. One theory for this is that the women were likely from lower socio-economic groups—slaves—and would not have been considered worthy of inclusion. We can only imagine their stories.

I hope you enjoyed imagining this one.

ACKNOWLEDGMENTS

I would like to express my gratitude to the many people who contributed to this book. My biggest thanks goes to my readers for taking a chance on a new series. Without you guys, I wouldn't get to do what I love. Next, a huge thank you to my rock star husband who supports and encourages me even though my writing takes time away from him. I love you to bits. A big thank you to Joanna Walsh from Saltwater Writers for your ongoing feedback and support. A big shout-out to my beta readers, who each brought a unique perspective. Your insights were fabulous. Thank you to Kristin and the team at Hot Tree Editing for polishing the manuscript into something beautiful, and to my proofreader Rebecca Fletcher for catching everything I missed. A round of applause for my cover designer, Domi, from Inspired Cover Designs, for this *gorgeous* cover. And finally, a huge thank you to my Launch Team for your encouragement, honest reviews, and being the final set of eyes on my work. You guys are amazing.

ALSO BY TANYA BIRD

You can find a complete list of published works at
tanyabird.com/books

www.ingramcontent.com/pod-product-compliance
Lightning Source LLC
LaVergne TN
LVHW091251150826
845673LV00006B/1387

9780648341130